TRUE LIES

John Halfnight

International Government Security Organisations

MI5 UK (Security Service). Britain's intelligence agency protecting the UK's national security against threats such as terrorism and espionage.

MI6 UK (Secret Intelligence Service). Collects Britain's foreign intelligence and provides a global covert capability to protect and defend national security of the UK.

DGSE. (Direction Générale de la Sécurité Extérieure). French Government equivalent of MI6

CIA. (Central Intelligence Agency). United States Government equivalent of MI6

MOSSAD. (Institute for Intelligence and Special Operations). National Intelligence Agency of Israel.

FSB. Federal Security Service of the Russian Federation.

SVR. Foreign Intelligence Service of the Russian Federation.

GRU. Military Foreign Intelligence Directorate of the Russian Federation.

MSS. Chinese State Intelligence Security Agency.

IISG. International Intelligence & Security Group. US/UK Private Group, Washington and London.

International Time: Time of the day is always local time. Readers should remember that Europe and Gulf countries can be 1, 2, 3 or 4 hours *ahead* of the UK, or in the case of the USA, or South American Countries 5, or 6 hours, *behind.*

Personae

Norman Spencer - Director IISG, ex Deputy Director MI6

Harry Baxter - now with IISG, ex officer MI6

Charles Urwin - First Secretary, Foreign & Commonwealth Office

Quentin Horncastle - Senior FCO official

Jack DeCosta - CIA agent, long standing friend of Harry Baxter

Paul Frere - CIA Section Head. Jack DeCosta boss

David Hadar - Mossad Head of Station London

Alain Dubois-DGSE agent Paris (*Direction Générale de la Sécurité Extérieure*)

Mikhail Fradkov - Director SVR Moscow

Sergey Lavrov - Foreign Minister of Russia

Jean Nemours - Banque Liban

Josh Morgan - Banque Roubert Saudi

David Khoury - Mossad undercover agent, Lebanon

Michel Yassin - DGSE undercover agent, Lebanon

Petro Dudnyk - previously Ukraine Security Service

Dimitry Durov - First Secty Russian Embassy London

Sir Robert Fordcombe - Foreign & Commonwealth Office

Stepan Volkov - SVR Russian Embassy London

Jan Glaus – Swiss Intelligence Service (Federal)

Lina Eblin - Swiss Intelligence Service (Military)

Alex Buhler - Director Swiss Federal Intelligence Service

Tom Denman – Serving Officer MI6

Prologue

Six months later. June 2008. London

Harry was sitting in the Reception of IISG (International Intelligence & Security Group) located just north of Oxford Street, London He had realised, for at least two months, that he was not qualified for anything else other than what had occupied him for the last twenty years.

The pain of December was still there. He had continued his journey to Tel Aviv.

Anna's funeral had taken place on the 27th December 2007. A small but senior group from Mossad had attended. Little was said, but his relationship with Anna was known, acknowledged, and sympathy was extended.

He returned to London on the 28th December and resigned at the end of the month. The Deputy had understood, his retirement was effective the same date.

Harry had sat around for a month, mourning in his own way. He had contacted his friends in Sussex and stayed with them on a couple of weekends.

Fed up with London he sold his flat in Clapham and moved down into Sussex, buying a small house in a quiet village, with a pub, a church and village shop.

Sometime in May 2008, an old US contact, Jack DeCosta, had suggested talking to IISG, (International Intelligence & Security Group). It was a US operation extending its reach through London and reinforcing its ranks with appropriate, and experienced recruits from the UK and European Government agencies.

United Kingdom Security Services were heavily stretched with existing numbers, and risk was rising exponentially.

In the United States government agencies were pulling private intelligence companies into the net to work with, co-operate, share and assist in order to counter the adverse pendulum swing. Expertise in specific geographical regions in USA Government agencies was also in short supply. The UK was close behind in adopting a similar strategy.

Harry was sitting in IISG reception, wondering what form the interview would take, when a familiar voice interrupted his thinking.

'Morning Harry, what brings you here, or need I ask?'

He rose, turning to see an outstretched hand, which he grasped and shook, smiling in recognition, and not a little surprise.

It was the Deputy.

***

I

June 2008

June 2008. IISG, London.

Harry sat in the Director's office, located in a fairly nondescript modern office block, being brought up to date with what had been happening with his erstwhile boss since the end of December 2007. Despite some internal whispering about 'revolving doors', there had been no Ministerial objection to the Deputy taking up the position as London Director IISG.

Realisation as to the level of co-operation that could, and would exist, countered any negative thinking. 'All on the same side' was the pragmatic response.

As Director he had taken up his appointment on Monday the 31st of March, initially spending three weeks in Washington being brought up to group speed, and, more importantly, discussing some of the gaps in the group's armoury, particularly those in Europe, Middle East and Gulf.

Relations in Washington between IISG and the important players, such as the CIA, NSA, Department of Defense, etc, were good and well-established. One of the Director's tasks would be to establish good working relationships with his previous Service, MI6, and also foster similar relations with MI5, GCHQ, MoD, etc. Phase II would include some European and Middle East agencies, such as DGSE and Mossad.

'Not my favourite activity Harry, but it will have to done. Perhaps sprats to catch a mackerel, who knows at this stage? We will have to show them all we can be even more professional than them, or certainly their equal,' he said, a small smile crossing his face.

Harry nodded, 'As we're outside the tent doesn't that make things doubly difficult? You know how they like to keep things very close to their chests, in some cases they are damn nigh paranoid.'

'True, but we have a different brief. Our relationships with UK government departments, or foreign government departments, will be where we can plug the gaps due to their lack of capacity and resource. We can be more flexible and opportunistic than some of the agencies, whether UK, or US. I can use you, Harry. It depends on whether you want to be used!'

Another small smile crossed his face, 'Incidentally, I cannot imagine what you would do, away from what you and I have been doing, most of our professional lives!'

On this occasion Harry gently smiled, albeit ruefully, 'Yes, perhaps, unfortunately, you may be right.'

He paused, unlocking his hands, and reaching into his jacket produced a pen, 'So, in that case, where do I sign, and when do I start?'

***

II

Monday 16th June 2008. IISG, London.

Harry had rented a small, one-bedroom apartment in Clapham, not far from the one he had previously owned. Convenient for London on the tube or rail. No point in selling his cottage in Sussex yet. Let's see how things pan out, he thought.

That Monday he had presented himself at IISG, where most of the morning was spent meeting colleagues, completing admin, registration, medical, insurances, laptops, mobile, working funds, etc, etc.

In the afternoon he had sat with the Deputy, now to be called Director, to consider where best he should be deployed after review of current ops, and as a result of that, then a possible agreed strategy. They were deep in discussion when it was interrupted by a knock on the door.

An agent, about 35/40 years of age Harry thought, apologised, but then spoke at speed,

'Director, you remember the example you discussed with us a couple of weeks ago concerning Charles Urwin, Foreign & Commonwealth Office?'

'Yes, and?'

'We understand from one of our contacts that he has disappeared, no trace is being picked up at present, and the proverbial is hitting the fan in the FCO. Our contact wondered if we had picked up anything.'

'My God,' Harry interjected, 'my old bête noire is still making waves, is he?'

'Do you know him?' the agent enquired.

Harry looked at the Director, smiling as he replied,

'Know him? Hm. More than a passing acquaintance! Perhaps I could contribute something on this, with your approval, Director?'

'Why not Harry, start with something you know something about!'

Harry left with the agent, who turned out to be an ex-Intelligence Corp WOII, Jim Bolton.

'Well Jim, what do we know so far?'

'He's just disappeared off the grid. Was supposed to be at an FCO meeting yesterday. No show. SO19 checked his apartment. No sign of any suspicious activity.'

'Meeting yesterday, Sunday?' Harry queried.

'Yes, some urgent concerns over border activity and escalation of words between Russia and Georgia. It's been building since April; all the news channels and wire services are monitoring it.'

'Yes, I'd seen some commentary, it's certainly building. Do we have any idea as to his specific role and country emphasis at present?'

'No, unfortunately.'

'Well, on past form and posting, Russia will certainly be involved.'

'It was agreed between them that, until further information was provided by their contact, there was little they could do, other than brief their agents to log and submit any detail that might appear relevant, however remote.

**

Friday 13th June 2008.

The Pig Country House Hotel, Brockenhurst, Hampshire.

Charles Urwin had checked in under an assumed name, paying in cash, and was sitting in his room running through the instructions he had received concerning his departure that evening.

He would be taken to Bucklers Hard at 1600hrs, a small yacht basin linked to the Solent. There he would board a boat for an evening cruise, probably a 45-foot Mooney, ketch-rigged. With the long summer evenings, staying light until 2200hrs, this was often done.

From the Hard, sailing down the Solent, and into the English Channel, a rendezvous would occur with a power boat, which would take him in a SW direction down the Channel for a further RV with a commercial freighter, boarding from the Southern side, thus avoiding observation from the shore.

With his disappearance there would be the usual reactions expected from government and security agencies. Watches would be mounted on all airports, Eurostar, private airfields, ferries to all ports on the continent, etc. However, nothing would be flagged at the hotel until at least lunchtime Tuesday, by which time he would be well into the North Sea, probably approaching Denmark at least, well on his way to St Petersburg.

He smiled wryly to himself. Sometimes the slowest routes provided the best cover.

The sacrifice or dedication of man for the greater good. Yes. That is what he was doing. He understood clearly, even if, in the fullness of time, nobody else would. You have to believe, that what you do is right and proper, and this certainly was, in the grand scheme of things. He knew, even if not one other person understood his actions.

He picked up a bag, similar in size and style to what many a keen photographer would carry, capable of carrying a couple of cameras, assorted lenses, filters etc, and walked downstairs to the main entrance, where a Skoda taxi was waiting for him.

It was 1600hrs.

In the drive to Bucklers Hard he reflected on what had happened earlier in the year following his 'arrest' by CTC SO15. Interminable meetings, under caution, all designed to trap him into some sort of 'confession'. Fairly pathetic, and with limited hard facts on which to base their assumptions.

They were hanging their hat on his attitude, his abrasive relationships, with both senior and junior colleagues, unless, of course, on those occasions, when he was using his well-honed manipulative techniques to achieve what he wanted.

Accusations of working spontaneously, outside of FCO accepted norms. Why not, if the situation demanded a rapid response?

Some old diary entries had been thrown at him, easily countered. Acerbic private observations. Not allowed? People in similar positions, Prime Ministers and below, did not keep diary notes? Published 'Memoirs', containing critical comments, had not appeared before?

All soon dealt with, and dismissed.

Whilst under suspension these meetings had been carried out for over four weeks, before he was advised that no further action would be taken against him, and he was to resume his functioning role.

Unknown to Charles however, Quentin Horncastle had been briefed to maintain a close 'helicopter' eye on Charles' attitudes, relationships, and application within his Permanent Secretary role. It was quite clear that there was a significant question mark hovering over his personal file. Discreet professional surveillance was required.

2200hrs. Mid-English Channel.

The RV had been made, and he was now on board a freighter, making its way, uninterrupted, up the English Channel, as he sat in a small aft cabin, wondering what the future would hold.

**

Tuesday afternoon 17th June 2008. FCO, London.

Senior Department officials were scrambling to keep a lid on the disappearance of Charles Urwin. Uncontrolled speculation by the Press, once news leaked out, was an anathema to a government department that revelled in its control of information and dissemination of news.

Quentin Horncastle was attending the meeting, chaired by a Deputy Under-Secretary.

It soon became clear that he was one of the targets for responsibility of the current situation, bearing in mind his clear brief to maintain a critical overview of Charles Urwin.

'Quentin, what is your view, currently, bearing in mind your brief to maintain some level of scrutiny of Urwin, following his in-depth performance review earlier this year?'

The tone and content were very clear in their allocation of responsibility, Quentin thought to himself, before choosing his words of response carefully,

'As you are aware, I was instructed by the Foreign Minister, following Urwin's review, to maintain an overview of his performance in a purely professional capacity. This was to cover his advisory briefs to Ministers, relations with Ambassadors, both here in the UK, and elsewhere, if either posted or travelling from the UK, and a clear adherence to stated UK foreign policies.'

The Deputy Under-Secretary opened his mouth to speak, but Quentin ignored this and continued,

'In addition, and where possible, and in person, I was to observe his style and relationship with colleagues and FCO staff, and to raise, as a concern, any issues which would fall under the heading of inappropriate, or unacceptable, behaviour.'

The Deputy Under-Secretary again opened his mouth, which, once again, was ignored by Quentin, who continued,

'Regrettably on reflection, my brief, for obvious physical constraints and time limitation, did not include a 24-hour surveillance operation. However, if such an operation, perhaps CTC SO15, who had previously interviewed Irwin, had been authorised and activated, it might have provided some sort of answer as to his current disappearance.'

Quentin felt quite satisfied that his response would, to some extent, restrict, or nullify, any possible apportionment of blame to him, or his section. The Deputy Under-Secretary, on seeing that Quentin had finished, did not choose to comment, but opened the discussion to the rest of the meeting to hear and consider their respective views and observation. After about half an hour, it became clear, that most, if not all comments were speculation, and until some hard facts, from Police, Security Services, Airports, Docks, Railways, etc, were available, further discussion was pointless.

The meeting broke up and Quentin made his way back to his office, mulling things over in his mind. Locking his door, he sat at his desk and put a single sheet of paper in front of him. He let his mind run over the investigation of Charles Urwin earlier in the year. There was no doubt that Urwin was very intelligent, albeit with a very high dose of intellectual arrogance. Let us assume, he thought, that Urwin had played us.

What if, the political passion of his youth had continued into adulthood, well hidden within professional FCO presentations, always laced with a mix of, intelligence, an urbane style of authority, and with discreet superiority/sycophancy in equal measure?

Quentin jotted down some brief headings on the sheet of paper, which he then placed in a locked drawer.

That afternoon Harry made a call to his old friend, Jack DeCosta, CIA, in Washington.

He had two on his list he wanted to contact soonest. One was Jack De Costa, the other Alain Dubois, DGSE, Paris.

They had not spoken for some months, and Harry wanted to tell him of his new assignment. Jack had previously spoken to Harry following his resignation from SIS, and the loss of Anna, and had returned to Washington the following month.

'Hi stranger, what have you been up to, and what are you doing?' was his response when Harry was put through. Harry briefly explained about IISG, which was well known to Jack, who congratulated him on his new appointment.

'Would not be surprised Harry, if we found ourselves working together again sometime. I know of links between us and IISG here in Washington; needs must these days, with the amount of escalation coming from the East, if you get my drift.'

'Definitely Jack. Russia, China, North Korea, uncertainty in the Gulf and Middle East. You name it; their name is legion, for they are many! More than enough to keep you and me occupied, without adding in any home-grown challenges. Thought I would touch base, so you know where I am.'

They finished their conversation with Harry giving Jack his various contact details, telephone, fixed and mobile, email, etc., whilst noting Jack's had remained the same.

His final comment was offering Jack his first drink, as and when he pitched up in London next. The one omission was any reference to Charles Urwin. Perhaps, if he had, everybody might have saved some time.

CIA, Washington, USA.

After the telephone conversation Jack went to update his boss, Paul Frere, about Harry's new role and their previous history. Paul had recently moved up a notch in the hierarchy, and listened closely as Jack filled him in.

He was fully aware of IISG, its international operations, and a close but informal relationship with the CIA. Often beneficial to both parties.

'Keep your friendship well buttoned Jack, who knows when that could be very useful.'

Neither, at that time, could realise how true that statement could be.

That evening, just before midnight.

The freighter was now NNE of Holland, heading up the west coast of Denmark, almost level with Esbjerg. Charles was bored. Meals were brought to him. He was confined to his cabin. Small, and starting to feel prison-like. Never mind, only a few more days, he thought. Friday morning latest.

Thursday 19th June 2008. IISG, London.

Harry telephoned David Hadar, Mossad London. He was put through immediately.

'Morning Harry. It's a few months since we last spoke. By the way Asher Roshal, Head of Station is now back in Tel Aviv, and I've been promoted. I am now Head of Station, London.'

'Congratulations David, good luck for the future. Reason for the call was to bring you up to date with my own recent moves.'

Harry then explained IISG and their role worldwide, and his position with them. As he explained, company, relationships, etc, he sensed a slight withdrawal or resistance from David. Nothing obvious, just a cooling in tone.

Wondering what was causing that, he decided not to raise questions now, but see if any clarity could be found in IISG. Notwithstanding such concerns, they parted amicably, with the usual suggestion of a meeting in the not-too-distant future.

Saturday 21st June 2008. St Petersburg, Russia.

The freighter had been delayed near Kiel. Too many ships. However, she was now tied up in St Petersburg, and Charles Irwin was getting impatient. He had woken at 0700hrs, and had been told by the captain that he would be taken from the ship at about 0900hrs. At 0920hrs a car pulled up adjacent to the gangway.

Two men, from the SVR, greeted him, and took him immediately to the local HQ, where he was reunited with some of his clothes and personal items that had been collected from a 'friendly' dry cleaner in Fulham, West London.

Once properly dressed, he was taken to the Senior Officer SVR in St Petersburg, Colonel Egorkov, who reports directly to Director of SVR, Moscow, Mikhail Fradkov.

As a meeting it was strictly formal, a welcome to Russia, a firm handshake, followed by a brief man hug. Then information as to his journey to Moscow. He would be travelling on a military transport to avoid, at this time, any risk of exposure. Any exposure would be strictly staged, at an appropriate time, at some unspecified time in the future, in Moscow to the media. The meeting was thankfully short, and he was taken by car to Pulkova Airport, Military side, and boarded a transport aircraft for the flight to Moscow.

His new life was about to begin.

Moscow. Prince Park Hotel, not far from SVR HQ, Yasenevo.

Charles Urwin had arrived at the hotel, being driven from Vnukovo Airport, about ten miles distance, arriving at about 1530hrs. It was a 4* hotel, (Russian 4*), and he was shown to his room, and informed that a security detail would be posted outside his room overnight.

He would be able to relax on the Sunday, prior to being taken to SVR HQ on the Monday morning. He slept fitfully that night.

Sunday passed slowly, and he felt nervous as to the possible scenarios that could occur on the Monday. No matter what scenarios had been indicated to him in London, there was always the risk that such promises would not be kept in Moscow.

Bearing in mind his own value, as perceived by him, such value could be traded, and clearly demonstrated, enabling interpretation of Western Governments thinking behind bland and, at times, obfuscating statements of policy. This was something no Russian could do, or so he was thinking.

Monday 23rd June 2008. London.

Harry woke that morning irritable, and with an upset stomach, which he put down to a suspect curry, and a well-lubricated group of four men on an adjacent table discussing the relative merits of Arsenal and Chelsea soccer teams.

He reflected on his first week with IISG, and wondered, hypothetically, whether he had made the right decision. Same problems and challenges. Different name on the door and different address.

Snap out of it. Get up and on, and give Alain a call at DGSE, Paris, and bring him up to date.

At 1000hrs, in the office, he called the last telephone number he had for Alain. After giving his name to an automated request, the system let him in and Alain answered,

'Mon Dieu, mon vieux! Hullo, Harry. How are you? Where are you? What are you doing? Are you in Paris?'

Harry interrupted him, 'I will answer your questions, but not necessarily in the same order!'

Alain laughed, 'D'accord, allez!'

Harry spent a little while bringing Alain up to date with his new role, and questioned whether Alain got over to London occasionally.

'De temps en temps,' was the response. 'Pourquoi?'

'Perhaps a discussion over a meal and some wine, French, naturally.'

'When? Give me a date!' Alain replied.

Harry laughed, 'Let me get back to you in about a week, and we can firm up something, whether in London or Paris.'

'D'accord, à bientôt copain!'

Harry sat reflecting on his past relations with Alain, and thought that a re-established official/unofficial scenario could only be viewed as beneficial for IISG. He would keep the Director up to speed, which he did later that morning.

'First steps, Harry. Top brass in DGSE may not like the idea, but it is well worth a try as they were happy to work with you in the past. No doubt you will be contacting some of your other past allies?'

Harry explained that he had already contacted Jack DeCosta CIA, and David Hadar, Mossad London, discovering his old ally was now Station Chief London, but that there appeared to be a little reserve in David's response.

'Possibly wants to run it past a higher level before discussion,' the Director observed, 'wouldn't read too much into that.'

Harry said he would leave both for at least a week before following up. If higher approval was being sought, then that would give them time.

He was thinking about possible lines of co-operation when Jim Bolton's head appeared round the door.

'Morning Harry. Got a minute?'

'Of course, come in Jim, grab a seat. What is it?'

'As you can guess we get some funny peculiar ones from time to time. This is one of them.'

'Expand.'

'We have been approached, through a third party, concerning a large investment deal in the Far East. Gulf funds being handled by a Swiss bank, which appears to be a little out of the ordinary.'

Harry raised an eyebrow, 'Investment deal, Swiss bank, Gulf funds, Far East, a problem? Surely not?' he enquired sarcastically.

Jim smiled, 'Hear me out. The original funds came from the Gulf, links to a ruling family, etc. Problem appears to be frozen funds that cannot be released, because signatory to provide authority has disappeared without trace. Request to us was, can we help?'

'Well, what does the boss think?'

'He suggested I have a chat with you, bearing in mind your Gulf and Middle East experience.'

'Well, who am I to argue with the boss. Let's see if we can get some more details.'

The rest of the morning was spent trying to build some sort of Sitrep, although details at this stage were scarce. Initial confidential discussions with the Swiss bank London office would be vital, in order to build some sort of event timeline.

Harry asked Jim to clear and establish any required protocols through the original request, in order that direct communication could be established between IISG and the Swiss bank's London branch initially.

Harry wondered if this was another wild goose chase, culminating in the Gulf investor being found safe and well in the South of France, merely resting from the Gulf heat, in a friendly and accommodating 5* hotel, with a suitable companion!

It would not be the first time, or the last!

1000hrs SVR HQ Yasenevo, Moscow.

Charles had been collected from his hotel at 0930hrs, and now found himself in the ante-room to small conference room on the fourth floor of the SVR HQ.

He was to meet the Head of SVR, Director Mikhail Fradkov.

He was led into the conference room to see Fradkov standing at the head of the table, who greeted him in both Russian and English, grasping his hand in a very firm handshake. It was widely assumed that Fradkov had been a long-standing member of the KGB, and had previously served as a Prime Minister, before being appointed by President Putin to be Director of SVR.

He smiled and indicated a seat for Charles, dismissing the two officers that had brought him from his hotel. He was offered tea or coffee, and was asked if he was comfortable in his hotel.

Charles was just expanding on his journey and hotel, when a separate door opened and a tall, erect man, wearing glasses, entered. Charles recognised him immediately.

It was Sergey Lavrov, Russia's Foreign Minister, well-known and well respected around the world, multi-lingual, a tough negotiator, but a man who aimed, generally, but extremely firmly, for a working compromise. Having shaken Fradkov's hand and exchanged some pleasantries in Russian, he turned towards Charles, now in fluent English,

'Mr Urwin, I am delighted to see you. Welcome to Moscow. I am so glad to see that you have made such a positive decision as to your professional career since our meeting in September last year.

Bearing in mind your accumulated experience over the years, it will, I am sure, greatly assist us in the interpretation of foreign policy, whether of the United Kingdom, the USA, the EU, or specific members of the EU.'

Charles had been so surprised to see Foreign Minister Lavrov in attendance that it took him a few seconds to respond, as he thought, in a professional manner appropriate to the situation.

'Foreign Minister, it is indeed a pleasure to meet you again, and I hope, no, I am sure, that my contribution within SVR, or any other area where you believe my skills are appropriate, will support the foreign policy ambitions of Russia.'

It was at this point that Lavrov shook his hand, saying, 'I will leave you now with Director Fradkov. I am sure that you have much to discuss.'

With that, Lavrov turned to Fradkov, exchanging a few further words in Russian, before exiting by the main door.

The meeting then resumed, in English.

Thursday 26th June 2008.1000hrs, Banque Roubert, London.

Harry and Jim sat in a small, but expensively furnished office, in the City of London branch of the Swiss bank, Banque Roubert. The bank had asked for complete confidentiality, both in writing, and now verbally.

'You do understand, I am sure, that complete confidentiality, involving our bank, is essential to protect our 200-year reputation with our existing clients.'

These words were uttered by a young man, Hugo Padgett, probably about 35 years of age, impeccably suited and cuffed, with a manner that could only be described as both superior and obsequious, at one and the same time.

Years of practice from an early age, Harry thought. Probably inbred, bearing in mind his research had shown that the uncle of this particular example was Chairman of the bank, its HQ being based in Lausanne.

Monkeys and organ grinders sprang to Harry's mind as he and Jim started their initial questioning.

'Will you please take us through the investment process from the very beginning?'

'Naturally,' was the response. And how detailed would that be, thought Harry.

'Our protocols for such transactions are robust, thorough and extremely detailed, developed over many years which have established our cast–iron reputation throughout Europe, and many other regions of the world.'

Harry interrupted at this point,

'I am sure that they are, and we do not need convincing of your international integrity, but we are here for a reason. Something, somewhere, within the system and protocols, has failed, and your bank is in a cleft stick. This is where we come in, and why we are meeting today. Now, can we go through, in as much detail as possible, the actual chain of events and processes that occurred from Day One until now?'

Hugo's face reflected his feelings only too well to the question, but he obviously thought that nothing could be gained by an over sensitive reaction at this stage. He took them through, verbally, what had happened over the period, Harry only interjecting once, to ask that copies of all instructions, emails, etc, be made available following the meeting.

At the end of his explanation of events, Hugo paused briefly, before saying, 'There is one issue that none of us in the bank understand, and have no idea, or evidence, as to how, or why, it happened.'

'Which is?' asked Harry.

'An amount of four and a half million dollars was transferred from the originally specified investment amount of three hundred and fifty million dollars to a small bank in Beirut, Lebanon. Correct protocols were used, but no originator is evident. That is the conundrum.'

'And you have no idea why, and for what purpose, the transfer was made?'

'No.'

'Bearing in mind this sort of transaction often involves commissions, could this be one?'

'No details as to any commissions have been given to us, and no reference was made within any documentation.'

'You have full details of the receiving bank in Beirut?'

'Yes.'

'Then please include that information with what we have requested.'

The discussion continued, mostly of a speculative nature, until it was clear that no further information was available from the bank and that forensic analysis of documentation, or more specifically, digital digging, in a number of foreign jurisdictions, might bear some fruit.

On the way back to the office Harry and Jim mulled over what they had been told. Jim was suspecting the usual scam of ripping off amounts from large transfers, but no action had been taken by the Lebanese bank, only advising Lausanne they had received it. At the same time, they had advised Lausanne that any attempt to move the deposit would be blocked.

Usual culprits sprang to mind, Hamas and Hezbollah among them, who were developing more sophisticated ways of acquiring funds for their operations. Shia Hezbollah, backed by Iran, controlled large areas of Lebanon, whereas Sunni Hamas, backed by the Gulf States, was essentially confined to Gaza. Both, however, on an inconsistent basis, put their religious differences to one side in their common goal of the destruction of Israel.

Harry listened, but, in his mind, the scenario made no sense at all. Let's see what data we have when all communications are provided to us by the bank, he thought.

*

CIA HQ, Langley, Virginia.

Paul Frere had called Jack into his office, 'Something caught my eye yesterday, which, connected with the conversation you and I had the other day, concerned your friend Harry Baxter.'

'The connection?'

'Yes. Our station chief in our Moscow Embassy pushed through a report that might have a bearing on your man. It appears from some overheard gossip, electronic digital that is, that there is somebody coming into Moscow from the UK.

Additionally, it is not someone from Government to Government, but somebody in their slang, 'under wraps'. Why don't you contact Baxter, unofficially, and see if he has heard anything which might be relevant?'

'I copy that. Leave it with me.'

Friday 27th June 2008.1300hrs. IISG London.

Harry's phone rang. It was Jack DeCosta. 'Afternoon Harry, can you move your phone onto a security level?'

Having complied, Jack then explained what had been picked up in Moscow, and wondered if there had been any indications in London that might make some sort of connection.

Harry took a neutral position, even though he wondered if there was one between the CIA query and the Charles Urwin disappearance. He promised to get back to Jack soonest, and thanked him for thinking of IISG, and himself, in this instance.

Jack replied, 'Well, bearing in mind it's early days with this piece of Intel, a conversation with an old working buddy seemed like a good idea, before we push it through official channels from Langley to London.'

'Less of the old, if you don't mind, but I do get your drift!'

Harry went straight to the Director. Outlining the conversation with Jack he then observed,

'Recognising the co-incidence with respect to timing, there may be no connection, but I would have thought we could put a few flies on the water with 5 and 6, and/or GCHQ, to see whether their trawls have picked up anything. But, as a new boy with IISG, I need your approval, or I hand it to you to cast the fly at a higher level?'

He looked questioningly at the Director, who paused before replying,

'Yes, leave that one with me Harry.'

***

III

July 2008.

Wednesday 2nd July 2008. 1000hrs. DGSE HQ, Paris.

Alain Dubois was sitting patiently in his Director's office as his superior scanned the file in front of him.

Finally, the Director looked up, 'Bien Alain, what do you want to do?'

'D'accord. I have worked very well with Baxter on several occasions in the past when he was an officer in their SIS.

He is now in IISG with his old boss from SIS who is Director Europe, but covering, as well, Middle East and Gulf. With the increased demands on all of us I would recommend that a working relationship and understanding is agreed. I understand that there can be no official acknowledgement of such an arrangement, but I trust him and his Director.'

There was a slight pause before Alain's Director replied,

'I understand and agree to your request, which will be noted in your file. However, please ensure your contact is aware, that if any situation arises that could compromise our public standing and reputation, then a full denial will be our official response. Understood?'

Alain agreed, and thanked his Director for his official/unofficial approval.

He called Harry later that morning,

'Bonjour Harry, remember our conversation last week? We never had it, but I think we can work together, but not officially. You understand? Anything gets too public, we deny everything. If you agree to that, then we can definitely co-operate!'

He laughed, 'Nothing like that stopped us in the past, eh?'

'Many thanks for that Alain, let's keep in touch on a regular basis.'

Harry put down his phone. Good, he thought, one down, a few more to go.

His phone rang. It was the Director asking him to come to his office.

'Morning Harry. Following our discussion last week, I have been trying to cast a few flies on the water with our ex-department, and others, to try and determine what is the current Sitrep and, perhaps more importantly, current thinking and potential reactions.'

Harry made no comment, merely retaining, he hoped, a facial expression of interest.

The Director continued,

'In summary, blocking at every turn. No comment, just evasive, a combination of pleading ignorance, and any comments or observations will be made in due course.

First we've heard of it, or, with the FCO, perhaps some confusion as to assignment, and/or leave/vacation! Usual short-term blocking whilst they race around trying to find out what's happened!'

'No surprises there then!' Harry commented, 'Leaked enquiry to us to see if we've heard anything, then denial, and trying to shut stable door after horse has bolted. Classic! I can see an egg on face scenario with this one!'

'O.K. Harry, let's not be too hasty. Let us do a little more digging, quietly of course, and see what we can turn up. I'll leave that with you then. Decide who you want to assist.'

Returning to his office Harry was trying to determine what, if anything, the Director had been able to extract from his previous professional contacts in 5, 6, GCHQ, FCO, etc. It was pretty obvious that the first reactions had been to close ranks, pull up the drawbridge, and keep the outsiders outside. Yet, the original contact had been made by the FCO, admittedly, by an old contact of Jim's, perhaps unofficially, in the initial concern of Urwin's disappearance.

The Russia/Georgia major standoff could be a player in this, bearing in mind Urwin's expertise and experience. Best get up to date with that first, thought Harry, as he lifted his phone to call Jim.

After confirming a meeting with Jim for that afternoon, Harry updated himself on the developing stand-off between Russia and Georgia.

By April 2008 a major crisis was looming between Russia, led by Putin, and the Republic of Georgia, with its pro-Western Government.

South Ossetia and Abkhazia separatists in Georgia, backed by Russia, were clamouring for self-determining republic status, and diplomatic relations between Russia and Georgia were in free-fall, a deliberate and intensifying programme fuelled by Russia. Current status was described as highly fragile, with outcomes ranging from 'civil breakdown' to 'military resolution'.

Not a pretty picture, thought Harry, as he reflected on the current update.

That afternoon

Jim and Harry were some way through their meeting concerning the Gulf banking brief, when Harry suddenly changed tack,

'I was thinking earlier today about our man Charles Urwin, and your contact at the FCO. Whilst respecting confidentiality on your part, can you give me some idea of the level your man/woman holds there? And secondly, was there a specific suggestion on their part for him/her to contact you for a bit of fishing?'

'No. As far as I could gather, my contact, who I have known well for many years, was not instructed to contact me. They merely wondered if the news had leaked out. I advised them that we had not heard anything.'

'I like the 'them and they' Jim,' Harry said, smiling slightly, 'What's a little more curious is the negative reaction by the FCO when the Director spoke with his contacts. Basically blanked, as far as I can gather. OK, put that to one side. Back to the Gulf.'

At this stage Harry decided not to include Jim on the content of Jack DeCosta's phone call.

Having gone through, in detail, all documentation, electronic and written, provided by the London branch of the Swiss Lausanne Bank, Harry was keen to provide the Director with an update, and plan 'next steps.' One unusual area was the Beirut bank and why an amount had been transferred there, with apparently no specific recipient, and with no record of transmission.

Thursday 3rd July 2008. 0930hrs. Director's office.

Harry had pulled electronic and physical files together for the Director, and had covered in detail, various facts, observations and opinions, following the meeting at the London branch of Banque Roubert.

'Right Harry, give me your summary and suggestion.'

'OK. Currently we do not have enough information. The London office merely acted as a Post Office. Lausanne would be able to provide more, I'm sure. And, they must have some more details, and info, as to why a particular transfer was made to the Beirut bank. We can request details, but I would think a face to face with the major players would be better. My Director, I know, could extract maximum information, I'm sure.'

Harry spoke the last line with a smile on his lips, but he was serious.

The Director smiled too. 'All right Harry, leave this with me. I'll get back to you once I've digested all this,' he said, waving at the file and his laptop.

Friday 4th July 2008. SVR HQ Yasenevo, Moscow.

Almost two weeks had elapsed since Charles Urwin first entered SVR HQ in Moscow. He was finding things frustrating, very slow, and very bureaucratic.

A number of discussions had been held with Mikhail Fradkov, Director SVR, as to where his skills and experience could be best employed. No firm decision had been taken as yet, but three Directorates had been identified as possible alternatives.

Directorate I.: Intelligence Data & Analysis. Daily summary for the President.

Directorate of Economic Intelligence: Country Specific.

Directorate PR: Political Intelligence: Country Specific.

Directorate I was certainly the preference in Urwin's mind. Daily Summaries for the President. A clear opportunity to demonstrate his value, expertise and intellectual rigour across a broad canvas.

Meanwhile he was being shown apartments. Very average, but early days. However, he would have to make a decision soon. Life was going to be very different, but, no doubt, very challenging living the true cause.

*

Tuesday 8th July 2008. IISG HQ, London.

'Come in Harry,' the Director called, as he waved Harry to a chair, 'I've been thinking about this Lausanne bank challenge. You will go to Lausanne, and pose all the awkward questions you can think of. I can, after you have dug out some facts, and they have complained that you were rather brusque and somewhat aggressive, then apologise on your behalf, excusing your actions as professional enthusiasm.

Now let's discuss some of the detail you will be after. First, request a meeting with the bank in Lausanne, and get that at the highest level you can. If you need me to push that. Shout!

Secondly, push and push with your enquiry and questions. Insist on, as wide as possible, discussions with everybody concerned and involved, whether in Lausanne or elsewhere. If we are to earn our fees we need to get under their collective skin. I'm sure you appreciate what I am saying. Understood?'

Harry was in no doubt.

That afternoon Harry made some notes to use in his telephone discussion with the bank in Lausanne, when arranging the future meeting.

Then he called David Hadar at Mossad London. On this occasion he felt that he and David were back to their old relationship, with no obvious signs of reserve.

'I'm starting to settle in and get my feet under the table here at IISG, and wondered if we could have a meal and a catch up, if you agree?'

'Definitely Harry, suggest a date.'

'What about Thursday?'

'Fine with me. Where do you suggest?'

Harry suggested a small Italian restaurant he knew, not far from David's base in South Kensington, meeting at 1930hrs. That was confirmed, with both indicating they were looking forward to a convivial update. Harry had just put his phone down when it rang, this time it being Jack DeCosta from Washington.

'Hi Harry. Surprise, Surprise. I'm going to be in London next week. Can we meet?'

'I think so, but I have a meeting in Lausanne coming up which might interfere, but unlikely. Give me a shout once you are in London, OK?'

'OK, I'll get back to you.'

After his telephone calls to Banque Roubert in London and Lausanne, it was agreed his meeting in Lausanne would start on Tuesday morning the 22nd July, this providing sufficient time for Lausanne to ensure that all individuals involved would be available. He would fly to Geneva on Monday the 21st.

Foreign & Commonwealth Office, London.

Quentin Horncastle was under the cosh. When the proverbial hits the fan, and responsibility is to be assigned, then there is nothing better to watch than a theatre of civil servants, top to bottom, left to right, covering themselves, as far as is possible, with an impenetrable fire-proof coating. Obfuscation rules, and the more impenetrable the better.

Checks at airports, docks, and railway stations had produced nothing concerning the disappearance of Charles Urwin. No evidence at his apartment indicated anything, other than that he was no longer there.

His mobile phone had been left on his desk, which was taken away for analysis, but nothing untoward was evident from that.

Nothing but blanks at present, and the finger of blame returning from time to time to focus on Quentin, and his ill-defined role of keeping a weather eye on Charles. Situations, such as this, guarantee that collegiate action is rapidly ignored in order to ensure personal self-preservation.

The slippery pole is getting very slippery, he thought.

David Knowles, FCO, career diplomat, unmarried, ornithologist, generally reliable, does not make waves, prepares excellent policy papers, third tour in Moscow, was out feeding the birds in the park near the UK Embassy.

As he passed the three-foot-high chess pieces on a giant sized forty-foot by forty-foot chess board, he felt a small vibration in his right pocket, caused by his receiver picking up the signal from the middle of the chess board.

He smiled to himself. No doubt confirmation of safe passage of a recent package from the UK. Good to know, a friend and fellow traveller was on board.

That evening. Italian Restaurant, Kensington, London.

Harry and David Hadar shook hands warmly. David even gave Harry a friendly slap on the back.

'Good to see you again, old friend,' said David.

'A little less of the old if you don't mind,' retorted Harry, 'Everybody, well you're the second or third in the last few days, has decided I'm an old friend, or an old colleague, or in French, just old!'

'OK, settle for mature?' They both laughed.

Over dinner they brought each other up to date with their respective roles, interspersed, from time to time, with observations on current theatres of operations. Harry spelt out what IISG were looking for in an on-going relationship, and, as far as could be determined by David's response, this would not be a problem with Mossad. In fact, it would be encouraged.

Harry described the current scenario with an absent senior FCO official, no name being provided, and asked that if any intel sourced by Mossad, even if it only indicated a tenuous connection, could he please be advised?

David confirmed that effective from now he had Senior Officer agreement for co-operation in most areas, and would liaise on a regular basis, which he expected would be reciprocated by IISG.

They parted after dinner, the relationship and confidence restored to a practical operational level. Harry would confirm that to the Director on Friday.

The parked car, about thirty-five yards from the restaurant, waited until they had disappeared, before starting its engine and moving slowly away.

Friday 11th July 2008. IISG HQ, London.

Harry brought the Director up to speed with what had been agreed with David Hadar the previous evening. It was clear that their future relationship had the approval of Mossad Control, so that IISG could liaise on a regular basis with exchange of intel and also flagging of potential joint interest scenarios.

The Director nodded as Harry finished, 'Good. Get some of these connections nailed, and operational, and it will almost be like the old firm, Mk II!'

Harry agreed, whilst also bringing him up to date on Jack DeCosta's visit the following week.

'I'll obviously meet up with him whilst he's here, and see if there is anything additionally, they have picked up on the 'under wraps' Moscow link. I'm sure you've seen the dates for my meeting in Lausanne. I can see that will probably take a few days, bearing in mind who they will be pulling in.'

'Fine Harry, just keep me posted, and up to speed. If anybody in Washington IISG HQ starts asking questions, I need the answers, or, at least, a very current Sitrep. Understood?'

'Completely.'

Tuesday 15th July 2008. IISG HQ, London.

Harry took the call at about midday. It was Jack DeCosta.

'Hi Harry, what about dinner tonight? And, before you answer, no excuses!'

'Alright Jack, no arguments. La Barca, Waterloo, 8 o'clock, don't be late!'

During their conversation over dinner, Jack was able to fill in Harry on the working relationship between the CIA and IISG in Washington. Not surprisingly, IISG contains a number of ex-CIA officers, well experienced in a number of international postings and assignments. The working relationship was excellent, with high degrees of trust extended by both parties to each other.

'What's top of your list currently?' Jack enquired.

'Two things at various boiling stages. The FCO one, which is currently quiet; a European bank investment investigation which involves KSA and Lebanon, very current; and whatever hits my desk tomorrow,' replied Harry.

'By the way Harry, there could be some connection between your European investment bank, and an ongoing investigation in the States.'

'Such as?'

'On behalf of the State Department we are investigating the international, and illegal, operations of two major French banks with Iran, Libya, Sudan, and Cuba. Perhaps there could be a link?'

'I'll certainly keep that in mind.'

'OK. So, Harry, what's your view on the current slugfest building between Russia and Georgia? Is it likely to calm down, or escalate?'

'From my limited overview, it is not looking particularly calm, as Russia is ramping up the rhetoric daily, and with various incursions into Georgia by South Ossetian forces, preceded by occasional artillery shelling. Whether somebody will intervene, I do not know. Perhaps Jack, you know more than me?'

'No sir, not me,' said Jack, raising his hands in mock surrender.

'Well, you would say that, wouldn't you?'

'Only if you asked me!'

Rapport established, Harry felt comfortable, so that if push came to shove, he could always rely on Jack for the helping hand.

Friday 18th July 2008. SVR HQ, Moscow.

The meeting was very tiring.

Charles was seated on one side of the table with his interpreter, whilst on the other side the Director of Directorate I was outlining the scope of his activities and responsibilities if Charles were to be selected.

Vetting in SVR was a slow, laborious, bureaucratic process, but hardly surprising he thought. A fourth man was taking notes as the meeting proceeded.

The Director pulled his papers together. He spoke in Russian which was translated by the interpreter, 'I will advise you of my decision next week.' He stood up and left the room with his note-taker, leaving Charles with the interpreter.

Monday 21st July 2008. Lausanne, Switzerland.

Harry had arrived in Lausanne, flying into Geneva, and then taking the train.

He had telephoned Banque Roubert, and was pleased to hear that a meeting was planned, starting at 1000hrs on Tuesday the 22nd, and that all relevant personnel would be available during that day for questioning.

He had prepared his basic dossier covering all the main elements, with a quartet of basic questions and various subsets, dependent on relevant responsibility and seniority of management being questioned. Should be quite interesting, he thought, dependent on the directness/evasiveness of the person being questioned.

Tuesday 22nd July 2008. Banque Roubert, Lausanne, Switzerland.

By midday Harry was feeling very disappointed. Nothing was forthcoming from his questioning. Even when venturing into the realms of speculation.

The only suggestion was to take up the issue directly with the Lebanese bank.

By 1630hrs Harry had finished and left the bank with copies of all documents, email communications, and transfer details and dates. He just made an evening return flight to London Heathrow from Geneva, he had to admit, in not the best frame of mind.

Not much more to go on, where does IISG go from here? Beirut?

That afternoon. FCO Westminster, London.

The internal investigation committee, formed following the disappearance of Charles Urwin, was becoming more fractious between its members, as the lack of any intelligence from the police or security services threw no light as to the reason, or possible locations.

Concern of collective 'red faces' is always a great stimulus within civil service structures, and this was no exception. 'In camera' meetings were scheduled with police and security services, but most committee members knew that this was just a holding action.

As always, things must be seen to be done.

*

Russian-Georgian Border

As the rhetoric, both public and electronic, increased between Moscow and Tbilisi, Russian military reconnaissance patrols, at night, were frequently venturing into Georgia, testing responses, if any, and determining military resources and dispositions.

*

Wednesday 23rd July 2008. SVR HQ, Moscow.

Charles Urwin had been called to a meeting scheduled for 1000hrs that morning. He was expecting, as a matter of course, to receive confirmation that his appointment to SVR Directorate I was agreed.

He was shown into the empty Director's office by the secretary, and sat down at the conference table.

He was more than surprised, but very pleased, when the Director entered, accompanied by Sergey Lavrov, the Foreign Minister. He maintained a pleasant, but inscrutable, expression on his face as they both sat down, Lavrov clearly taking the senior position on the table.

Lavrov opened the discussion, 'The Director speaks highly of you, and your position in Directorate I, in his opinion, should be confirmed.'

Charles half-opened his mouth to respond, but checked himself as Lavrov raised his hand, a small smile playing on his lips,

39

'However, Mr Urwin, I have overruled the Director. I have a more specific and challenging initial role for you on behalf of Mother Russia. Before taking up your position in Directorate I, you will be lecturing and briefing our officers at the SVR Institute on all matters covering UK foreign policy, the structure of your FCO, career path planning, and most importantly selection of candidates, not only for the FCO, but also for your Security Service MI5, and Secret Intelligence Service MI6.'

Charles' face started to turn puce, whilst at the same time his anger was only just held in check. He tried to collect his thoughts and composure in order to make a civil response.

He replied, with an obvious edge in his voice,

'How can I do that? I am not a university lecturer, nor would I wish to be. This assignment was never discussed, and would have been rejected by me if it had been mooted. It has all the appearance of reneging on our agreement.'

There was a pause before Lavrov replied, on this occasion his voice carrying an icy but obvious tone,

'I think Mr Urwin, you should realise by your recent choice of leaving the UK, that at this stage any choice as to your role and activity is to be decided by me. And that is final.'

Lavrov then finished by saying that full details would be discussed with him within a few days. Meanwhile, he suggested, Charles should start preparing some basic notes and format for his potential role at the Institute, located north of Chelebityevo, about 20 miles outside Moscow.

Friday 25ᵗʰ July 2008. Moscow.

For the first time since his arrival Charles was left to his own devices that Friday, so asked if he could go for a walk in the park adjacent to his hotel. His personal security and movement were rigidly enforced so a formal request had to be made. This was finally given, but his 'minder' would be accompanying him.

They left the hotel at about 3.00pm, the minder keeping station about ten paces behind. After about half an hour Charles started to feel a pain in his stomach which increased over the next ten minutes. A possible food poisoning, something doesn't agree with me, he thought. He indicated to his minder that he wished to use the public toilet situated about 100 metres away close to the far perimeter of the park, near an ornamental access gate. The request was acknowledged with a curt nod of the head.

Charles entered one of the cubicles and locked the door. After about three minutes he thought he heard a muffled thud. The sort of sound you associate with a closing door. He ignored it. His stomach pain had ceased. He was relieved. After flushing the toilet, he unlocked the door and started to exit.

The first thing he saw to the right of his cubicle, was the body of the minder stretched out on the floor, apparently unconscious. He glanced quickly to his left to see a balaclava clad figure moving very quickly towards him, who bundled him back into his toilet, a smelly gloved hand now over his mouth, followed by a painful jab into his left arm, causing him to start to lose consciousness. Before he passed out, he could see another balaclava clad figure appear behind the first; then blackness descended.

Monday 28th July 2008. Location unknown.

Charles Urwin lay strapped on a bed, sweat pouring off him. His mental condition, recognised by himself, was not good. He had regained consciousness, but had no idea how long he had been drugged. He had no idea how long he had been there, and with no window in the room whether it was night or day.

41

Masked armed men came at regular intervals with food and water. No words were spoken. There was a toilet in the corner of the room. When it was needed a masked armed man stood and watched him. He assumed he was still in Russia, kidnapped for what purpose he could not imagine, by whom, and with no idea as to what would eventuate. From time to time his mind raced over a number of frightening scenarios, creating, by panic, uncontrolled body tremors, sweating and shivering cycles.

His scrambled mind tried to examine his situation. Was this a straightforward kidnap for money, which if denied would result in his probable death? Or, was this something orchestrated by Lavrov/SVR which if broadcast would embarrass the UK Government? Was this what had been planned all along? What options did he have? Nil or less. Lavrov would be dictating everything, over, or in which, he would have no influence or control.

Two obvious and conflicting scenarios filled his mind, dependent on whether Lavrov wanted to chronically embarrass the UK Government, or to continue to infiltrate it. His mind raced around a number of permutations based on the two contradicting options. React, as best I can, as events unfurl, was the only thing he could do. Such a thought did not fill him with any degree of confidence, certainly not at this stage.

Wednesday 30th July 2008. SVR HQ, Moscow.

The Director SVR, Mikhail Fradkov, was speaking in a slow icy tone, that left no room for doubt as to his opinion of the debacle of Charles Urwin's disappearance,

'From the evidence so far, and verbal description from the injured security, this is a typical Bratva kidnapping. How they obtained sufficient intelligence to carry this out will result in a full investigation to determine where such an accidental, or deliberate, leak occurred.

I have instructed specialist teams to pursue local known Bratva connections, both high and low, without exception.'

At this point he glared at his Directors, 'I hope my orders are quite clear. No exceptions.'

All, without exception, had their heads down, and were writing furiously.

Thursday 31ˢᵗ July 2008. FCO Westminster, London.

An internal flap was building as a result of the situation in Georgia. A Red Alert was flagged. Intelligence coming through from the UK's Georgian Embassy was indicating a significant escalation in the skirmishes between Russian backed separatists and Georgian military.

Russian radio was pumping out inflammatory news broadcasts accusing Georgia of aggression against South Ossetia, and threatening that such actions 'would not be tolerated, and that Georgia should expect a hard response if continued.'

Various Foreign Ministers of a number of European countries, and the USA, were in regular contact and consultation, each being fed intelligence from their respective embassies. Pressure was increasing, as they could not see a way for this situation to be cooled down in the short term, particularly with the current rhetoric being employed.

IISG London. Update on Banque Roubert.

Harry explained, as quickly as he could, what had not been achieved by his meeting with Banque Roubert. The Director looked disappointed, which he expressed, but commented,

'Frankly in some ways I'm not surprised. Let me think on this, bearing in mind our clients' requests. I'll get back to you shortly.'

***

IV

August 2008.

Friday 1ˢᵗ August 2008. UK Embassy, Tbilisi, Georgia.

Intelligence being gathered by the UK Defence Attaché indicated that Russian forces, contrary to international laws, had crossed the Russo-Georgian border and advanced into the south Ossetian conflict zone.

Initial Russian units were now being augmented by additional forces on a daily and nightly basis, and were clearly working to an agreed military strategy with South Ossetian military units.

'Extreme Concern' was being flagged back to London, and shared with friendly, and similarly concerned Governments. If the situation were to spiral into conflict it would, in all probability, be imminent.

With the public Russian declarations and accusations of aggression by Georgia against South Ossetia, it could be triggered in the next few days. Russia kept repeating their threat of 'Peace Enforcement' unless Georgia responded quickly with a 'Diplomatic' solution acceptable to both sides.

Monday 4ᵗʰ August 2008. SVR HQ, Moscow.

One team had been fortunate. SVR had hit the streets of Moscow targeting known or suspected members of Bratva. With their Director Mikhail Fradkov's order clearly recalled, subtlety was removed.

About 10 kms from the HQ, at roughly midnight, a small restaurant, clearly closed for the night, suddenly found its door smashed down, as a balaclava wearing team entered, shouting instructions, all carrying a mix of small arms.

The owner of the restaurant was 'entertaining' some friends in a back room.

The operation was over in less than ten minutes, as eight people were arrested, blindfolded, and bundled into SVR armoured vehicles. Shouts of protestation were met with gagging, or a heavy punch.

A number of similar actions took place in various areas of Moscow, but it was the one at the restaurant that bore fruit.

Tuesday 5th August 2008. FCO Westminster, London.

Quentin Horncastle was being put on the spot by the UK Foreign Minister, David Miliband.

'Quentin, I have been advised that you had, what could be described as a mentoring or overview role for Charles Urwin? Is that correct?'

'Yes, Foreign Secretary.'

'His most recent appointment was as First Secretary to our Embassy in Moscow, and was on some UK leave when he disappeared?'

'Yes, Foreign Secretary.'

'Can you throw any light at all, on what may have happened to him, and any other observations that you may have, that could indicate any possible reasons, or connections, as to his disappearance?'

'At the present time Foreign Secretary, none whatsoever.'

'Disappointing,' Milliband observed.

'Foreign Secretary, currently we have a number of specialist staff, Police, and both Security Services, investigating his disappearance, and I would assure you that I will report back immediately on receipt of any information that will explain this unfortunate set of circumstances.'

The Foreign Secretary looked up from the file he was reading,

'Thank you, Quentin. I look forward to your updates on a regular basis. Good luck.'

Quentin walked back to his office, confident that a holding action had been achieved, but for how long? The one thing he knew, was that at some time in the future, the full story would emerge, and on that occasion would the UK Government give thanks, or disapprobation?

Thursday 7th August 2008. SVR HQ, Moscow.

Interrogation had, after two days, increased in severity, and one person in particular was beginning to talk. He was one of the 'diners' arrested at the restaurant.

He was a driver of one of the 'Special' cars owned by certain members of Bratva. Special meant a number of things, or options. Large, with more powerful engines; bullet proof bodies, windscreens and windows, and a hidden compartment for weapons, drugs, or a person. This was normally located under a raised boot floor and extending under the rear seats.

During his physical interrogation he admitted that he had driven a Special containing a hidden person from Moscow to a house southeast of the city, about 50kms distant, and yes, he could remember its location. He provided the address and was then thrown into a cell.

Two SVR teams left Moscow for that address.

*

Friday 8th August 2008. 50kms SE of Moscow.

At 3.45am Friday morning the lead SVR team smashed down the front door of an unprepossessing house located on the edge of a village, and stormed in. The second team were covering the rear.

46

Despite curtains, furniture, and evidence of recent occupancy, no evidence was found to link the building with either captors, or Charles Urwin. The two SVR teams then returned to Moscow after details had been passed to their HQ.

Georgia

On the morning of the 8th, August, Russia launched a large land, air, and sea invasion on Georgia on the pretext of 'Peace Enforcement'.

The Russian Navy blockaded part of the Georgian coastline, and Russian Air Force attacks were also made on areas not in dispute.

The diplomatic channels between Western European countries and also the USA, were feverish with activity, with an urgent need to resolve such a tinderbox scenario as quickly as possible.

Monday 11th August 2008. IISG, London.

The Director called Harry to his office at about 1030hrs,

'Things are never what they seem,' he said, with a small smile on his lips.

Harry adopted a querying look as the Director continued, 'Banque Roubert is, according to our client, the tip of the iceberg. The transaction, that resulted in the receipt by the Lebanese bank, was probably a mistake, by persons unknown, trying to organise, what might be described as 'commissions' for services rendered. What has subsequently come to light, courtesy of an internal whistle-blower, is a money laundering/hot money transfer from various sources into, and through, safe Western Europe banking havens.

Essentially Harry, this has developed into a major investigation as to sources, receiving banks, and credibility of those banks. There will be not only banking, but political repercussions, as a direct result of

47

this operation. Once I have clear instructions and the scope of the investigation we will be carrying out, I will brief you fully. Suffice it to say Harry, clear your desk. This is a 24/7 operation.'

He paused,

'Good Lord, I hate that 24/7 description. Stop me next time you hear me say it.'

'Copy that Director, I think we're done!'

'Don't you start Harry!'

**

Monday 11th August 2008. SVR HQ, Moscow.

The meeting was not going well, Mikhail Fradkov SVR Director was in his most quiet and deadly mode. His senior officers had their eyes fixed on their pads as they wrote furiously, thereby avoiding the possibility of any eye contact.

He was summarising the situation as he saw it, from levels of incompetence to the possibility of collusion with enemies of the State. Not an area of discussion in that any of them wished to be involved.

He reconfirmed his original instructions, this time ordering that the net should be spread wider, with oblique suggestions as to possible reassignments if no satisfactory results were achieved. Everybody was under no illusions as to consequences of failure.

Monday/Tuesday 11-12th August 2008. EU HQ, Brussels.

24-hour activity had occurred over the weekend at the HQ of the European Union, the current Presidency of which was held by France, in the person of President Nicolas Sarkozy. It was hoped a Cease-Fire Agreement could be negotiated between Russia and Georgia, and all diplomatic actions were being taken to make this happen on Tuesday 12th August 2008.

Finally, on Tuesday it happened, and a collective, but nervous sigh of relief, was heard around Europe.

Wednesday 13th August 2008. IISG HQ, London.

Harry was called by the Director for a meeting at 0930hrs. The Director was reading a report as Harry entered.

'Sit down Harry, but pour yourself a coffee whilst I finish this,' he said waving the report.

Silence was maintained for about five minutes before the Director looked up.

'Hmm', was the noise made, as the Director expelled air.

'Right Harry. This is quite complicated, but you will be able to read this report at your leisure when we are finished, and I hope you and I will share the same interpretation.'

Harry made no comment.

'You recall our discussion last week concerning Banque Roubert?', he continued, without waiting for a response, 'We have been provided with more information which only increases the complexity of the investigation, and which will make our position and actions all the more difficult and riskier. Let me take you through what is understood so far, although I think understood might be stretching a point.'

The Director rose and poured himself a cup of coffee before continuing,

'Remembering what I said last week Harry, the transaction which finished up in Beirut, was assumed (a) to be a mistake, and /or (b) probably/possibly a payoff for services rendered.'

Harry nodded in agreement.

49

'What we have now is a labyrinth of actions and transactions that are all part of the same murky mix.

Banque Roubert, in their further internal investigations, believe there could be a link between the Lebanon receipt and another major transaction that is giving them an additional headache.

I will explain. They had received a major transfer of funds from Jeddah, Saudi Arabia, the covering information described it as a potential investment in South East Asia.

Source of funds was described as a minor member of the ever-increasing number of the Saudi Royal Family. Onward transmission of the funds depended on the authority and sign off by the Saudi Royal.'

At this point the Director sighed before continuing,

'However, this Royal has disappeared over five weeks ago, and the transfer has therefore not taken place.'

He paused again, 'Bearing in mind the position of this Royal in Jeddah, eyebrows were raised in the bank at the amount that was being transferred as an initial investment in South East Asia.

The amount was in excess of $350m dollars, a considerable sum for the individual to call on, and secondly, what was the investment in South East Asia? No information to hand, currently. With me so far Harry?'

Harry nodded, 'With you so far. Where does it go from here?'

The Director smiled, 'Prepare for further bumps in the road, it gets quite bumpy! We now move into the rather grey areas of international banking, where, in certain countries, discretion and fees overcome good banking practice, checks, balances, and probity.

Another connection in all of this is the knowledge that there are a number of routes for the transfer of funds from former soviet bloc

50

countries, now stand-alone, and theoretically independent, to European mainstream bank subsidiaries operating in these countries.

I do not have to spell out to you Harry, I'm sure, where most of these deposits come from. Such is the complexity and sensitivity of this information, that I am keeping it, at this stage, solely between you and me. I will be considering how we can proceed to assist our client, meanwhile read this report which I will send you on our internal network. Understood?'

'So far, and hugely complex. And, may I say, probably more than a one-person assignment.'

'Yes Harry, that's why I need some thinking time on how we can handle this with our current team capacity. We will discuss further on Wednesday, same time.'

Harry left, thinking that one should never be surprised at what comes down the road. Complex variations on a theme. Their name is definitely legion, for they are definitely many!

Friday 15th August 2008. Bratva (Russian Mafia), Moscow.

As is well known the reach of Bratva extends through all levels of government and society in Russia; information is rewarded in many ways; however, loyalty, if broken, carries the ultimate sanction.

Rumours of a kidnapping gone wrong were starting to circulate among a small group of Bratva members, with instructions from the centre ordering fast resolution.

Otherwise, having to resist attacks by SVR would prove costly to Bratva, and bring summary resolution to the kidnappers.

*

Tuesday 19th August 2008. Somewhere unknown.

On Saturday, Charles Urwin awoke from a deep drug induced sleep, confirming the date as the 19th from his watch.

He looked around the room. Basic furniture, one small window with external blind, also what looked like a walk-in shower bathroom with toilet.

He raised himself into a sitting position fighting the nausea as he did. He tried to stand, and eventually succeeded, stumbling into the shower room where he retched into the toilet.

The noise he had made had obviously alerted someone who appeared at the door of the bedroom carrying what looked like a 9mm hand weapon.

Charles responded, in a hoarse voice in English, by asking where he was, and could he have some drinking water?

The man turned, left the room, and locked the door.

Within ten minutes the key turned in the lock, and a new man appeared, who immediately spoke in English,

'Mr Urwin, you are in Russia. You will be given food and water.'

With that he turned and left the room, locking the door as he did so.

Charles felt a surge of panic pass through his body. He rose quickly from the bed in order to retch again in the toilet.

About ten minutes later the key turned in the lock, and the door opened. One man came in carrying a tray of food, a glass, and a bottle of water.

Wednesday 20th August 2008. IISG HQ, London.

0930hrs and Harry was sitting outside the Director's office.

At 0940hrs the Director came bustling out, 'Apologies Harry, telcon with IISG Washington. Updates, etcetera.

Right, banks and their games. How to proceed?

Two steps. One, you go to Beirut, Banque Liban, and see what we can find out from that end. Two, then to Jeddah. I will clear your trip with the Foreign Office, diplomatic visa, etc. The F.O. are aware of the current bank problem, but it is not part of their remit, yet!

After that, you may be going to visit one of the Baltic States, if current thinking confirms. It's a one-man band at the moment Harry. I'll tack on some assistance as soon as I can. Understood?'

'So far, Director. Still fairly woolly round the edges, but only to be expected at this stage. Incidentally, may I ask who is our client? Having some idea of that could help, or hinder, my line of questioning.'

'I'm sorry Harry, but I can't reveal that at this stage. At some point when I can, perhaps clarity will assist. However, at present my hands are tied.'

'Well, let's hope mine aren't literally, when I'm diplomatically asking awkward questions in foreign lands!'

'Harry, that's bread and milk to you! Plan on leaving this weekend or early next week. I'll get back to you within 48 hours.'

FCO, Westminster, London.

That Wednesday a further meeting had been held to update all persons involved as to whether any further details had arisen concerning the disappearance of Charles Urwin.

Nothing of any substance had been received, other than the usual platitudes from police and security services that teams were still active in their search for any information or sightings.

Sunday 24th August 2008. Beirut, Lebanon.

Harry flew by MEA from Heathrow, landing at about 1930hrs, and was in his hotel the Al Bustan by about 2100hrs. The following morning, he contacted Banque Liban to agree a convenient time for their planned meeting.

Feelings were still running high in the country between the Government and Hezbollah factions, but most of the fighting was taking place near Tripoli in the North of the country. In Beirut an uneasy peace seemed to be holding.

Harry was sitting on the hotel terrace at about 1030hrs, drinking coffee, and watching people on the road outside going about their business. He was not particularly focussed, just passing the time of day, when his eyes, nerves and body jolted into gear.

He looked again, this time with deliberate focus.

He must be wrong, his mind was playing tricks, and his body felt both numb and electrified at one and the same time.

The image had disappeared, and he reached with he noticed, an unsteady hand for his coffee.

His mind was telling him he had just seen the back of Anna or someone almost identical to Anna. The person had been walking quickly, and had then broken into a run around the corner of a building.

His brain was saying it was Anna; he'd recognise her walk or run at any time. But she had been killed in December '07. He shook his head. It can't be, but his eyes and brain were saying something else.

He finished his coffee and went to the front of the hotel to take a cab to Banque Liban in the centre of Beirut.

As the taxi made its way downtown, he tried to focus on his line of questioning to Banque Liban and whether, face to face, more information or an explanation might be gained. Focus Harry, he told himself. Pushing the thoughts of Anna from his mind he recalled various bank issues he had discussed with the Director. He hoped there would be some clarity soon.

Banque Liban, Beirut, Lebanon.

The meeting did not get off to an auspicious start.

The Director, Jean Nemours, involved with the account in question was extremely defensive, clearly anxious to defend his position, the bank, and extent of responsibility.

Harry tried another tack.

Recognising that the Beirut bank had no control or responsibility for the incoming deposit, which was resting in limbo-land at present, Harry extended an invitation for dinner to the Director.

Purpose? In order to discuss, off the record, any or all thoughts, assumptions, possibilities, etc, which, as a result of the dinner, would produce no records on file, etc, of the likely reasons and sources for such a deposit.

After an initial hesitation the Director agreed. 2000hrs at the Al Bustan.

2000hrs. Al Bustan Hotel, Beirut.

Harry met Jean Nemours, the Banque Liban Director, in the hotel reception, and took him into the bar, where they sat adjacent to the French doors leading out onto the terrace.

'Jean, may I call you Jean?'

'Of course.'

'Please call me Harry. May I ask you a number of questions that would not fall under the 'official' designation?'

'Yes, but whether I can answer them is another matter.'

'Fine. Putting to one side this deposit, with no name or source, what would be your best guess as to likely suspects both as a source and as a recipient?'

Jean smiled gently before replying, 'With the sort of transactions happening daily in our region, the Middle East and Gulf, then suspects, as you call them, would probably add up to several hundreds or thousands in total. When you look at other regions, such as Eastern and Western Europe, then you could add at least the same number of major dealers.

Although the amount of this deposit is small, the trail back to Switzerland shows an initial large transfer. For an 'investment'!' The inflexion in his voice clearly indicated sarcasm.

'You refer to Eastern and Western Europe. Have you seen any transactions from this region, Gulf, etc, that have raised queries or questions in your mind?'

On this occasion Jean raised a quizzical eyebrow,

'Harry, the driver for all banks is income. Of course, numbers of transactions do raise questions, but if we don't handle them, then another bank will, and zero income for us.'

The discussion continued through dinner, and Jean became more open and relaxed over a good meal and some very reasonable Lebanese red wine.

Harry told Jean that he would be travelling to Jeddah to follow up on the initial transfer from a Saudi bank to Switzerland for the so-called 'investment', following that back to the UK, unless returning to Beirut.

If that was the case, could they meet again for an update and to compare further notes?

Jean was happy to agree.

*

Tuesday 26th August 2008. Russia.

Although Charles had been told he was in Russia he had no confirmation that this was true. No view of road, traffic, or any external markers confirmed that. He had to trust what he had been told. He lay on his bed at about 2100hrs and fell into a troubled sleep.

It seemed he had only been asleep a short while when the door burst open and two balaclava clad men burst in, one swiftly gagging him, the other tying his arms and legs. No lights were put on.

He was then thrust into a body bag, and before it was zipped up, he was injected in his right arm, losing consciousness almost immediately.

*

Wednesday 27th August 2008. Moscow, Russia.

Charles could hear voices. He was still quite heavily drugged, but could feel the body bag being dragged roughly over ground. He tried to shout but no sound came out. His hip hit something which caused a sharp pain. This time sound came from his mouth. The dragging motion stopped. He was lying on his side. He felt the zip of the body bag being pulled down.

Hands turned him over onto his back, and he looked up into some concerned faces looking down at him. It was dark, morning or evening, he had no idea.

The men looking down at him were suddenly pushed aside, and a uniformed policeman was now looking at him, who, seeing his eyes were open, knelt down and started undoing the ropes binding his arms and legs.

He called out in pain as they were released, and the officer and another man helped him to his feet, whereupon he almost fell over before being caught, and made to sit on the kerb.

He looked around, slowly, at the small crowd which had gathered, before looking behind him at a low wall, on which a sign declared it was the British Embassy.

He looked to see if he still had his watch. Yes, he had. It showed 27, and he assumed it was about 2130hrs. He spoke hoarsely to the police officer, explaining that he was British, and could he be taken into the Embassy. No, in English, was the short reply. The Police Officer spoke good English,

'First, you are being taken to a hospital for an examination, and following that, questioning as to identity, and reasons for discovery in a body bag outside the British Embassy.'

Charles was then carefully put into a police car and driven to a hospital, still very weak, sick, and groggy.

Thursday 28th August 2008. Jeddah, Saudi Arabia.

Thursday 28th August 2008. Jeddah, Saudi Arabia.

Harry had flown on Saudia direct from Beirut to Jeddah arriving at about 1800hrs. After the usual slow Immigration Passport and Visa procedure he was in his hotel, the Intercontinental, Al Hamra Corniche, just before 2000hrs.

He would not be able to contact banks until Saturday, Friday being Holy Day, so took the opportunity of sending a brief report to the Director in London. Pretty general in content, but Harry felt that Jean Nemours, of Banque Liban, could prove useful as events move along. He certainly felt that he was getting to grips with some of the banks' M.O., and flexible responses, even if the only driver was income, come what may.

*

Hospital, Moscow.

After his examination Charles had been mildly sedated, and did not wake until 1030hrs Thursday morning.

At about 1130hrs doctors pronounced him fit enough, to be taken by police escort, for questioning by the State Police at their station, close to the British Embassy. The questioning was firm but reasonable, as the two officers were clearly aware that he was British.

Charles had stated who he was, and his position in the Foreign and Commonwealth Office. Also, that he had been kidnapped, drugged, and then dumped outside the Embassy. Details were non-existent as to why he had been kept prisoner in an unidentified room and frequently drugged. However, no passport, or any other document to prove identity, was obviously causing considerable problems.

What he had decided to say, and which would provide the reason for his appearance in Moscow, would be drip fed over the next 24 hours.

Charles spoke clearly and slowly,

'If you submit a photo of me and a written statement by me to the British Embassy, you will soon be provided with confirmation as to who I am, and with a request that I be handed over to the Embassy.

The Embassy will also issue a temporary passport for me within 24 hours. May I request that this action is started?'

One officer left, obviously to seek approval or otherwise from a senior officer. Charles sat motionless, maintaining an expression of tired neutrality.

In about half an hour the officer returned, this time accompanied by a photographer, who took several photos from different angles.

After that, Charles was asked to print out his statement on plain paper, and sign it with his date of birth and address in London, and full description and title of his position in the FCO.

Then he was taken by the second officer to a holding cell, which contained a bed, washbasin and toilet. He was brought some food and bottled water, and the door was locked. He looked at his watch. Almost 1515hrs. Nothing would happen until Friday.

He sat on the bed and picked at his food.

*

Friday 29th August 2008. British Embassy, Moscow.

Robert Jones was on duty that Friday morning when a meeting was requested at reception by a Russian Police Inspector. Probably some parking violation by an Embassy vehicle, he thought, as he entered the room.

That thought was very quickly dismissed when he was presented with the photographs and written statement by Charles Urwin, senior FCO official, missing for over two months.

Asking the police officer to wait, he took the details immediately to the Deputy Head of Mission. To say the Deputy Head of Mission was surprised was not to exaggerate his response. Briefing notes on Charles Urwin's disappearance had been circulated to all embassies and consulates world-wide.

After two months the initial high interest had faded, but now Moscow was suddenly taking centre stage.

Thoughts of beneficial media coverage, TV preferably, of the UK Embassy, crossed the Deputy's mind as he looked at the photos and the hand-written statement.

'Robert, take the Inspector to our main meeting room, I will join you there after a telephone call to London. The FCO needs to be updated if this turns out to be credible, or not. We need to cover all bases as they develop.'

Robert hurried down to re-join the Police Officer, and take him to the meeting room, making small talk to cover the gap before the Deputy's arrival.

After about five minutes the Deputy entered, carrying the photos and written statement.

He shook the policeman's hand, and waved him to a chair, as he greeted him in fluent Russian,

'Inspector, if this is true and correct,' he said, 'then you will have succeeded in solving, at least in part, a mystery that has occupied our Foreign Office, for over two months, since Mr Urwin's initial disappearance in the United Kingdom.'

The policeman nodded before replying,

'Perhaps we should consider firstly what we require from you, in order to determine, whether or not, the man in our custody, is, who he says he is.

We will require your government's official response to our request for specific information concerning initially, his blood group, dental records, any recent doctor examination and report, together with copies of his UK Passport, Photographic Driving Licence, etcetera.

We, in turn, will be taking a blood sample which will be checked against your data, and our dental surgeon will also check his teeth against your UK dental records. Photographic comparisons between what we have taken, and what will be provided by you, will assist in our verification procedures.

Following these initial checks, we will decide if anything further is required to confirm, or otherwise, whether this man is indeed Charles Urwin.'

The Deputy looked disappointed at the formal requests made by the police, but responded by agreeing that he would initiate, immediately, such requests to London, and that such information must be provided as soon as possible.

However, in the meantime, could he please be allowed to visit the man held in custody? The Inspector thought this would possible, and promised to revert later that day. Hands were shaken and the Inspector escorted from the Embassy.

Robert who had been taking notes, then asked whether the Deputy would like him to prepare the detailed request to the FCO London.

'No Robert,' the Deputy replied, somewhat testily, 'I shall be handling this situation personally from now, until a satisfactory, and or, proven result is achieved.'

Robert handed over his written notes, saying, 'If there is anything you want me to do, no doubt you will tell me.'

'Noted Robert, but very unlikely. However, thank you.'

That afternoon the Police Inspector telephoned, advising that the Deputy Head of Mission could not visit the detainee the next day, Saturday the 30th August. The earliest convenient opportunity would be at the start of the following week.

Saturday 30th August 2008. Jeddah, Saudi Arabia.

Banque Roubert Saudi was situated in the commercial district in Jeddah, and, at about 1100hrs, as Harry stepped out of his air-conditioned taxi, he quickly appreciated it was not the best place to be in August, as the temperature approached 40°C. However, entering the bank he was met with a blast of ice-cold air conditioning, which certainly helped.

Entering the office of the GM, Josh Morgan, a Canadian, Harry was offered coffee, and exchanged generalities before starting a Q & A session.

Harry explained his, and IISG's position, the confidentiality clause covering his client, and the basic banking transactions that had predated this enquiry, including Beirut.

It was very evident, from his demeanour, that the GM was extremely concerned as to the bank's position, and its prime status when the original major transfer took place. Their discussion, on first name terms, had to start from when the first transfer was originally mooted, and Josh obviously led.

'I have known the family concerned for some time, medium sized players in the KSA markets, and it was fairly obvious that one of the younger brothers, Sheikh Ahmed, was keen to strike out on his own.

He'd bought and sold some small to medium sized operations here, trading companies with some international brands or services, you know the type of thing.'

Harry nodded but did not interrupt.

'He was always talking about getting involved in an international operation, external to Saudi Arabia, which would give him a reasonable size footprint to develop in other countries, and hopefully Europe. An international brand, pizzas, ice cream, soft drinks, who knows. Obviously suitable for all Arab and Western markets.'

He paused, and turned a couple of pages in the file sitting on his desk,

'About six months ago he came to see me to discuss such an opportunity.

The major problem was that he said he had signed a confidentiality agreement with the international Franchisor, based in the Far East, and could not discuss the product or service, but that he was very excited he said, about the huge potential.

He told me the amount he would have to invest, some of which would be to purchase shares in the Franchisor, this giving him a favoured position, the remainder being the fee for the franchise covering a number of countries.

The initial amount to be transferred was $350million to an account in our Lausanne Head Office. From there a subsequent transfer was to be made, instructions to follow, to a bank in the Far East.'

Josh paused again, then continued,

'Two very strange things happened, one very serious, the other, how and why?

The route of the how and why was a transfer of $4.5m from the Lausanne account to our bank in Beirut. No one can see how this was done and why? Incidentally this has been parked and frozen.

The very serious situation was the complete disappearance of Sheikh Ahmed. Initial thoughts were that he was off on vacation, South of France, wherever, so airlines and airports were checked. Nothing.

He had two mobiles, no usage, complete silence, and that overall situation has now existed for over two months. His family have no idea where he is, or what has happened, and are desperately worried, meanwhile keeping a low profile, and with no public acknowledgement of his disappearance.

We have no information concerning the franchisor, name, location, product/service, nothing. And what is also surprising, is that there has been no contact from any organisation to Lausanne Head Office chasing up a potential transfer of $350m. to the Far East.'

Josh partially slumped back in his chair, 'As you can see a Grade A problem!'

Harry commented, 'I'm assuming nobody in his family knew of any of the details of the Franchisor, history, reputation, etc?'

'Nothing, his family knew nothing. He kept everything very close to his chest.'

'OK. I have an idea, but would like to run it past my Director before I put it to you. Could we meet tomorrow? Say about 9.30am?'

Josh nodded his head in agreement. 'Great.'

As Harry taxi-cabbed back to his hotel, he wondered whether his idea was too hare-brained, or whether it might draw out some of the other players in this, inevitably, dirty game. That afternoon he put through an encrypted call to the Director.

'Sorry to bother you Director, on your weekend, but you may recall that some working weeks and hours are slightly different in other countries!'

'I get the message Harry, and the purpose of this call is?'

'I have had a meeting with the bank here, and wonder if you could organise a little media exposure, which could possibly generate some interest and activity from those whose identity is not currently known.

Not necessary to give the name of the bank, just an indication of significant sums sitting, unclaimed in Swiss banks, initially going to be an investment overseas, SE Asia/Far East. Just enough to generate some interest and comment. You know the sort of thing.'

'Can be done Harry. Send me some draft words and music, and I will tap a friendly journalist, or three, on the shoulder to call in a few IOUs. Bearing in mind a few of our friendly European banks, with their questionable activities over the last few years with some restricted regimes and countries, I am sure some of our media chums might like to stir the pot a little. Leave it with me. I await your song sheet!'

Harry did just that, sending the encrypted package via his satellite linked laptop. On Sunday morning at 0930hrs he met with Josh, and outlined what he was proposing by way of media coverage. No names of banks would be revealed, just a varied catalogue of slightly suspicious banking activity in Europe, and elsewhere, and unclaimed amounts of serious money that might bring out a few mice, or rats.

**

V

September 2008.

Monday 1ˢᵗ September 2008. FCO Westminster, London.

The encrypted messages received from the Embassy in Moscow on Saturday had produced a flurry of activity, not least with the weekend communications staff, but also telephone calls to junior ministers, the Foreign Secretary and Security Services.

The FCO had complied with all requests, save those concerning Urwin's dentist, who was not available until Monday.

Total surprise and bafflement followed the news. Why Russia? How and why had he surfaced there? Gossip over coffee was at an enhanced level. Even for the FCO who are not often surprised, nor admit to it, they were.

Instructions to the Embassy included following through with all data requested, but in turn maintain pressure for access to the person detained. If true, vital; if an imposter, perhaps even more so.

At 0915hrs Quentin Horncastle was called in to see the Foreign Secretary.

David Milliband was standing by his desk looking out of the window.

'Quentin, you have obviously heard the latest news concerning Charles Urwin, his surfacing in Moscow, and that currently he is a guest of the State Police.'

'Yes, Foreign Secretary.'

'A rum show, don't you think?'

'It certainly appears that way, Foreign Secretary.'

'I suggest you fly out today, if you can, and try to get to the bottom of it. Push for an early meeting at the Police HQ, and fully brief me with, I hope, the facts, as soon as you have them.'

'Of course, Foreign Secretary. I will do my best.'

Quentin hurried back to his office, his thoughts, concerning Charles Urwin, confused to say the least.

He checked with flights, and saw that a BA flight from London Heathrow was leaving at about 1500hrs, arriving in Moscow about 11.00pm, local time. He could make that easily.

However, instruct the Ambassador, and Deputy Head of Mission, to hold back on pressing for a face to face with the purported Charles Urwin, currently held by Moscow State Police. He would like to be present for that. He knew Charles Urwin probably better than anyone.

The BA flight arrived on time in Moscow, and he was met by the Defence Attaché, who had organised fast diplomatic clearance, arriving in the Embassy shortly after midnight, where he met the Deputy head of Mission.

It would be fair to say that the Deputy was feeling a little put out by the arrival of Quentin. He had been anticipating an interesting meeting with the detainee. Now the FCO was taking over.

Quentin was then updated, not much in addition, if anything, other than a repeat of what London had received.

A request had been made for a meeting at the Moscow Police HQ, situated at 38 Petrovka Street in Tverskoy District, Moscow. and a confirmation was expected Tuesday morning.

Quentin slept fitfully in the Embassy that night, thinking tomorrow could be quite an interesting day, no doubt involving some even more interesting revelations!

Acknowledgement of the request to see 'Charles Urwin' was received at about 1000hrs with the time stated as 1430hrs.

It had been agreed that Quentin would be accompanied by the Deputy Head of Mission, with Quentin taking the lead role for obvious reasons.

All copies of passport, driving licence, medical information including blood group, had been provided to the State Police, dental records being the last.

At 1430hrs that afternoon, Quentin and the Deputy presented themselves at the State Police HQ.

They were treated with utmost courtesy, the police recognising and respecting their diplomatic status. They were also advised that checks were ongoing by the Police, but that they were fully aware of the concern shown by the Embassy, if the man currently detained was shown to be Charles Urwin.

They were then taken to a small meeting room, no windows, containing a table, four chairs, and a small cabinet on which sat four glasses and a bottle of water. No doubt somewhere would be a digital microphone.

Quentin and the Deputy sat down, and after a few minutes heard footsteps coming down the corridor.

They rose as one as the door opened, and Charles Urwin, looking pale and undernourished, was led in by a policeman, who left immediately, closing the door behind him.

Quentin and the Deputy greeted him kindly, Quentin shaking his hand gently, and indicating a chair.

Charles spoke first, testily enquiring, 'How much longer do I have to stay in this damn hole before the FCO confirms it's me, and I can get a decent meal, and a decent night's sleep?'

Quentin turned to the Deputy with a smile, 'If any further confirmation is required that this is indeed Charles Urwin, then I don't know what it is!'

The Deputy smiled, shook Charles's hand, and then turned to continue his note taking.

Quentin continued, 'Are you being treated properly? Do you have food, water, bathroom, toilet, etc?'

Charles nodded, 'Yes, but all I want to do is get out of here.'

'Agreed,' said Quentin, 'But there are a million questions both from the Moscow Police as to your arrival at the Embassy in a body bag, and then from us, the FCO, as to what has happened to you over the last two months, starting from your disappearance on the 15th June. You do appreciate the seriousness of your situation, I trust?'

'Of course,' Charles replied, this time in a note of flat resignation.

'We are hoping that you will be released to us, no later than tomorrow morning, followed by a full medical check-up, and then get some decent vitamins inside you,' Quentin explained in a sympathetic tone.

A short conversation, covering his drugged arrival in the body bag followed, before Quentin stood up, left the room, and asked to see the Police Inspector.

'Assuming all questions concerning Identity are confirmed from your side, medically etc, I would like to add my own incontrovertible confirmation that this Charles Urwin, a man I have known and worked with over a significant period of years, and hope that he can be released into our care tomorrow, Wednesday the 3rd September 2008.'

'We would hope to agree to this, subject to a final questioning as to the circumstances leading up to his arrival, in a body bag, outside the British Embassy.'

Quentin spoke again, this time with a slight edge to the tone he adopted, 'As I understand he had been drugged by his captors, it is unlikely he can provide any worthwhile information whatsoever, and would strongly suggest, and request, that he is released to Her Majesty's Embassy tomorrow.'

'We will advise your Embassy tomorrow morning.'

Quentin advised both Charles and the Deputy as to the current position, and stressed that the strongest representations would be made at the highest level, if the release was not made on Wednesday.

Quentin also said he would return at 1000hrs Wednesday to apply further pressure, before getting the Ambassador involved with the Russian equivalent Home Secretary, or Foreign Secretary, if necessary.

Wednesday 3rd September 2008. Jeddah, Saudi Arabia.

Harry had called Josh at Banque Roubert Saudi,

'Morning. Can we meet for lunch somewhere? Out of the office. Just want to kick a few things around. You can? Good. Where, and what time.'

They met at a small restaurant near the bank, which Josh used from time to time, where he was known by the manager. They were able to sit at a quiet table, on one side, without being overheard, or disturbed.

Harry opened, 'I spoke to my boss yesterday, and I've got a draft here, of what is going out to some friendly and unfriendly media contacts.'

He handed over a single sheet of paper to Josh, who proceeded to read it, initially showing no reaction.

Press Release: Day: Date: Source.

Significant amounts of unclaimed money lying in banks in the UK, and Europe. Banks remain silent on source and destination. Questions should be asked.

Investigations, some through the Financial Ombudsman in the UK, have revealed a significant number of international banks, British, European (majority French and Swiss), US, and some in the Far East, have large sums of unclaimed money held in their accounts.

Bearing in mind the length of time some of this money has been lying in limbo, and the reluctance of the banks to reveal its source, it is hardly surprising that public confidence in the probity of banks is at an all-time low.

Questions to a number of banks have been completely rebutted, 'no comment', or 'client confidentiality' being the usual response.

It is therefore likely that a groundswell of adverse public opinion may well force the banks to reconsider their public reply to legitimate enquiries.

Bearing in mind the level of information that we have obtained in our research may, perhaps, provide a more effective and speedy reaction by areas of the banking world in general.

END

Contact: IISG London. <u>Tel:0207 345 6789</u>.

Email: <u>reception@IISG.co.uk</u>

As Josh read it, Harry noted that he had only winced once. Not too damning then, he thought. But at least starts the ball rolling.

Josh looked up, 'Why the IISG contact details? Couldn't this be non-attributable?'

'It could be, but my Director thought that with our group highlighting the situation, then those who know something may come knocking on our door?'

Josh nodded, 'All right, I take your point. What happens now?'

'Well, when this starts hitting the streets next week, who knows, but I'll bet there will some contacts made to our London office! Absolute certainty.'

Josh smiled, 'Rather you than me. I'll bet there will be a few uptight bankers come the end of next week!'

Police HQ, Moscow.

Due to diplomatic pressure from London, Quentin Horncastle did not have to present himself at the Police HQ at 1000hrs to demand the release of Charles Urwin.

At 0905hrs, on that Wednesday, the Embassy had been contacted by the Chief of Police Moscow, advising that Charles Urwin would be released to its representatives at 1015hrs.

At that time Quentin and the Deputy were happy to sign all necessary release papers produced by the Police HQ, and rode back, in comparative silence, with Charles Urwin in an Embassy vehicle to be greeted by the Ambassador.

'Delighted to see you, Charles. Obviously, this has been an extremely worrying time for both you, and the FCO.

We must, in short order, commence the necessary questioning in order to fully understand what has been the reason behind your disappearance over the last two months. Until that has been completed, with complete satisfaction, both here and in the UK, your position is one I will describe as purdah, which I hope you fully understand.

I will now leave you in the capable hands of the Deputy and your colleague, Quentin Horncastle.'

The Ambassador then left to return to his office, thinking to himself that he was very glad he would not be involved in, no doubt, a long and turgid investigation covering more than the last two months.

Quentin turned to Charles, 'Go and have a check-up with the Embassy doctor. Then relax, get some proper food inside you, then some proper sleep, and we can start our discussions tomorrow morning. Understood?'

'Regretfully yes, Quentin. See you tomorrow.'

Thursday 4th September 2008. British Embassy, Moscow.

Quentin and Charles met in a small meeting room in the Embassy at about 0930hrs.

Charles, thought Quentin, looked a little less wan than the day before. At least two regular meals, and a good night's sleep must have helped, he thought.

'Shall we get started?'

Charles nodded in agreement.

'I must point out to you Charles, that all our conversations in this debrief must be recorded, and, any questions I ask you, must be responded to verbally, not with a nod, or shake of the head. Is that quite clear?'

'Yes.'

'You should also be aware that another full recorded debrief will be carried out once you are back in the UK. This will, in all probability, either include officers of SO15, Counter Terrorism Command, or, if they insist, carry out a separate investigation under their jurisdiction. You do understand the processes that are now starting?'

'Yes.'

'The recording is now on.

Starting from the day of your disappearance, 16th June, can you please indicate, if possible, how this occurred, and what happened subsequently?'

'With difficulty Quentin, but I shall try. You will have to excuse me if the odd date is wrong, but when you hear, what I think happened, you should not be surprised.'

'Please proceed Charles.'

'I had decided to take a couple of days away in the country, down towards the South Coast, getting away from London, a little walking on the Downs, fresh air, recharge the batteries.

I was going to take a train to Lewes and then find a decent quiet little country hotel for my stay. Early on that Sunday morning I was walking to the Underground from my apartment, about a ten-minute walk. The streets were deserted at that hour.

Then suddenly a car coasted up alongside, I hadn't heard it, and two masked men leapt out, grabbed me and bundled me into the car. One, I remember, had a hand over my mouth to stop me shouting.

As soon as I was in the car, I felt an injection in my arm, and lost consciousness immediately. When I awoke, I found I my hands were tied, I was gagged, blindfolded, and had a hood over my head, and was obviously not in a car.

I could hear a throbbing, an engine throbbing, and with a slight motion thought I could be on a boat or ship.'

At this point Quentin interrupted,

'On regaining consciousness, what was your first reaction? Did you hear your kidnappers talking, and were they speaking English, or another language?'

'I had not heard any talking at this point, and I could not guess as to any reason for my kidnap, except possibly ransom.'

He paused, 'Frankly it was a nightmare. No idea why, no idea where I was. No idea of what was going to happen. From time to time I was injected, and immediately fell unconscious.'

He fell silent.

'And then?' Quentin queried.

'It seemed a very long time, and for some of it, I was either asleep or unconscious, but eventually I realised I was in some sort of vehicle. I could hear voices, certainly not English, but impossible to determine, very muffled and distant.

After another long period the vehicle stopped, and I was carried out and put in a room where the hood and blindfold were removed, but my hands left tied in front of me. My captors were all wearing masks or balaclavas, and did not speak, either to me, or between themselves. At this point food and water were provided.'

He fell silent again.

Quentin spoke, 'And you still, at this stage, had no idea why you had been kidnapped?'

'None at all.'

'Did you have any idea as to which country you were in?'

'No.'

'How long was it before your kidnappers spoke to you?'

'The next day. Fortunately, I still had my watch and the date indicated would have been Wednesday the 18th.

A masked man, I assumed the leader of the group, spoke to me at some length in an accent I could not place, although I thought it had an East European ring to it.'

'What did he say?' asked Quentin.

'He explained that they knew who I was, where I sat in the FCO, my previous postings etc. He was well briefed.

This was a kidnapping for money, a significant sum, if I was to be released safely. Regrettably, if no money was paid, he could not guarantee my safety. He was very clear.'

'But,' Quentin said, 'No contact was made, either to the FCO, or UK Police, indicating a ransom demand for your safe release. What he said, and what had happened, do not appear to match.'

'You're right Quentin, because he said that no effort would be made as to ransom demands until they felt that sufficient pressure, and concern, had been reached. That did not give me any confidence, as I am aware that in such cases, after a period of time, initial resources and priority are reduced,' he paused, 'if not stopped.'

Quentin did not respond.

Charles continued, 'After about three days of no activity I still had no idea where I was, and was becoming concerned at the group's likely reactions if no effort was made to demand a ransom, and if they did, whether they would be taken seriously. As a consequence of that, what would be their actions towards me?

On the Saturday, I think, they suddenly bundled me, tied, gagged and hooded into a vehicle. I could not see, so had no idea where we were, or in which country. That is until, on one occasion when the vehicle stopped, I heard a voice with an accent I think I recognised. It was Polish. I'm reasonably confident.'

'Polish?'

'Yes, but the journey continued for at least another day.

At night I was ungagged, fed and watered, but only allowed out of the van on a tied rope for, …. well, you can imagine.

It was either the 21st or 22nd when we reached our destination and stopped. Still gagged, tied and blindfolded, I was led into a room, pushed onto a bed, untied, blindfold removed, but ankles shackled, and left. One locked window, wooden shutters on the outside. Location, absolutely no idea.'

Charles paused, Quentin made no comment,

'Can I have a coffee please? Black with sugar. Brown if possible.'

His voice sounded flat.

Not surprising if he had been through what he was talking about, thought Quentin.

'Shall we have a break for fifteen minutes? '

'Thank you, Quentin.'

Quentin left the recorder running,

'Changing the subject Charles, will you be taking some safe holiday time when all this is over?'

Charles smiled wanly, mixed with a shade of exasperation, 'Yes, if it's ever over, judging by what you said earlier.'

'I am sure that what is said today, will shorten, to some extent, the subsequent enquiry in London.'

'Hmm.,' was Charles' response.

After finishing their coffee, the enquiry continued.

*

Banque Roubert Saudi, Jeddah, Saudi Arabia.

Mid-morning on the 4th September and Harry was wondering where the investigation was going, when he received a call from Josh.

'Morning Harry. A transaction was initiated this morning online, all security checks, passwords, code verification, everything. It went through without a hitch, but having been tagged was highlighted to me.

It was the transfer of $350m from our Lausanne Head Office, originally destined for the Far East. However, the destination bank was changed; it has apparently been sent to our sister bank in Riga, Latvia.

The sister bank acts as our branch in Riga, but operates under a different name, BSR Banka. (Banque Suisse Roubert). Bearing in mind that the only person with all the necessary security to effect the transfer is Sheikh Ahmed, then it was either carried out by him, or if not, frankly the alternative does not want to be considered.'

Harry was momentarily speechless,

'All necessary data checks were carried out, including change of destination bank, which would require top-tier authority, and all codes, etc?'

'Yes, apparently so.'

'If all that came in electronically, what was the source, cell phone bank app, bank website? If so, does the bank have any tracking as to source, location, etc?'

'Regrettably, not as far as I know.'

'Can you please check, and see if there is anything that can give us a clue; country, city, anything!'

'Leave it with me Harry, I'll see if I can do some digging.'

Harry put down the telephone, possibly even more confused than before he answered it. Let's hope Josh's digging might bear some fruit, however small, he thought, before a particular thought hit him.

He immediately contacted the Director, through his satellite encrypted telephone, with a detailed request,

'If one was able to identify time of payment instruction to a bank, made from, for example, a cell phone bank app, was it possible for an organisation, such as GCHQ, to trawl back through the available electronic data, and then by reverse engineering, to determine, at least, in/from which country the instruction was made?'

The Director promised to find out soonest, and revert.

That afternoon, British Embassy, Moscow.

Quentin switched on the recording machine again.

'Can we please continue Charles? Thank you.'

Charles continued his explanation as to what had happened over the previous weeks, but with scant detail, as he had been kept literally in the dark, and, on many occasions, heavily drugged.

However, one episode made Quentin sit up.

Charles was saying that on one occasion he was spoken to by the balaclava wearing group leader, in poor, and very broken English.

Charles imitated the brief conversation,

'Because of change plan, we soon hand you to your country.

We know you. We follow you UK. Take you Europe. Sell you. Last stop Belarus. We good connection Russia, you UK Government. Very interest to Russia. Lot of talk, no deal. Change plan.'

Charles changed his tone,

'Then I asked him where we were. He would not say, but I was thinking if they wanted to return me to the UK from Belarus, then they would have to go back through Poland, Germany, Belgium/Holland. I could not see that.

I can only assume they then entered Russia. I tried to keep him talking, as I was trying to work out his nationality, and suggested he was Russian. He responded very sharply, and told me he was Albanian.

Bearing in mind the control of many areas of organised crime in London is by Albanians, perhaps it is not surprising that I was on their radar, and hit list.'

Quentin, extremely surprised by this information, merely said,

'And then?'

'A further day, at least, tied, blindfold, gagged, locked up in the dark, in a vehicle, travelling from where to where, I did not know.

One night as I lay in the vehicle, they drugged me again. As I came to, I was being dragged over ground, which turned out to be Moscow. The rest, I am sure, you are fully aware of,' he said, smiling grimly.

Quentin said nothing, as he reached over and switched off the recorder, then sitting back in his chair.

Silence followed, for almost a minute,

'Almost unbelievable Charles. You should appreciate how lucky you are. In a similar setting, and with no success, most criminal Albanians would have shot you, and left you on the side of a very deserted road.'

'I count my blessings Quentin, despite being an agnostic.'

Friday 5th September 2008. Jeddah, Saudi Arabia.

At about 1400hrs Harry received a short message from the Director.

Yes, instruction can be traced, but can take some time. Date, time, receiving bank details, including payment instructions, were obviously necessary. If, up to three, possible countries were suggested, then this could shorten elapsed time of investigation.

The Director also cautioned that such 'favours' were pretty thin on the ground, but, if vital, would pursue.

Saturday 6th September 2008. Banque Roubert, Saudi Arabia.

Harry called Josh first thing,

'I'm sending to you, as we speak, a short list of details I require, which, I hope, may assist you and me, in tracking down Sheikh Ahmed, on the one hand, and assist in pinning down the 'how and why' of the particular transfers we have discussed. Can you get them to me soonest?'

'Once I've received them, I'll get back to you straightaway to advise whether yes or no, OK?'

'OK.'

Harry received them by text mid-afternoon, thinking Josh clearly had his areas of influence, and after adding three countries, KSA, Lebanon, and Switzerland., he sent them, by encrypted email, to the Director in London, with a request that the favour be called in with GCHQ, as soon as possible.

Progress at last, albeit slow. Never mind, small steps still count.

That evening. London Heathrow.

The BA flight, carrying Quentin and Charles, landed, on time, at about 2315hrs. They then made their way by FCO car to London. Quentin heading home, Charles staying at his club on Pall Mall. Quentin had advised, unbeknownst to Charles, SO15 CTC to keep a weather eye on him over Sunday, and until they would meet again at the FCO on Monday morning.

*

Monday 8th September 2008. FCO Westminster London

Charles Urwin arrived at Quentin Horncastle's office at about 1000hrs, still looking somewhat below par.

Quentin closed the door after coffee had been brought.

81

'Well Charles, one down, and one to go.'

'Yes.'

'The recording of our meeting in Moscow is currently being transcribed, which will obviously form the basis of the second interview, which, as I advised, could well include SO15.

This, hopefully, would then be the end of the enquiry, unless SO15 has other thoughts.'

Charles remained silent.

'Any observations Charles?'

'None I can think of presently,' said Charles in a tired voice, 'When can we start?'

'2.00pm this afternoon, if you agree.'

'2.00pm it is.'

SVR HQ Moscow, Russia.

Signal had been received that Charles Urwin was now back in London at the FCO.

1400hrs. FCO Westminster, London.

Charles was looking tired before the interview process got under way, and, no doubt, his mood was not helped by the eager and aggressive line of questioning coming from the two SO15 officers.

His responses, in the main, reflected what he had said in Moscow, only in one area did he expand, with cursory detail, that really added nothing. Bearing in mind the long periods in isolation, blindfolded, tied, and on many occasions drugged, it was not surprising that there was a lack of detail.

This aspect was pointed out, on many occasions, by Charles to the SO15 officers, in a polite but exaggerated manner, clearly indicating his annoyance at an irritating, and repetitive, line of questioning.

At about 1645hrs the recorded interview came to an end, the SO15 officers, as always, leaving the door open, for further 'discussion', if any additional information came to light.

Charles sat slumped and quiet in his chair, tired and irritable, whilst Quentin, on the other hand, quickly said,

'Well, that is now out of the way for a few days. Reports etc, to be written, reviewed, discussed, and filed, I hope.

And you, Charles, get a few days' rest, and then re-join your team in the FCO. Work to be done!' he commented, jocularly.

Charles replied, somewhat dourly, 'As you say Quentin, work to be done.'

Thursday 11th September 2008. Jeddah, Saudi Arabia.

Harry received an encrypted message late on Thursday from the Director.

From the initial trawls by GCHQ, it appeared that the first source of transfer instructions originated in KSA. Namely the transfer to the Banque Roubert H.O. in Lausanne. Brilliant, thought Harry sarcastically, we know that already!

Reading on however, he was delighted to see that the recent instructions, concerning the transfer from Lausanne to Riga in Latvia had been identified, and sourced from Lebanon, believed to be somewhere North of Beirut, near Tripoli.

At last, something positive to work on, Harry thought. Clearly, he should get back to Beirut a.s.a.p. He sought approval which was given immediately; rang Josh, thanking him for his help, and promising to update him once he had further information. He booked his flight on Saudia leaving Jeddah at about 1300hrs Friday.

Maybe those small steps were getting larger, he thought.

Saturday 13th September 2008. Beirut, Lebanon.

Harry was back in the same hotel, the Al Bustan.

He contacted David Hadar, Station Head of Mossad in London, for an introduction to their local Chief in Beirut. On the secure satellite telephone, they exchanged cordial greetings before Harry made his request.

'Understood Harry, but officially no Chief in Beirut. Operations handled in a slightly different way. Group Leaders in major cities, also broken down by City areas.

Leave it with me, someone will make contact with you. Al Bustan Hotel? Fine.'

Harry decided to contact DGSE, knowing their ongoing activities and interest in this part of the world, and the good working relationship they had with Mossad.

He called Alain Dubois in Paris on his cell phone, and heard a chuckle down the line, as his friend obviously realised who it was.

'Bien, mon vieux, what is the problem that you have, that requires my assistance?'

Now it was Harry's turn to laugh, 'Not today, my friend, but maybe tomorrow. I just want to make contact with your local man here in Beirut. Can you help? I'm staying at the Al Bustan Hotel.'

'Pas problème. Leave it with me. Somebody will contact you. And if you need me there to assist, call me. HQ in Paris can be quite boring!'

Harry laughed, 'Perhaps I might. À bientôt!'

Sunday 14th September 2008. Beirut, Lebanon.

At about 1100hrs Harry had a call from the hotel reception. Someone to see him. Someone from the Lebanon Wine Cooperative.

They met in the foyer. He introduced himself as Paul Khoury. They had a mutual friend in David Hadar, in London.

They shook hands and took a small table by the window for coffee.

Harry explained that he needed, perhaps, some local assistance. Hence his call to David. Although he was looking at a number of things at present, he would be grateful if he could have Paul's cell phone

'No problem,' was Paul's response. 'Call me when you need me.'

Harry filled him in on his own previous connections with his 'company', and the excellent working relationship he had experienced.

He made no reference at all to Anna, although thinking, that no doubt, Paul's company file would include most details.

They got on well, and Harry said he would keep Paul posted as to his investigations, results, and certainly any assistance he required at short notice. He spent that afternoon working through all the potential options involving Banque Roubert and Banque Liban and decided to contact Jean Nemours the next day.

**

Monday 15th September 2008. Banque Liban, Beirut.

They met in Jean's office, and Harry updated him, specifically concentrating on the location of the electronic bank instructions being somewhere near Tripoli, in the North of Lebanon.

'Do you have any specific contacts in that region who could assist us in trying to track down Sheikh Ahmed, or who would have a good idea of any possible groups involved in kidnappings, and subsequent ransom demands?'

Jean smiled sadly, 'At the present time, that region is effectively controlled by Hezbollah, and which is in almost daily conflict with government forces.

These actions die down for a time, and then flare up again. No reason, just flexing of Iran's muscle by proxy, which keeps their profile high in the region.

We have a branch in Tripoli. However, it is not open every day, for obvious reasons. And, if you are proposing to go to Tripoli, exercise extreme caution.

Besides the fighting, between Government troops and Hezbollah, that can break out at any moment without warning, kidnappings are rife.

It is not recommended to travel alone.'

Jean gave Harry the bank address in Tripoli, and said he would contact the manager to advise that Harry may contact and visit him, at some time in the near future.

When Harry got back to the Al Bustan, he found another message waiting for him, from a Monsieur Michel Yassin, Import/Export, France-Liban, Beirut, Liban. A mutual friend in Paris had suggested they should meet. Please call me, was the request.

Harry called the number, and arranged that they could meet at about 1000hrs the following day, Tuesday, at the local office of France-Liban. 'Merci Alain', Harry thought.

Just to keep the Director up to speed Harry sent a brief encrypted update and possible meeting in Tripoli.

*

Tuesday 16th September 2008. France-Liban Office Beirut.

Michel Yassin was very similar in temperament to Alain Dubois, although completely different in appearance.

He had, what could be described as a generic Lebanese 'Look', including a moustache and small beard.

His attitude, conversation, and general demeanour, reminded Harry very strongly of Alain Dubois. He was sure they could work well together.

He explained to Michel, without too much specific detail, what had brought him to Beirut, and why he needed to go to Tripoli to visit Banque Liban.

Michel shook his head,

'Not a good idea, at present. Hezbollah and Government forces are fighting almost on a daily basis, although I have heard they are trying to get a truce in place within 48 hours. If that holds, then maybe a quick 'Bonjour' and 'à Bientôt' could be possible.'

They discussed, at some length, the current situation in Lebanon, and the devastating effect on the country's infrastructure and economy by the guerrilla warfare tactics adopted by both Shia and Sunni backed militia groups. Historically, never a clear winner, just carnage, and then a long period of reconstruction, hindered by the continual carping and objections of political parties, divided on Sunni and Shia belief grounds.

They agreed to contact each other in 48hours to confirm, or otherwise, whether a truce had been established in Tripoli. If so, then a quick in and out would be arranged.

As additional security Harry contacted Paul, at the Lebanon Wine Cooperative, and brought him up to date concerning Michel of France Liban, and the possible visit to Tripoli, if the truce was established.

Now we wait and see what develops, thought Harry.

Following the enquiry on the 8th September, Charles had taken a few days away from London in the Lake District, walking, sleeping better as each night passed, along with good food.

His colour came back, along with energy levels, so that when he arrived back at the FCO on the 16th September, it was the Charles of old who entered.

After bringing himself up to current status, and reviewing issues marked 'Urgent', he was contacted by Quentin on the 18th, for a general discussion on future role and location.

They sat down with tea and closed doors. No interruptions.

'Good to see you looking like your old self Charles, the rest and exercise obviously did you no harm! Now the question is where best to apply your undoubted talents!'

Charles smiled, but made no comment.

Quentin continued, 'There is no doubt, in my mind, that your extremely fortunate recovery, from a situation that can only be described as horrific, provides us with an unparalleled opportunity.'

Charles nodded, but made no comment, a questioning look on his face.

Quentin continued, 'Reflecting on your recent role as First Secretary,' adding hastily, 'and Deputy Head of Mission in Moscow, there were particular and personal meetings that you held with the Russian Foreign minister, Sergey Lavrov.

During those discussions, as you have told me, he touched on your days at university and your own personal political leaning, which could be described as 'left of centre'.

Clearly, he was investigating to see if that political inclination had been maintained into your mature years. If we assume, initially, that your leaning has been maintained, and with that as a starting point, I have an idea that the FCO could use as a basis for a level of disinformation of UK foreign policy.'

'How is that to be achieved?' Charles asked.

'I need to give it a little more thought, but perhaps you and I could discuss it further in a few days?'

'Why not Quentin?' replied Charles, in a measured, but tired tone.

*

Tripoli, Lebanon.

A truce had been declared, effective 0001hrs Friday morning, so that both groups, Sunni and Shia, could attend Friday Prayers.

Sitting in Beirut, Harry could only appreciate the tragic irony of the situation, when it was pointed out to him, by both Aaron and Michel, that there were many instances of Sunnis on one side of a street, and Shias on the other. Warring neighbours separated by about twenty to thirty metres of tarmac.

*

Friday 19th September 2008. Foreign Secretary's Office, London.

Quentin had been asked to present a personal briefing to the Foreign Secretary, David Milliband, concerning the full background of the Charles Urwin kidnapping, and ultimate safe release and return to the UK.

Arriving in the Foreign Secretary's office he was greeted with, 'Good day Quentin, tea or coffee?'

Having chosen coffee, they both sat down in two armchairs, Quentin carrying a file.

'I will leave any questions until you have finished, Quentin. I do not want to interrupt your flow.'

'Thank you, Foreign Secretary.

There is a fully detailed report on file, but several large sections are redacted, if any application is made by the public under the FOI (Freedom of Information Act), for very obvious reasons.

Charles Urwin, you will recall, was posted as First Secretary and Deputy Head of Mission, to our Embassy in Moscow, and during that time had the opportunity for at least two or three, one on one, meetings with Sergey Lavrov, Russian Foreign Minister.

You will also remember from his personal file, that whilst at university, he held significant left wing, if not embryonic communist views, which were noted and forwarded to Moscow by certain academics and Russian sympathisers. It is fair to assume, and perhaps comment thus, that his current political views, if expressed, are probably left of centre.'

He paused, whilst smiling gently, before continuing, 'Not dissimilar to a considerable number of people that I know.'

There was no reaction, verbal or facial, from the Foreign Secretary.

Quentin continued,

'Over recent years we have involved ourselves in a policy of 'Seeding'; this being an indication of mutual thinking on certain international matters, and Western reactions.

In the case of Charles, we freely distributed copies of his views and analysis, to a number of media outlets and, as an extension, to a number of embassies, including Russia.

Lavrov appreciated this, and hinted, during one of the one-to-one meetings, that it was clear that Charles was still holding to some, if not many, of his ideals from his university days.

This started us thinking of a different scenario, certainly carrying risk, but which could reap rich rewards if successful.

What if a First Secretary was 'sympathetic' to Moscow, still covertly driven by political ideology held since his university days, co-operating with, for example, local SVR?

Such an entrée could provide us with incredibly valuable intelligence, as to where Russia was heading, both in thinking and action. Naturally, MI6 would have to be fully involved from Day One.

The downside would obviously be significant personal risk to the First Secretary, and perhaps, eventually, complete miss-interpretation if our actions became public. We believed, however, that this was an opportunity that should not be missed.

However, events overtook us with the kidnapping of Charles, and the subsequent farrago.'

Quentin turned to another note in his file,

'Whether Moscow had a hand in Charles's kidnapping we shall never know, but it would not be the first time Russia's SVR has worked with organised crime, such as the 'Mafia' of Albanian gangs. Bearing in mind the activities of Albanian criminal gangs across the whole of Eastern and Western Europe, including London, it was comparatively easy to arrange the final stop in Moscow.

The extreme downside for Charles was his treatment, and drugging, during the journey, but I am happy to report he is almost back to 100% fitness.

Therefore, it is suggested that Charles will send, on an irregular basis, analysis of our Foreign Office strategy, direction, and proposed implementation, which, of course, will not be official policy.

Naturally, this will have to be finessed, so that solid credibility is maintained.'

He stopped talking, and looked enquiringly at the Foreign Secretary, who opened his mouth to speak, changed his mind, closed and then opened it again,

'Incredible Quentin. I don't really know where to start. Firstly, it is a minor miracle that Charles is still alive, knowing the usual reactions of Albanians in situations like this.

Secondly, do you honestly think that credibility can be maintained for any length of time, before the Russians rumble what we are up to?'

'Yes, Foreign Secretary, I do. But I would agree that the proof of the pudding, as they say, is in the eating, and that is something we can only demonstrate over a period of time.'

Milliband stared at Quentin for several seconds, before speaking,

'Be it on your head Quentin, and very good luck.

One major condition, however.

I require you to fully brief MI5 and MI6 as to this operation, also what has occurred vis-à-vis Charles's kidnap and recovery, and what is planned from today's date. I do not want to be briefed again on a First Secretary's kidnap. Security must be in place to counter such an occurrence.

But understand this. If anything goes wrong that could bring embarrassment to H.M. Government, this department, or my office, then you will be described as a 'rogue' unit, operating without permission or knowledge, and will be judged accordingly.

Risk/Reward ratio, is, to my mind, extremely high. Do I make myself clear?'

'Perfectly, Foreign Secretary.'

**

Saturday 20th September 2008. Tripoli, Lebanon.

That morning Michel took Harry by car from Beirut to Tripoli, a distance of just over 80 kms.

It was not an easy journey. Frequent roadblocks, of either Government Forces, or Hezbollah militia, meant that what should have been an easy 1hr 30min drive, developed into a 2hr 30min crawl, queues at checkpoints, checking ID or passport, doubling the time taken.

They arrived in the centre of Tripoli, and booked into the Via Mina Hotel, one of the few apparently operating.

The atmosphere in Tripoli was noticeably tense. Many shops, cafes and restaurants were still closed, and road blocks were evident, mostly on ethnic/religious grounds.

Michel had a hidden compartment in his car, located behind the rear seats, holding three automatic weapons, two semi-automatic HK P30 9mm pistols, and one HK MP7 Machine Pistol 4.6mm.

If push came to shove, then deployment.

Over dinner, somewhat brief and limited due to recent fighting, Harry outlined further what he was investigating, and why Tripoli was now on the schedule.

He would contact Banque Liban in the morning for a meeting. However, Michel was insisting he took him there, and brought him back to the hotel. Under the truce, and with no idea if it would hold or break down at a moment's notice, Michel insisted, blaming, with a smile, Alain Dubois, who had said he must look after Harry, as if he were his brother.

And that, he said, was exactly what he was going to do.

*

Sunday 21st September 2008. Banque Liban, Tripoli, Lebanon.

Having telephoned first thing, Harry had agreed a meeting with the bank for 1130hrs, Michel dropping him at the door, and giving him some words of advice if the truce were to break down during the meeting.

93

'OK Michel, I've got the message. You will be no more than 25 metres away, I must stay inside, keep my head down, and only come out when you come in! Fine.

Can I go to the meeting now? Good. See you shortly, I assume!'

He met the manager, Gilles Arnaud, and pursued the usual line of questioning, including the question as to whether a Sheikh Ahmed had an account at the bank.

Gilles checked his records with no success, whilst Harry commented,

'Not at all surprised, bearing in mind bank transfer instructions were made from a cell phone, or satellite laptop. The location was fixed as somewhere close, but South of Tripoli.'

After discussing all options with Gilles, and agreeing to keep in touch, Harry left and joined Michel in the car.

They stopped at an open café, a short distance down the road, and sat near the open front. Whilst lunching Harry suddenly gagged on his food.

His eyes were playing tricks again. The woman who had appeared around a corner, and was walking quickly down the street could be/was Anna.

He leapt to his feet and ran down the street after her, as the first rattle of automatic gunfire hit his ears. The noise increased in intensity as responding gun fire started, and he saw chips of masonry flying from the building in front of him.

Throwing himself to the ground he rolled in the direction of the deep kerb, and lay motionless as the exchange of fire continued. It was an exchange from an upper floor to ground level about 30 metres away, and ceased as quickly as it had begun.

He looked for whom he thought was Anna, but the woman had disappeared. Possibly into a shop, close to where he had last seen her.

He ran across the road into the only open shop, which sold home hardware, pots, pans, paint, and tools. An old man was sitting behind the counter, his head in his hands, clearly affected by the recent gunfire.

At this point Michel joined him, grabbing his arm, and enquiring in extremely harsh tones,

'Mon Dieu, are you completely stupid? You could have been killed. Never, ever, do anything like that again, or you will be on your own, and I will tell Alain that his friend is totally mad and suicidal.'

Harry realised that he was completely in the wrong, and apologised to Michel, agreeing that such a situation would not occur again, ever.

Turning to the old man, he asked if a woman had run into the shop, a few minutes earlier.

Yes, was the reply, but she had run through the shop, into the small warehouse at the back, which has an exit onto an almost parallel street. And No, he did not know her.

Harry and Michel thanked him, and left, taking the car back to the hotel.

Once there Michel said, 'D'accord Harry. I think we need to start at the beginning concerning Anna, and you must explain to me everything.'

Harry did just that, but in précis form, up to, and including, her death in the previous December.

Michel remained silent for a minute or two when Harry finished.

'Harry, I can understand your sadness, having lost a woman you love. But, and I may sound cruel, you will have to live on some happy memories. The reality is, she will not come back, and if you continue to react like you did today, then you might die as well. That would not be sensible. Do you understand what I say?'

Harry nodded and paused, 'Yes, you're right. Let's get on with chasing Sheikh Ahmed down. I've got an idea, but will have to talk to London first. Let me send a request, and then I will discuss it with you. At least my Director will know I'm active when he sees my communication tomorrow morning!'

*

Monday 22nd September 2008. IISG HQ, London.

The Director read Harry's request, and telephoned his GCHQ contact to see if such a particular detail could be released to him, following the tracking and approximate identification of the area of transmission, near to, but South of Tripoli.

Transmissions carry their own unique code, and if known, and if further transmissions are made, can narrow down the location, by a comparatively simple electronic triangulation/and or satellite positioning, within 25-30 metres or less, using specialist software.

He received the detail that afternoon, and arranged to send the software by encrypted transmission to Harry's satellite laptop.

*

Tuesday 23rd December 2008. MI6 HQ, Vauxhall Cross, London.

The team assigned to Charles and Quentin had read the file before the meeting, so were well briefed on background, events, and results, including clear instructions from the Foreign Secretary.

General questions were raised as to proposed M.O., and the 24-hour security detail to be established. Few observations were made during the meeting, but after Charles and Quentin left, certain comments were made.

The team leader spoke first, 'How the hell does this fit with our current investigation as to leaks from the F.O. to Russia? If this is an official source, are we now looking at two potential feeds?'

No one answered.

'OK, we have two feeds now. One official, one unofficial. Work on that assumption.'

**

FCO Westminster, London.

Charles and Quentin were heavily involved in, what at times, could be described as, a moderately heated discussion.

Taking clear guidance from FCO policy documents, they were working on a number of scenarios, both in the short and medium term, where credible disinformation would be fed to Moscow, via the London Russian Embassy, by Charles.

Credibility and verification were paramount in what was being planned as to current UK Government and FCO thinking in a number of world regions.

In order to ensure both criteria, then UK media would be fed sufficient information to register suitable comment from home grown journalists in the UK, but which, in turn, would, no doubt, be picked up by European and regional broadsheets.

A delicate balancing act, sufficient to be credible, but not necessarily of a size to destabilise equilibrium, unless that was the UK Government's intention.

'Charles, I clearly recognise your far greater experience as to Lavrov's strategic thinking, but do you think that what you have just suggested is likely to be accepted by him at face value?'

Charles paused before replying,

'My credibility at present has to be at least 90% plus, bearing in mind, perhaps, his knowledge of what I have just been through recently.'

Charles then fell silent.

Quentin, recognising the current strength of Charles's argument, continued their discussion along hypothetical FCO policy lines.

At one point Charles suddenly interjected across what Quentin was saying,

'I've been thinking whilst you have been talking. Firstly, do you think that what has been achieved so far in terms of deception is both credible and feasible?

Secondly, do you also think that we have sufficient finesse within the FCO to provide a regular, but at times, contradictory foreign policy brief, that will assist us, and both our allies in Europe and the United States, in keeping Russia on the back foot?

Finally, do we need to brief at least the Americans and the French at the outset, otherwise international confusion, and a certain amount of testiness could arise?'

Quentin paused before replying,

'Bearing in mind the Foreign Secretary's ambivalence to our current proposal I think we need to keep it 'in house', certainly until we can see some positive results. Perhaps an opportunity for a verbal brief may present itself sometime in the interim.'

Charles said nothing.

12kms South of Tripoli, Lebanon.

Michel was driving, whilst Harry was studying the screen of his satcom kit, which now included the software sent from London.

Michel was understandably nervous of the region, bearing in mind the unpredictability of sporadic attacks by Hezbollah against Government forces, or vice versa.

As they drove along the road, passing Haret Al Fouwar, a short, sharp sound, and a rumbling sensation, indicated a blown tyre.

Coasting to a halt, Michel got out to inspect which wheel had been affected.

Almost immediately four figures rose from the roadside ditch, faces covered with the keffiyeh headscarf, all carrying automatic weapons pointed at Michel and the car.

Harry got out of the car and stood next to Michel.

One man stepped forward and spoke to Michel in Arabic.

Harry understood the gist.

Two men would change the wheel, Michel and Harry would be taken by the speaker and the fourth somewhere.

When outnumbered 2:1 in such a situation he thought, agree and re-group springs to mind. Harry indicated that he wished to take his laptop with him which was accepted.

They were led by one Arab in front, the other at the rear, through some olive trees, towards a small farmhouse, about a kilometre from the road, sitting on a small knoll, which gave an elevated view of the surrounding terrain.

Entering the farmhouse, they were pushed into the main room where one man sat at a large table, on which lay several automatic weapons, and a number of ammunition boxes.

Harry presumed the man was a local Hezbollah leader.

Passport and Identity Card were handed over.

Michel was asked a number of brusque questions in Arabic, which he answered in a measured tone, occasionally indicating Harry.

Harry, interrupting, spoke in English,

'Look, I had a stopover in Beirut, and telephoned Michel in Tripoli, who promised to show me some of the country outside of town. I've never been here before.'

The leader then spoke in English, glancing at the passport,

'Mr Baxter, my country at present is not stable, with many people very unhappy with the Government, and the way it is treating them.

Your friend Michel is stupid to treat you as a tourist, and I have told him so.'

He paused.

'Why your laptop?'

'I take photos to take home, and write some comments on the views.'

'Show me.'

Harry opened his laptop and pulled up some photos he had taken in Beirut. Street scenes, and the hotel,

'I had not taken any photos today, before your men stopped us. When I get back to London I try and sell them to magazines.'

The leader gave them a cursory glance.

'Go back to Tripoli. Now. You understand?'

He said the same thing in Arabic to Michel, who nodded vigorously in agreement.

Identity Card and Passport were handed back, and they were escorted back to their vehicle, with the punctured wheel having been replaced.

They did not speak until they had started back towards Tripoli.

'That was too damn close,' Harry muttered, 'Thank God he didn't want to go exploring in my laptop.'

Michel nodded, 'We were fortunate today. Next time we might not be so lucky.'

'By the way,' Harry said, 'That new tracking software had picked up nothing before the tyre was punctured.'

They continued towards Tripoli in silence for a time, both locked in their thoughts as to what had happened, and what might have happened.

As they reached the outskirts of Tripoli, Harry saw the flag on his laptop indicating a received email.

The Director was telling him to get back to London soonest. Significant developments which could have a strong connection with current investigations had arisen.

Harry brought Michel up to speed with his change of plan, who turned the car South towards Beirut. Arriving in Beirut Harry found a BA flight leaving on Thursday morning at about 0800hrs, which would get him into London Heathrow at about 1100hrs local time.

**

Thursday 25th September 2008. IISG HQ, London.

Harry knocked on the Director's office door at about 1430hrs that afternoon.

'Sit down Harry. I'm guessing a good strong black coffee would be acceptable?'

'No contest!'

'Right,' he said pouring a cup for Harry, 'An update which includes some quite extraordinary connections and activities. You will recall the investigations that have been going on since 2006, across several jurisdictions, involving two major French banks.

These cover breaking UN and US sanctions, and dealing with certain proscribed countries, Iran, Cuba, Sudan, the amounts involved running into many billions of dollars.

As yet no legal case has been brought against them, but when it does the repercussions will be significant. Keep that in mind. We now have information of a further investigation which involves another European bank.

This time money-laundering is the activity. Indications, so far, show that large sums of money, from Eastern Europe, and it is certain to include Russia, have been funnelled through a small LLP [Limited Liability Partnership] in London, reputedly owned by companies in the Seychelles, and other offshore locations.

A small branch of a European bank in Eastern Europe was transferring, every day, very large sums of money, equivalent to many millions of pounds, through the London LLP. Such actions clearly consistent with money laundering.

Although both investigations are apparently not connected, there is a line of thought that says there might be a link, albeit at this stage tenuous, with our Saudi transfer and disappearance.'

The Director then sat back with a querying look on his face directed at Harry, waiting for a response.

Harry shrugged, 'Only tenuous? Before I reply, where has all this information come from?'

'Sources at present not approved for disclosure.'

'All right. If we are involved in this, my first question would be, where do we start?

Do we have the necessary resources on the ground as IISG, and how far can we tap our good friends in Europe, the USA, and the Middle East? Maybe, and it's a big maybe, if we had a first team of all those available, who I've just mentioned, and, by the way, let's throw in the UK's 5 and 6 as well, then we might be able to make a start.

If not, then not a cat in hell's chance of getting off first base.'

The Director slapped the desk with the palm of his hand, and then said,

'Good response Harry, exactly my thinking. But what if we were to break it down and focus on one or two areas.'

'Different ball game, Director. But which one or two areas?'

'Sixty-four-Dollar question Harry. We need to put our very selective thinking caps on. Let's look at some of the detail.'

'For example?'

'What if the Saudi transfer and Sheikh Ahmed disappearance were just the result of a money laundering transaction going wrong, for whatever reason.? Sticky fingers, no honour amongst thieves?

The amount of the Saudi transfer was very small compared to the East European daily amounts I've just referred to, going through the LLP. Maybe our initial focus should be on East Europe and the London LLP?'

The Director fell silent, obviously waiting for Harry to respond.

'Well, Harry replied, 'at least that could be a starting point depending what other intel we can collect in the meantime. Can I tap a few of my European friends to see if they have any nuggets?'

'Yes Harry, but make sure your questions have an oblique angle to them. Understood?'

'Of course. I'll start with the LLP on Monday, when I've caught up with all the file details you are going to give me?'

'A little light reading for you Harry. That'll probably take care of Friday, and most of the weekend.'

'Thank you, Director. I hope you have a good weekend too!'

**

Monday 29th September 2008. IISG HQ, London.

Harry was going over again some elements in the data given to him by the Director the previous week.

The memory stick on his laptop gave him all information provided from the confidential source with additional comments or observations added by the Director.

Not surprisingly there was no clue as to source of the Intel, although one or two sentences and phrases gave an indication that a translation had occurred. However, no idea as to language or country.

What was clear however, was the location and description of the LLP, not far from IISG HQ. It was situated in a nondescript street just to the east of Kings Cross Station.

It had one of those all-embracing names, International Financial Services.

Harry decided to visit that Monday, and presented himself at 1100hrs at Reception. No one was in attendance, but an electric pushbutton invited visitors to PUSH, which he did.

A young man with a bored look appeared, and enquired 'Yes?' in a similar tone.

Harry's story was that a friend had recommended them as a suitable commercial operation for providing a 'bed and breakfast' service for a small trading company, which he was starting.

The response did not surprise him. They were full up and could not take on any additional companies. Perhaps in at least six months' time there might be a slot. Suggest he contacts them then.

Harry thanked him and left.

If the intel was correct then obviously it was a straight cover for the laundering operation. Monies in, and monies out.

But, as an LLP, how were the transactions handled? What was the M.O.? Electronic transfers handled in the UK, or elsewhere? Probably receipts into numbered accounts, no names? Onward transmissions, similar, or using two-step process in UK, or elsewhere? Could we bug, or hack the company? Options, various. Discuss!

Harry took a gentle stroll down the street, and up a parallel one, to see if there was a possible rear access to the building. Yes, but not easy. A traverse across a single storey garage roof would give access to the rear of the property. That might be the only option for an access team. Just a minute, he thought, IISG does not have access teams as yet. He was still thinking of the 'Old Firm'. Fresh thinking required Harry!

He made his way back to the office and filed a report including his questions.

Clearly access is required to bank accounts. How can this be achieved? Official Frontal Fear approach, or black ops? Hacking the LLP network has to be an option. Legality, official support?

This is definitely one for the Director, he thought, and signed off on that suggestion.

Tuesday 30th September 2008. IISG HQ, London.

The Director was reading Harry's report and observations as he entered the office and sat down. The Director looked at him quizzically,

'As you observe Harry in one section, we do not, as yet, in IISG, have the same level of resources that we could call on previously, and I am sure that Washington Head Office would not be too happy for you to start freelancing.'

Harry nodded, 'I'm not arguing Director, I fully appreciate our new style of operation. I'm just thinking how we can crack that particular nut with our limited resources.'

'Harry, in these early days we are confined to legwork, and contacts. We will have to be extremely careful that none of our investigations cross the line, and result in our organisation being investigated. Do I make myself clear?'

'Absolutely. But, if information came to us from a third party, who was not working under such restrictions, would that be acceptable?'

The Director looked at him suspiciously before replying, 'For example?'

'I don't know, I'm just exploring possible scenarios.'

'Fine Harry, explore, but clearance with me first.'

'Definitely, of course Director.'

***

VI

October 2008.

Harry telephoned Alain Dubois in Paris,

'Bonjour mon vieux,' Alain responded, 'And what can I assist you on today?'

'It is slightly delicate Alain, so was wondering if you are coming to London in the near future?'

'Give me an indication of what you mean by 'delicate'.'

'Well, with your team in London, and remembering their flexibility in the past, was wondering if a small incursion could be arranged, which I think could be of benefit for both of us, and therefore our bosses.'

'Where?'

'In London.'

'A possibility, certainly. Let me call you later on your mobile. This evening?'

'Perfect.'

Harry next telephoned his old CIA friend in Washington, Jack DeCosta. After the usual greetings, and old friends insults, Harry ran the same scenario past Jack that he had outlined to Alain.

'Why?' was Jack's first response.

'Well, you must be aware that IISG does not have the same capacity and resource as my old firm, so hence the question. Incidentally, I have also asked Alain Dubois if he can assist, and he's calling me this evening.'

'Well Harry, if you can give me some sort of outline, no names I understand, I might be able to get our local man interested, if there is some intel benefit.'

'Oh, there's that for sure, Jack. I'll email something by this evening. If you can't assist, I'll understand, but it certainly has enough specific content to warrant your interest.'

'I look forward to the read later,' Jack replied.

Remembering what the Director had said, Harry decided to wait until he had either positive or negative responses from Alain and Jack. He had an oblique conversation with Alain that evening who indicated that he thought some assistance was possible, and that he would be in London the following Tuesday to properly discuss.

One plus, one to go. Had all the makings of the old firm partnerships, he thought.

Friday 3rd October 2008. IISG HQ, London.

Harry had spent Friday doing more digging and research on bank trading and international transfers.

With fast electronic connections and 24-hour trading, control and governance, by either banking or government institutions, was always going to be miles behind the events, and as the current situation clearly demonstrated, often required a 'whistleblower', in one form or another, (fear, or favour, being the norm.).

Back in his apartment that evening, at about 2100hrs, his telephone rang. He answered in the usual way, giving his name, expecting a voice in response. Nothing, just silence for a few seconds, although he thought he could detect a sound of breathing before the line went dead.

Wrong number he thought, and gave it no more thought.

Monday 6th October 2008. IISG HQ, London.

Jack's response was waiting for him when he arrived in the office.

The man who would contact him was Phil Mason. Currently sitting in the US Embassy in London. His official designation was Liaison Officer, Office of Defense Cooperation. A broad enough title, and department, for him to fly under most radar.

He telephoned Harry at about 1100hrs. The conversation was circumspect, merely arranging a meeting for Wednesday, 1400hrs at IISG's office, at Harry's suggestion, so that he would have Alain's reaction to add, or subtract, to their discussion.

Tuesday 7th October 2008. South Kensington, London.

Harry met Alain at noon in a small restaurant in South Kensington, to be greeted by,

'Mon vieux copain, plus ça change, plus c'est la même chose!'

'Unfortunately, mon ami, you're right again! Let me bring you up to speed. A little complicated, but……'

Harry took Alain through all the recent events, and then concentrated on the huge, clearly illegal, bank transfers from Eastern Europe through London, to points West. He touched on, briefly, the fact that two major European bank groups were also under investigation, concerning illegal operations with proscribed countries.

At this point, Alain's eyes widened slightly, and he cut in,

'Yes, Harry, without naming names, I am aware of this. Very sensitive, and very stupid by the banks. It will be very ugly when it is concluded.' He shook his head at this point, 'Just greed.'

Harry nodded in agreement,

'Very unfortunate, but not the one, or ones, we are after. The East European transfers are coming through a small LLP here in London. IISG is hugely restricted in terms of field ops, and what we can do. We do not have the flexibility of the old firm, or your souplesse!

What I was hoping for, is that you or your team, could pay a little visit to determine what they were doing, and leave, giving the impression it was just a typical opportune burglary. Incidentally, I will be discussing the same thing with our US friends tomorrow.'

'Is that with your good friend Jack?'

'No, but one of his team based here in London, Phil Mason.'

'Don't know him, but would like to. Could I come to your meeting?'

'I'll have to get clearance from him, I'll call you tomorrow, mid-morning. But first, could you help us, in what form, etcetera, with this LLP?'

'D'accord! Nous sommes une équipe!'

Wednesday 8th October 2008. IISG HQ, London.

Clearance was agreed with Phil Mason, conveyed to Alain, and advised to the Director.

Phil Mason turned out to be a well-grounded individual, with a flexible attitude, and no apparent hang-ups. The discussion flowed, additional comment concerning the investigation of two European banks being provided by Phil, who intimated that certain UN members had kick-started that one.

'Perhaps not in on the deals,' he noted somewhat cynically.

He offered to work closely with Harry, commenting on Jack's long-standing relationship with him, but, thought that Alain's team were probably, on previous performance, best suited for the 'Entry' request!

Contact details were exchanged, and frequency, on a need-to-know basis.

Following the meeting Harry briefed the Director who listened closely.

'Fine Harry, but a couple of observations, no, make those instructions.

We cannot have any clear connection with Alain's team, and at this stage I need to have no detail. How they gain entry to the LLP is none of my, or your business. I do not need to know whether they are using UK or French teams, or whether someone gave them the key to the front door.

We must keep our noses very clean, and with no risk to the reputation of IISG, either here, or in The States. Is that understood?'

'Completely.'

'Excellent, just keep me up to speed.'

Thursday 9th October 2008. IISG HQ, London.

Harry briefed Alain, in detail, as to what the 'Entry' project was looking for. Obviously, physical documented evidence, files, diaries, etc, but even more importantly, computer log files of transactions both in and out, and, if possible, source locations of inbound transfers, and, possibly more easily recognised, destination locations.

From Alain's perspective the team may not be able to acquire all this information and data in one visit, so the first must give no indication of entry, in order to allow for a second if required. Alain planned on a team maximum of three/four, two being computer specialists with diverse skills, including hacking, deep network penetration, and specific international digital bank operation experience, the other three or four being masters in clean entry and withdrawal operations, including power systems and control.

In terms of timing, he proposed that the first entry would be carried out overnight Saturday/Sunday 17th/18th October, commencing no earlier than midnight Saturday, and withdrawal no later than 0400hrs on the Sunday.

If a second entry was required, at least two weeks should elapse before any further attempt was made.

Harry contributed all the information that was at his disposal, pointing out that clearly all evidence uncovered would be shared between them.

It was very clear from information to date, that there was huge sensitivity attached to this operation, both from the illegal transfers that had already taken place, but also from the political connections implicated therein. Public disclosure would have significant, and damaging, repercussions around the globe.

Alain then outlined his plans for a recce of the office, precise location, front, back, and sides. Any residential units adjacent, traffic flow, possible access points, installed security systems, electronic location and identification. Power supplies, electricity particularly. Possible stand-alone power generation if mains supply failed, etc, etc.

Harry commented, 'Well Alain, all that is your bag. Just don't start a small war when you do it!'

'Moi? Never! They will never know we have been there.'

'Can I have that in writing please Alain?'

'We both need this information, Harry. I will be very careful, pas problème!'

Tuesday 14th October 2008. French Embassy, London.

Alain had invited Harry to the meeting to provide some background data to the two specialists who would be attempting to crack access codes and download data from the systems installed at IFS.

Harry outlined countries and banks of interest, and any or all, that were flying under obvious aliases. Consistent large-scale transfers, both in and out of IFS, to any points, east or west would be of interest, and over the last two/three years would be ideal.

The two experts indicated that if access to the systems were to take some time, then total acquisition of data would be reduced. Alain countered this by saying that, if necessary, a second entry would be carried out, after analysis as to what had been secured, and downloaded.

Harry thanked them in advance for their actions on his, and Alain's behalf, this being met with a wry smile, a gallic shrug, and 'Pas problème!'

Back at base Harry briefed the Director, who looked a little apprehensive as details were revealed,

'There can be no connection back to IISG? Is that clear, and correct? If so, fine.'

Harry explained again, that the same data was required by Alain and DGSE, to see if there were any cross-links to the current investigations into two major French banks. In many ways IISG were merely riding piggy-back on a major DGSE investigation.

'Right Harry, I look forward to your further report after this weekend, hopefully with all being achieved in one entry, but I have a slight suspicion it might take a second!

If a connection can be shown, linking some of these transactions, or, for that matter, one transaction, with the mystery in Saudi Arabia then we will have made a little progress. Plus, DGSE will be piling up the evidence against a number of international banks. And, not before time!'

That evening at about 2000hrs Harry went back to his apartment, taking the Underground from Oxford Circus to the Elephant & Castle, where he changed trains, to continue south to Clapham Common.

As he left the station, and started walking in the direction of his apartment, he became conscious, or so he thought, of a tail. As he passed some shops, he suddenly stopped, turned, and backed up to shop window three units back. He could then see who was following, whether innocent or guilty.

One man had turned quickly into a shop doorway and disappeared. Harry smiled. A shop specialising in ladies' garments, and with a large display of underwear!

Harry waited in the doorway of his adjacent shop, and a few minutes later the man appeared, with no package or parcel, and started off down the street in the same direction.

As he passed, Harry stepped out and tapped him on his right shoulder. As the man turned to the right, Harry moved left and tapped his left shoulder, so he now swung to the left, facing Harry who immediately grasped his right hand in a very firm handshake.

'Simple question. Firstly, why are you following me, and secondly, if you try anything, I will break your wrist. Do you understand?'

The man nodded his head.

'Right. Why are you following me?'

The man started to speak; the accent was East European,

'We need to talk.'

'Why.'

'I know who you are, and what you are looking for.'

'You're talking rubbish.'

'I am not. I have good connections.'

'OK, so what am I looking for?'

'Sheikh Ahmed.'

Harry was so surprised his grip momentarily slackened, at which the man immediately broke his grip, turned, and walked quickly away.

Harry stared after him, thinking furiously. So somewhere in the web there is an East European connection, he thought.

Clearly the man did not want to fight, but to trade. But to trade what? How did he know about me? What connection does he have with some of the other players? Curiouser, and curiouser. The Director will love this when I tell him!

He walked to his apartment, turning things over in his mind, and frankly not getting very far. His street was packed with parked cars. As he walked towards his apartment, he was not paying attention to any of them.

As he started to pass a car facing towards him, the driver's door violently swung open and hit his legs and lower stomach.

He grabbed the door to stop himself falling, as the driver started to exit, balaclava clad, a glove fist raised.

He was not fully out of the car as Harry slammed the door, using his full body weight against one of the driver's legs which produced a muffled scream of pain. Meanwhile the passenger, also balaclava clad, was circling the front of the car, approaching Harry from behind. Harry spun round, and, with no obligation to Queensbury rules, placed a well-deserved kick in an area where it hurts the most.

The driver, meanwhile, had pulled himself back into the car, started the engine, and drove away, leaving Harry with one sobbing, balaclava clad, thug.

Harry called the police, and waited, having pulled off the balaclava, and viewed what he thought were classic Slavic features. It being Clapham, a Police car quickly appeared, took a statement from Harry, and carried out a formal arrest of the individual.

The arrival of the police with flashing lights, brought out some residents, curious to find out the cause. Harry meanwhile kept a low profile.

As Harry entered his apartment, he was wondering what the connection was. First, East European accent, and then secondly, Slavic features. Too much of a coincidence. And why the supposed connection with Sheikh Ahmed? Frankly, bloody confusing. Never mind, bring the Director up to date tomorrow.

Meanwhile a nibble and a glass of something. And never mind the developing bruises and cuts on my shins, and the faintly aching stomach!

Thursday 16th October 2008. IISG HQ, London.

Harry saw the Director at about 1000hrs.

He had written his report covering events the previous evening, so decided to let the Director read it, before, no doubt, he started throwing questions at him.

'Hmm. What the hell is going on Harry? And before you answer, I think we need to do some basic analysis, review, and dare I say, some conjecture, as to what we are apparently facing on several fronts.'

He paused, 'Well? Firstly, I hope only your pride was dented, and not your knees and gut! What is your interpretation of these events, and why have you been singled out for attention?'

'To be honest, I have no idea,' Harry replied, 'But the first reference to Sheikh Ahmed might be a clue. The second is, if the man currently held in custody by Clapham Police sings a little, but,' he added hastily, 'as IISG, we can't exert any pressure. On the other hand, unless, of course, some old colleague of yours could do a bit of digging on our behalf?'

'Yes Harry, I get your drift, but at this stage a little unlikely. I will, of course, on your behalf, be making enquiries to the police to see if they have gleaned anything. To mitigate his position the man currently detained may provide some information. We'll see.'

When Harry arrived at his apartment that evening, he found a note pushed through the letterbox, giving a mobile telephone number, and two words, 'Ahmed business'.

He rang the Director, leaving a message that he would follow up the following day unless advised otherwise.

Friday 17th October 2008. London.

At about 1030hrs, not having received from the Director any instruction to the contrary, Harry called the mobile number.

It rang a few times before answering, 'Yes?'

'A note was left in my apartment yesterday with this number, and a two-word message. How do you think you can assist?'

'We have to meet,' the caller said, and then suggested a small café on the edge of Clapham Common at 1500hrs.

Harry agreed. Following the call, he then telephoned the Director to bring him up to date.

'I'll find out as much as I can, without compromising our position, and then brief you.'

'Fine Harry, but take care, we know what form East European discussions can be!'

At 1500hrs Harry walked into the café, a small number of people at tables, but one individual, with slight Slavic features, seated on his own.

Harry approached, and asked, 'You can assist with a particular location, you say? I'm Harry Baxter.'

The man looked at him, and gestured towards a chair, 'Yes, I can. Me Petro Dudnyk.'

The man looked at him silently for a few seconds, before starting,

'First, you have to understand the various problems in countries in the East of Europe, I am Ukrainian.'

Harry nodded.

'Second, I do not want money for information I give you.'

Harry nodded again.

'A man you worked with in Government was brought back from Russia recently. His name Urwin.'

Harry just controlled his facial expression to remain in neutral.

'He arrived British Embassy Moscow.'

Harry's brain was running in top gear, 'Where was this going?' he thought.

'He was doped for all journey, but sometime talk. Your name spoke twice.'

Harry put his hand up and spoke bluntly, 'How does any of this connect with location of Ahmed?'

'Please, connection through bank in Latvia. Big transfer money made by Ahmed. But he stupid. Not pay commission. Some people very angry. He disappear.'

'But, why contact me? And why did your friends try and beat me up the other night?'

'In Ukraine we have people who are friends with Russia, I am not friend.'

Harry paused, before replying. It did not make proper sense.

'Ahmed, a member of a wealthy family, making a business investment. Why should he pay commission?'

'He could not raise money from family, so talk with people who had good friend in Latvia mafia. They make deal with bank but want commission. He not pay. He disappear.'

'So why contact me?'

'I know certain people want to stop investigation into banks connected with Ahmed loan. Your name is on file. Russians and Russian friends want to stop investigation. That is why you attacked by home.'

Petro fell silent, waiting for a response from Harry, who by now was completely nonplussed, and just about grasping the various angles within the situation.

'How long will you be in London, because I think we have to have a meeting with my Director at my office in London?'

'A few days, no more. I then return to Kiev.'

'OK. If I can organise, can we meet tomorrow, Saturday?'

'Yes, telephone me.'

They parted, Harry immediately contacting the Director.

Harry quickly explained that a meeting was necessary and urgent based on Petro's schedule, whilst recognising the inconvenience of a Saturday.

However, on the bare bones provided by Harry, and his clear pressure for a meeting, the Director agreed. 1030hrs Saturday morning IISG office.

The Director was polite when meeting Petro, but was wearing his 'I'm prepared to listen, but I will need convincing,' facial expression.

Harry filled in the background that had preceded his initial meeting with Petro, plus a summary of the detail that Petro had provided the previous afternoon.

The Director listened carefully, whilst still maintaining his facial expression, to all that both Harry and Petro said, only, on one occasion, turning towards Harry with a raised eyebrow.

When both had finished silence reigned, for almost a minute, before the Director spoke,

'I am sure Petro, that you are aware, of both my and Harry's previous positions, within the UK government's security service. Needless to say, I ran a few checks overnight, both here in the UK, and the USA.

The information I received, indicated that you previously held a similar position, within the Ukraine security service, before resigning.

However, my US sources indicate that you still have a continuing, friendly working relationship with them, including intelligence being provided in both directions. Would you care to elaborate?'

Petro smiled, 'If you had not run checks on me, I be surprised. The situation is difficult with political problem with Russia, and groups in Ukraine, some pro-Russia, others more national Ukraine. With big crime in Eastern Europe, Russia Bratva, Albania gangs, Turkish, Italian Mafia, now start Vietnamese.'

He fell silent for a few seconds,

'What we have, and the Ahmed bank crime is good case, is where a government, or people in a government, and a crime family are linked. Corruption in government. It must be stopped.'

The Director turned to Harry, a small smile on his lips,

'I will give you one opportunity. Who do you think is Petro's handler in Washington?'

'No. You are joking, I hope. Not Jack DeCosta?'

The Director nodded,

'Yes, Petro comes recommended, and he has been working with Jack for over three years.'

'Well, I suppose we should be grateful. At least we don't need to run any further checks on Petro, do we?', he said, turning to shake hands with Petro.

They shook hands and the brief/debrief continued.

The Director then said,

'Before we go any further the major, and critical subject, we must discuss is the kidnap and return of Charles Urwin to the UK. How much detailed and verifiable intelligence do you have of that incident?

You made certain comments to Harry. Are these rumours, or, do you believe factual? What, or who, was your source? This we need to verify. Do you have any connections or sources that can provide detail, or fill in any obvious gaps, from start to finish of that incident?

Are there, to your knowledge, any specific UK contacts or connections, that would have been involved in his kidnap, and/or his subsequent return?

Before you answer, please be aware that this is a highly delicate political situation, which involves both the UK Foreign & Commonwealth Office, and MI6. Before any statements are made, we must be 110% sure of our facts.'

Petro replied, after clearly marshalling his thoughts.

'Because of problems in Eastern Europe we develop safe relation with certain people in other country's intelligence. One contact of mine is from Belarus. He is friend of the West, but he is also friend of officer in Russian intelligence station in Belarus.

They talk, and exchange information to help each other. He told me of diplomatic package coming to Moscow. He did not know then what was in package. When your man found outside UK Embassy in Moscow, then he knew.'

The Director and Harry looked at each other, Harry speaking first,

'This is going to cause a lot of unfriendly stuff to hit the fan, both in the FCO, and our old firm, don't you think?'

'No doubt about that Harry, it has catastrophe written all over it, even if the original version was true, and this is Russian spin to cause major embarrassment to the UK government.'

They both fell silent; this being broken by Petro,

'If I can help, and you want me to, then I will. I do not like Russia and the games they play.'

The Director looked at him squarely,

'Thank you for your offer, Petro. Any additional horsepower is always welcome, but obviously I shall require approval from IISG HQ in Washington. You do understand?'

'Yes, call me when you have Yes, or No.'

The discussion then briefly turned to their respective results in pursuing the various bank connections in Europe and Lebanon with the Ahmed transfer, and current holding positions which would need to be resolved with sensitivity and diplomacy, bearing in mind their updated intelligence.

After Petro left, the Director and Harry discussed, and reviewed, the new information received, and what should be their first steps. The room became quiet from time to time, as each was turning over in their mind, what the impact would be, in various Government departments, if such information was to be made public.

The Director tried to sum up,

'Whichever way you look at this, and the possible actions or reactions, the outcomes could be catastrophic. The number of players involved are legion, countries several, integrities in many cases doubtful, validity of intelligence not yet confirmed.

Other than those few concerns, and to what extent our security services are up to speed, it means that this situation is a huge morass, into which a significant number of reputations, including intelligence and Government, could fall.'

Harry looked at the Director,

'Well, I suppose on that basis, a few telephone calls, a couple of meetings with the right people would put the whole thing safely to bed! But, there again, I think not!'

The Director smiled, somewhat strained,

'I need to sleep on this Harry, before I update Washington. And that is going to be an interesting conversation. Lord knows what the reaction is likely to be! Sleep on it as well Harry, next week could be a very demanding week!'

Harry went back to his apartment, regurgitating, mentally, all the information, much contradictory, and decided that he would go down to the country pub run by his friends, for the rest of the weekend. A battery recharge for the next week was necessary.

*

Saturday/Sunday 18th/19th October 2008. East of Kings Cross Station.

The 'Entry Team' of three specialists, organised by Alain Dubois were on station just before 0100hrs, having run a 'blind' recce of the adjacent area shortly before midnight.

There did not appear to much activity, vehicles or pedestrians, the area being mostly small offices, two four-storey office blocks, and one small factory with yard. Street lighting was poor, ideal for their purpose, and what was intended.

The three men clad in black jeans, sweaters, and balaclavas, swarmed silently up to a back window, which was apparently alarmed. The entry expert quickly isolated that, and the team were in on the first floor within minutes. What surprised them was the overall lack of building security, but when discussing this after the event they came to the conclusion that the company, IFS (International Financial Services), had concentrated their investment on the hardware/software, data, and comms units, which proved to be a significantly harder nut to crack and open.

It took a good ninety minutes before they were accessed, several layers of encryption, some blind alleys, but finally success.

A huge mass of data was downloaded, going back several years, providing significant levels of information as to original sources of money transfer, personal names and banks, inwards and outwards transmission information, and significantly, full details of accounts in receiving banks in the Caribbean and Indian Ocean.

The team left as easily as they entered, leaving no physical trace, whether on the building itself, or on the banks of IT and comms units, clearing the area by 0400hrs.

When Alain was briefed later that Sunday, he congratulated the team on the huge volume of information, which would greatly assist both IISG, and DGSE. He looked forward to the analysis of this in due course, which would be shared with IISG.

Monday 20th October 2008. Foreign Office, London.

Quentin and Charles were discussing certain elements of UK Government foreign policy covering specific areas in Eastern Europe, and the particular or general emphasis that should be applied within briefs to the Foreign Secretary.

It was obvious, that during such discussions a certain amount of contention arose, as both men, well versed in shades of grey, and any shade in between, would debate from their own intellectual perspective, and attempt to ensure their own view or emphasis prevailed.

From Charles's position, he needed to demonstrate, when the Foreign Secretary made a public statement, that no attempt was being made to either insult or antagonise current Russian foreign policy.

For him, very much a thin ice position.

'Quentin, I do find this way of doing things extremely frustrating, and intellectually debilitating. Could we not prepare on the basis of my draft submitted to you, returned, hopefully, with minimal commentary, and then forwarded to the Foreign Secretary for his sight?'

'Charles, I know you are fully aware of the clear advice, nay instruction, given to us both, as to how we should prepare the policy document for consideration, However,' he added hastily, noting the exasperated expression on Charles's face, 'I am happy to submit your proposal for consideration, so that we can continue our enjoyable working partnership.'

Charles did not reply, his facial expression conveying everything.

1530hrs IISG HQ, London.

Harry had been called to the Director's office.

The Director was standing behind his desk, looking a little tired.

'Sit down Harry. I'm starting to wonder, again, if I'm getting too old for this fun and games. I've spent a long time on the telephone to

Washington, obliquely indicating what has transpired, and, essentially, the resultant demands likely to be placed on our organisation.

Despite our unofficial links to previous partners, US, French etc, this current situation is moving up the scale significantly. If we are to get involved, then we need additional funding to increase our capacity, particularly good men and women on the ground.

Our income stream is likely to be reduced due to the advice concerning Sheikh Ahmed, and we cannot rely on other operations cross-feeding what you and I were discussing this morning. Washington has asked us to look at other possible income streams, or arm's length Government funding, for areas they would find too sensitive, whether political or intelligence based.

If anything blows up, particularly in our face, the Government can merely tut-tut from a distance, with no risk of damage to their reputation.

I also suggested. that as the IISG UK subsidiary is active in the UK, Europe, Middle East and Gulf, it would also be appropriate for them in Washington to make the same sort of representation to their own particular Government Department which has similar parallel interests.

They said they would look into it, and I suggested they might have a conversation with Jack DeCosta, CIA, who knows us, and you particularly well. I've left it with them, and they promised to revert soonest. We shall see.'

Harry nodded, 'With your agreement I'll keep the situation warm with Petro, until you hear back from Washington. I want to find out how much he knows about Charles Urwin. The FCO sometime may have to get involved.'

'Agreed Harry, but no trips until we know what will be happening from Washington.'

'Understood.'

Harry decided, without informing the Director, that he would be a little bit pro-active.

He telephoned Jack DeCosta in Washington. After the usual exchanges Harry outlined why he had called.

'Jack, we are getting involved, no, are actively involved, in a very big, and I mean very big, exercise here. Cannot give you any details over the phone, but I do know that IISG Washington may be contacting you shortly concerning our activity, and a pressing need for some funding. If you are over here anytime soon, I can obviously fully brief you at that time.

The data coming out will also be of significant interest to you and your boss, so hope our request will be looked at carefully. OK?'

'Fine Harry, I copy that, and by the way will probably be in London in about ten days. You can fully brief me at that time; however, it's playing out.'

'Wilco.'

Tuesday 21ˢᵗ October 2008. FCO, Westminster, London.

A flap was building. Both internally and externally.

A senior member of the Russian Embassy located in Kensington Palace Gardens, London W8, had presented himself at Kensington Police Station, seeking political asylum.

The police had gone through all the necessary formalities, including advising The Foreign & Commonwealth Office, and, as a consequence, such information was passed to the security services.

All that was known at that time, was that the individual concerned was a First Secretary. Which particular sphere of responsibility was not known currently. However, the normal reaction in such circumstances is for the Russian Ambassador, or his nominated representative, to request an early meeting with the individual concerned. Such meetings, which can be denied by the UK authorities, are invariably a waste of time. The mind was made up by the presentation of self at a Police Station.

The name given to the police was Dmitry Durov. Area of responsibility could be determined by searching the Russian Embassy list. However, in many cases area of responsibility was purely a cover for intelligence work, whether active, or counter.

A meeting was called hastily at the FCO, senior civil servants together with the Foreign Secretary, and members of the Security Services, 5 and 6.

Background information on Dmitry Durov was scarce as he had only recently taken up his position at the Russian Embassy. Prior to that, the only information concerning his activities was a senior admin role in Moscow at the Kremlin.

The consensus of the meeting determined that there would be no haste in responding to the Russian Embassy, and gentle interrogation would be the first step with Dmitry Durov.

Quentin Horncastle had attended the meeting, and briefed Charles on his return.

'Another Russian who has decided that that the UK fleshpots are more attractive than Moscow,' commented Charles, with obvious sarcasm, 'Probably weighing up a semi in Wimbledon against a block of flats on the outskirts of Moscow.'

'Who knows indeed?' responded Quentin, 'No doubt all will be revealed in due course.'

Little did they know, that in a few weeks' time, how true or false that comment could be.

*

A meeting had been arranged for an update, and partial data evaluation, between IISG and Alain Dubois, following the 'intervention' at Financial Services International.

Alain was delighted with the performance of his team, 'all hand-picked by me,' he proudly claimed.

Even more graphic was the huge volume of data acquired, and which would take several weeks, to analyse and format into some reasonable order.

However, there were some interesting headlines concerning some of the transfers, particularly from Russia to Latvia, then via London, to the Caribbean. Other destinations included tax havens in the Indian Ocean.

Analysis had shown that the original source of transfers from Moscow reached into the higher echelons of privileged Russian society, some with links into the Kremlin. If such information became public in Russia, one can only imagine the implications for those involved.

Total sums over a period of years ran into the equivalent of billions of dollars, such a tempting financial flow to be targeted for 'commissions, or handling charges.'

Detailed information, once compiled, would be shared between DGSE and IISG, both organisations benefiting from such specific intelligence, and which could assist in both their individual investigations.

After the meeting the Director and Harry discussed where emphasis should now be placed, once full analysis was available, and which would also be dependent on existing, or enhanced future resource.

Harry opened,

'Dependent on what you think, and also what Washington thinks, I need to refocus. But the question is where should one either pick up the threads, or start a new line based on what is now to be available?

Clearly on the intel from Petro, chasing the Ahmed shadow is now a dead end, literally, if his assassination is true. But there is still a significant unclaimed amount of dollars sitting in a bank, which, I am sure, would be quite happy for it to sit there indefinitely.'

The Director had nodded on a couple of occasions as Harry talked,

'Yes, we are fumbling in the dark currently. I hope that when Alain's team complete their detailed analysis, we may find one or two leads, or people to investigate. Meanwhile, I suggest you follow up with Petro, and see if any of his detail fits in with our jigsaw.'

'Agreed,' Harry replied, 'Although I do feel a little frustrated after some of the time we have spent down various cul-de-sacs!'

'Not arguing Harry, but often occurs where we are involved. Have patience!'

Friday 24th October 2008.

Harry met Petro on Friday at 1000hrs in the café on Clapham Common.

'What I would like Petro, at this stage, is to discuss what you know about Charles Urwin and his recent kidnap, and subsequent return to the UK, via our embassy in Moscow. You indicated that what we understand is the official line, is not necessarily the real one?'

Petro was quiet for a few seconds, obviously collecting his thoughts.

'As I said in our meeting, I get information from my friend in Belarus State Security in Minsk. He gets information from his friend in Russian Embassy, possible SVR.'

'Can we have their names? There might be something in our files on them.'

'I know my friend, but not name of Russian. I will ask, but he may not give.'

'Understood, but I have to ask,' said Harry smiling, 'If you can remember, what did your friend say, exactly?'

Petro paused again,

'If I remember right, your man named Urwin, arrived in Russia from the UK by ship. Not good deal with Moscow, so drugged, and arrived in Moscow outside UK Embassy. My friend was on duty when it happened so saw all details. After confirm it is Urwin, he was released to UK Embassy.'

Harry responded, 'Could I ask that you speak to your Minsk friend, and see if he can get any information from his Russian friend about Urwin? It is important for us, so would appreciate your help.'

'I will try, but maybe too difficult.'

'I understand Petro, but please try.'

They went their separate ways, Petro flying back to Kiev, Harry wondering if this was a typical no result goose chase.

'Who knows,' he thought, 'But we have to keep trying.'

*

Tuesday 28th October 2008. IISG HQ, London.

Harry kept the Director up to speed with his discussions with Petro, and his gentle pushing for more details.

The Director, in turn told Harry, that he had been told, confidentially, by an old friend, that a senior member of the Russian Embassy had recently claimed political asylum.

Such wheels grind slow, but the friend had promised an update, as, and when, further information was available.

Thursday 30th October 2008.

Harry received a call at the IISG London HQ at about 1645hrs. It was Petro calling from Kiev.

'Harry, I speak with my friend who has Russian friend in Moscow. You understand? Good. Russian friend in embassy in Minsk knew of Urwin from before.'

'What do you mean from before?'

'Last year, I think in Moscow.'

'Can you find out anymore for me Petro?'

'I will try, perhaps I am in Belarus next week.'

Friday 31st October 2008.

Harry received a call from Jack DeCosta, 'Good day Harry, I'm in town. When can we meet?'

'If you're free Jack, dinner tomorrow.'

'I'm never free Harry, but yes, let me know where, and what time!'

'Why not our usual Italian in South Kensington? About 7.00pm, I know you Americans like to eat early!'

'Done deal Harry, See you then.

But I would guess we've got some updating to do between us, haven't we?'

***

VII

November 2008

Saturday 1ˢᵗ November 2008. 1900hrs. Italian Restaurant, South Kensington, London.

After their usual mock insulting greetings, Harry started to bring Jack up to speed with what was happening on several fronts.

'With the data that has been collected, and is currently being processed, we believe there will be a raft of information covering these international hot money transfers through Latvia to many off-shore bases. You will not be surprised to hear that my good friend Alain Dubois, and his team, were able to collect all this data, on our behalf, but it will also provide significant evidence for current investigations DGSE are pursuing.

And, do not be surprised that, when that information is shared with you, it will probably plug a few gaps in what was originally kicked off by the UN, and identify one or more persons that you would like to interview, or at least keep tabs on!'

'Sounds good Harry, anything else on the immediate horizon?'

'Some gossip that a senior Russian diplomat at the embassy here is seeking political asylum. No details yet, but could add a little excitement for the FCO. Plus, some interesting contacts made by yours truly with some operators in Belarus, with some further links into local SVR. All a bit sketchy at the moment, but will share once I have something solid. It will be the least I can do, after you've picked up the tab for a superb meal!'

Jack laughed, 'I should have seen that one coming, but it is my turn, and intelligence never comes free!'

Wednesday 12th November 2008. IISG HQ, London.

That afternoon Harry received a telephone call from Petro.

'I speak you Harry from Kiev. Now back. I speak with my friend, who also speak with his Russian friend. You remember Russian friend; he say he know Urwin in Moscow?'

'Yes.'

'Well, Russian friend name is Stepan Volkov.'

'Are you sure. I know a Volkov. If it is the person I know, he is an SVR officer.'

'I just give you his name. I do not know his position, but he is in Russian Embassy in Minsk.'

'Petro, many, many thanks for that information. It could help us here greatly.'

'OK Harry, we keep in touch. Maybe you do me favour one day?'

Harry briefed the Director immediately.

'It's certainly a small world isn't it, Harry? Gets smaller by the year. However, that information is useful, because if needed and because of the two of you working together previously, would certainly assist in some way, even if we are not aware in which way, currently. Log and file Harry. A useful nugget I think!'

Thursday 13th November 2008. FCO, Westminster, London.

A small meeting was being held to determine next steps with the asylum seeking Russian, currently held in a safe house, under 24-hour protection and supervision.

The Chair of the meeting, a senior civil servant, Sir Robert Fordcombe, was running through the process which would determine the scope of questioning of the diplomat, to determine the truth of his request, complete scope of his position, level of intelligence to which he was party to in the embassy, family commitments, and what would be the details of his request for a new identity.

'Initially, we can delegate, from this group, two persons to conduct the initial questioning, and to form a view as credibility. Following that, we may need to bring in a more suited forensic team such as SO15, but I hope that will not be necessary. Any questions? No?

The two who will be carrying out the initial investigation at the safe house, are Fitzroy and Clements. This will be carried out on Friday the 14th and Monday 17th, with an initial review of the Q & A by this group on Tuesday the 18th.'

Fitzroy and Clements left to put their Q & A in order, using a previous template as a basic model, based on, co-incidentally, a former SO15 investigation. Naturally they were very pleased with such an opportunity, which must be grasped enthusiastically in the Civil Service. The opportunities to shine, if only in front of one's peers, are strictly limited.

Friday 14th November 2008. 1000hrs. Safe House, West London.

Fitzroy and Clements were admitted by the Security detail at the Safe House, and taken to the living room in which the interview would take place. The process was always designed to put the individual at ease, and to try and reduce any feeling of interrogation.

Dimitry Durov, a tall, slim man, in his late forties, joined them. His demeanour was confident, and he spoke impeccable English, with only a soft trace of accent.

The questioning took the usual form,

Question One. Why was he seeking political asylum? What did he hope to gain?

Question Two. Bearing in mind his senior position in the Russian Embassy, why?

Question Three. Did he have a family, and were they in London?

Question Four. If asylum was granted, did he not realise he would be a marked man by his action?

Answers came, slowly and with, apparently, clear thinking as to cause and effect.

Durov proffered one point, quite early on in his questioning, which caused Fitzroy and Clements to glance quickly at each other. Although he had said that his was a typical First Secretary role, his real responsibility was as Head of the SVR operation in the UK.

His consistent explanation for seeking asylum was his complete breakdown of trust in the present structure and control of the Russian Government. Corruption appeared endemic at almost every level, and within that buzzing hive you were either in, or very definitely, out.

It was apparent that he carried an overriding cynicism of the whole government structure, and frankly, wanted out.

Although he was married, and with no children, his wife, the daughter of a previous administration's commissar, was not in London, preferring her friends in Moscow to a formal, hierarchical atmosphere, in the embassy.

Durov said he understood their line of questioning, but his real value would be in his knowledge of SVR operations and agents in the UK, plus European and USA connections.

He smiled gently, when he said he looked forward to further detailed discussions, once all aspects of his asylum application had been agreed.

Fitzroy and Clements completed their questioning in line with their proforma, recognising that further discussions would require a more senior level, a person, or persons, permitted to give an indication of what might be offered, in exchange for what Durov suggests he could provide. Clearly very sensitive, not to be rushed, and no doubt, verification could take some time.

Upon returning to the Foreign Office, they verbally briefed Sir Robert Fordcombe, Chair of their small group, who listened without interruption.

When they had covered all their points and summary, he commented,

'I wonder how many times I have heard an identical, or similar explanation, to justify a request for asylum? No, don't answer that. I doubt if you can, as I'm carrying a few more years than both of you.

It's almost the SVR crib sheet to start negotiations. Don't misunderstand me. He could well be genuine, but for all our reputations', at this point, fixing his gaze on both of them, 'we will have to be doubly certain of his motives, and the value of what he has to offer.

Question him again, on Monday. Be quite repetitive, see if you can get him irritated, or obviously frustrated, with how slowly our process is moving. You may see a side of Durov you haven't seen before. Dependent on what happens on Monday, we can then consider how we wish to escalate the negotiation.'

Tuesday 18ᵗʰ November 2008. IISG HQ, London.

Harry was working his way through some irritating admin reports and fairly bland political overviews, when the Director called him for a meeting. Happy to put both to one side, he went the Director's office.

'Thought I would update you. My friend has put a name to this Russian seeking asylum. Dmitry Durov. A First Secretary, but that is obviously just a diplomatic cover. Not a name that jogs the grey matter, but the woods are full of them.'

'Status?' Harry enquired.

'Early days. Questions concerning reasons for seeking asylum, plus the usual fifty back up questions, which no doubt will be repeated more than once. I was thinking that perhaps some of your contacts may have some background on him which could fill in a few blanks. Also increase our street credibility with 5 and 6.'

'I'll see what I can find out, and let you know when, and if, I know.'

'Fine Harry, good luck.'

FCO, Westminster, London.

Fitzroy and Clements had repeated their questioning and gentle interrogation of Durov in the safe house on Monday, and were now outlining the responses to Sir Robert Fordcombe, who was listening patiently to their presentation. One point they omitted was the obvious anger shown by Durov during their meeting, when he clearly stated this was just time wasting, and he would only speak to a more senior F.O. official.

As they finished, he sighed, 'As I thought, no real progress, or depth, in terms of response.'

He sighed again, 'Reluctantly I shall have to pick up the cudgel myself. Please leave a copy of both sets of your questions and responses. I will advise you of my success, or otherwise, in due course.'

He smiled sadly and indulgently, with a gentle shake of the head at Fitzroy and Clements, in the style that both would have recognised instantly from their tutors at university.

He picked up his phone to organise a meeting at the safe house with Durov, waving his other hand in a dismissive gesture at Fitzroy and Clements.

Thursday 20th November 2008. IISG HQ, London.

Harry took the call from Alain who said he had some excellent news, and could Harry come to a meeting at the French Embassy soonest?

He readily agreed. 11.30am was confirmed. Harry thought to himself that perhaps the log jam was starting to break up, and yes, they definitely needed a break.

French Embassy Knightsbridge London

Alain met him in reception and took him immediately to one of the upper floors, where two members of the 'Insert' team were seated behind a bank of computer screens.

'Bien Harry.

I will say immediately that we have some excellent intelligence from our investigation. Henri and Guy will cover some of the details already analysed, but in terms of international activity it is global and highly sensitive. If any of this is released there are going to be some very embarrassed politicians and bankers in a number of countries around the world.'

Henri and Guy then detailed some of their early analysis of encrypted records, amounts, source, recipient, bank details, names or purely account number, etc.

On his return to HQ Harry briefed the Director, who also suggested he should also update Jack DeCosta in broad outline.

Safe House, West London.

Sir Robert Fordcombe smiled at Dimitry Durov as he shook his hand, and gestured to two armchairs situated either side of a small coffee table.

'I think it would be preferable' he said, 'if we addressed each other by our first names. At least that removes some of the formality from my questions, your responses, and my observations.'

He smiled again, 'Anyone who has taken the step that you have, needs to be put at ease, otherwise neither party will be able to determine what mutual benefit could arise from our discussions.'

'I would not argue with that suggestion,' replied Dimitry, allowing a very small smile to momentarily cross his face.

The conversation continued, Sir Robert initially covering again most of the items pursued by Fitzroy and Clements. He then changed tack.

'Clearly in a situation such a this, whilst recognising the basic facts that determined your wish for asylum to be granted, from our position there are a number of very important factors we must consider.

Amongst those is confirmation as to the integrity of your request, or is your action designed to embarrass the UK government in some way? Are your real motives well hidden for a specific reason?

And finally, if all such areas are forensically examined and proven, then the key question is, 'what is the overall benefit to the United Kingdom if your asylum request is accepted?

As you can see, I am sure, there is considerable ground to covered before any decision can be made.'

Sir Robert fell silent at this point, retaining a quizzical look at Durov. After a short pause Durov looked directly at Sir Robert,

'I cannot disagree with anything you have said Robert, and if positions were reversed, I am sure I would be replicating what you have just said. Let me provide something which falls under your heading of 'benefit to the United Kingdom', and which, I hope, will indicate a level of cooperation, and some value.'

Sir Robert nodded his head, 'Certainly Dimitri.'

Durov, looking directly at Sir Robert, spoke deliberately,

'Within your Foreign Office you have a senior leak, the individual concerned working actively over a number of years with our SVR. I do not know his or her name, but the quality of what has been made available to Russia has been high.'

Sir Robert had great difficulty in retaining his composure, but somehow it held. He played a straight bat back to Durov.

'Dimitry, I have to say that this is not the first time I have heard such an accusation from someone requesting asylum. Assuming it is true, I am sure you can imagine the length of the investigation to confirm or otherwise, and therefore the impact that would have on the process of approving, or otherwise, your possible asylum.'

Durov nodded, and quietly replied, 'Of course, which is why I have raised it now, at the beginning. Not something to be put on the table at the end of your current investigation.'

There then followed a brief discussion on how this would be examined, and Sir Robert returned to the F.O. to seek higher approval as to how the investigation would proceed.

Friday 21st November 2008. Russian Embassy Minsk, Belarus.

Stepan Volkov received an instruction from SVR HQ Moscow late on Friday. Report 0900hrs 24th November Moscow HQ for reassignment.

He nervously wondered what could cause such a rapid reassignment, but felt his performance in Minsk had been considered, certainly by the Ambassador, excellent.

Putting his doubtful thoughts to one side, he packed and travelled over the weekend to Moscow.

Foreign & Commonwealth Office, London.

A meeting had been hurriedly arranged with key players to discuss the recent meeting between Sir Robert and Durov at the safe house.

Sir Robert had not advised anyone of Durov's disclosure as to the FCO intelligence leak working over a period of time with SVR. This piece of intelligence he was keeping very close to his chest at the present time.

Discretion is vital in such a case. The statement could be true, or possibly a lie to hasten events, which could result in an immediate internal investigation. This would create significant confusion within the FCO whilst such an investigation takes place, either to confirm or deny authenticity.

However, he had made various additions to the group, including Quentin Horncastle. Bearing in mind the recent experience of Charles Urwin in Moscow, Quentin suggested he should also attend, to which Sir Robert agreed.

Included in the meeting were representatives of all interested parties, including both MI5 and MI6, and SO15 CTC. What became clear, was the wish of the various interested parties to be at the forefront of questions to be asked, something Sir Robert found irritating. After all points had been logged, Sir Robert advised that the meeting was now closed, and he would consider a best course of action for subsequent meetings with Durov the following week.

He caught up with Quentin and Charles as they walked down the corridor,

'May I have a quick word?' he enquired.

'Of course,' said Quentin, 'My office? It is the nearest.'

Once seated Sir Robert opened,

'With a number of very disparate positions expressed at the meeting, an idea crossed my mind as a first step.'

'Which is?' Quentin enquired.

'After I have introduced both of you to Durov, the two of you could then alternate, perhaps from different perspectives, with a series of questions, which perhaps, would either substantiate, or otherwise, his claim for asylum. What do you think?'

Charles looked at Quentin.

After a short pause Quentin replied, 'Well, it could produce some fruit, or, it would irritate him, and make him edgy. That in itself may assist in getting to the truth, whatever that is!'

Charles added nothing.

'Fine,' said Sir Robert, 'I will contact you on Monday.'

Monday 24th November 2008. SVR HQ, Moscow.

Volkov's senior officer was explaining details of his redeployment.

'Your time in Minsk produced a good report and review, including one from the Ambassador.

You are being posted to our Embassy in London. A traitor officer from SVR, Dmitry Durov, has requested political asylum from the U.K. government. At present we understand he is being kept under house arrest. We do not know where.

Your task is to find out all information about his location, status of his application for asylum, etc. All such information to be submitted to your Senior Officer in the Russian Embassy.

Any subsequent actions will be carried out by an appropriate team; such a decision to be taken here in SVR HQ. Is that understood?

Here are the complete files on Dimitry Durov. You will leave for London on Wednesday, and report to your Senior officer on Thursday. Udachi!'

Volkov left with some bulky files on Durov, thinking, 'Twenty-four hours to catch up on Durov and then London. Wonder who my Senior Officer is on this posting?'

He sighed as he sat down at his desk and opened the first file.

IISG HQ, London.

Harry was catching up on some boring admin when his phone rang at about 10 o'clock. It was Jean Nemours, Banque Liban, Beirut,

'Harry, an odd transaction occurred in the bank a few days ago. It was spotted through regular monitoring. You remember the deposit, connected to Sheikh Ahmed that had no recipient? Right. Well, about $1.5m was transferred from our bank to a bank located in South Lebanon adjacent to the Gaza Strip. No details as to issuing instruction from our bank. Questions raised internally, no knowledge as to who, why, and for what. We are continuing the investigation, but thought I would update you.'

Harry could offer no comment but thanked Jean for the update, and asked to be contacted if further data came to light.

Thursday 27th November 2008.Russian Embassy, London.

Volkov sat in front of his Senior Officer, Artur Baranov, as his career and latest review was read.

Baranov looked up,

'Now I have read details of your previous postings here in London, certain other recent intelligence given to me confirms why you have been sent here from Minsk.

The traitor Durov must be found and sanctioned,' he smiled grimly at this point, 'Such sanctions are neither your, nor my responsibility, merely to provide location.

Your file indicates a working operation with an MI6 officer, Harry Baxter, now apparently recently retired, but now active within IISG, a US operation with UK activities extending into Europe, Middle East and Gulf. Perhaps a re-connection might be an idea?'

Volkov nodded, thinking there was no point in disagreeing at this early stage.

Baranov handed over two files, 'Absorb these two files, and other details on our database. We can discuss specific actions tomorrow or Monday.' Volkov nodded agreement and left for his office, thinking to himself, that on this occasion, Harry Baxter might be surprised when he makes contact!

Friday 28ᵗʰ November 2008. Banque Liban, Beirut.

It being Friday, Holy Day, no banks were open.

At about 10.00pm a rear security door of Banque Liban was unlocked with a pass key, the person entering quickly and overriding the security alarms with the necessary code. No internal lights were switched on as he/she made his/her way to the first-floor admin offices.

A computer was switched on and entered with the appropriate code for the network. A fast scroll revealed the account required. An amount of $1.5m was chosen, destination account details chosen, and sent.

Probably fifteen minutes covered the complete operation, including access and departure. A total of $3.0m had now been transferred in the last seven days to a bank in South Lebanon adjacent to the Gaza Strip.

***

VIII

December 2008

Monday 1st December 2008. FCO, Westminster, London.

Sir Robert had fully briefed Quentin and Charles both verbally and written. It had been decided how their respective positions would be defined in discussions with Durov, and a meeting was scheduled for 5.0pm that day. The late start being a useful tool in the expectation that Durov's patience would be tested, perhaps.

Quentin was interested to see how the proposed 'interview' would play out. On the other hand, Charles' reaction could only be described as ambivalent. Quentin put this down to the fact that Charles had neither thought of, nor proposed, such an initiative. His ambivalent reaction therefore being somewhat predictable.

IISG HQ, London.

Harry took the call from Jean Nemours, Banque Liban, at about noon. He sounded tired,

'Good morning, Harry. A brief update. As you know we are keeping a constant overview on the deposited amount connected with Sheikh Ahmed.

Last Friday, when the bank was closed, a further amount of $1.5m dollars was transferred to the same bank close to the Gaza Strip that I referred to last Monday. Our requests to that bank for clarification, both last week and now, have gone unanswered. This is now a serious matter, and I have called in all security resources from our group. My own thinking now is that this is definitely connected with Hamas in

146

the Gaza Strip, as similar thefts have occurred in other banks in this region.'

Harry expressed a few words of sympathy, but beyond that could not add anything. He then went to update the Director, with an additional thought in his mind.

After providing the update Harry then said, 'I've been thinking about Banque Roubert, particularly their Head Office in Lausanne, and was wondering what the official view was of their operations.'

'In what way Harry?'

'Does the Swiss Government think that Banque Roubert is squeaky clean, or perhaps only some of the time? Are some of their international operations viewed with scepticism?

I was thinking that a few questions to the Swiss Embassy here in London might give us a few leads.'

'Hmm. They may not be very open in their responses. You know, Swiss banking confidentiality etc. Very proud of that, but various activities in the last century did not enhance their reputation.'

'Agreed, but worth a question or two. Nothing ventured, nothing gained?'

'Yes, and why not, Harry? I can always apologise for your line of questioning!'

Harry returned to his office to put through a call to the Swiss Embassy to find out which department would deal with his questions.

He provided his name and company, and was put through to an unnamed department. The man who answered, after listening to what Harry was referring to, said that a meeting would be necessary if the department Director felt it to be appropriate. He would revert within two days.

We shall see, thought Harry.

Safe House, West London.

At 5.00pm Sir Robert, Quentin, and Charles, arrived at the safe house, where Sir Robert made the official introductions to Durov, who looked quizzically at Quentin and Charles, a slight smile playing on his lips.

'Is this a case of bringing your own cavalry Sir Robert? He enquired.

'No Dimitry,' he replied, 'Let me explain.'

Sir Robert then briefly described the background and experience of both Quentin and Charles, placing particular emphasis on Charles recent appointment as First Secretary and Deputy Head of Mission in Moscow, and his kidnapping and recovery. He emphasised the seniority of both men, and his hope that Durov would therefore feel more comfortable in the questions and response that would follow.

Durov listened carefully, his head motionless, giving no indication of agreement or otherwise. As Sir Robert finished, Durov gently smiled again, 'We will just have to see Sir Robert, won't we?'

Sir Robert at this point rose and left, leaving two questioners and one responder to their exchanges.

Although Quentin and Charles had discussed, in some detail, the line of questioning of Durov, they opened with a question as to a choice of drinks. Tea, coffee, or something stronger?

Coffee was chosen by all, and Quentin opened the discussion,

'Why do you want to claim asylum?'

'I suppose you need to ask the basic questions in order to obtain consistency in reply, but I would have thought all such information would have been in previous reports given to you by Sir Robert?'

Charles interjected at this point, 'Yes, we have both read the reports, but frankly we would like to hear your reasons in full, not some civil service speak, all for the sake of brevity.'

'Understood,' Durov replied, 'let me expand.'

After three hours it was clear that Durov was tiring, and it was agreed they would continue at 10.00am the next day.

On their way back from West London Quentin raised a basic issue.

'Do you think he is genuine from what you have heard so far?'

Charles was slow in replying,

'A challenging question Quentin. If we assume that he is lying, then what is his purpose in asking for asylum?

Is it a case of gathering as much information as he can concerning UK foreign policy and intentions, Security Services current and future strategies, and then disappearing back to Moscow to a hero's welcome?

Or, if he is telling the truth and his application is genuine, what real value is he to the UK in the field of Russian foreign policy, and more specifically SVR agents, and their operations on a world-wide basis?

Clearly, from a UK, and friendly nations perspective, the second option is obviously preferable. However, the devil is in the detail, and that I am sure is going to take some time to extract.'

Quentin nodded, thinking Charles' last statement was certainly accurate.

Tuesday 2nd December 2008.1000hrs. Safe House, West London.

Quentin and Charles sat down with Durov in the same room, the atmosphere generally cordial.

Quentin reminded Durov that all conversations were being recorded, and therefore verbal answers were always required.

At about noon Durov suddenly interrupted the general flow of questions and answers, which themselves had frequently changed tack by a comment or a question from left field, introduced by either Quentin or Charles.

'I am curious about one thing that neither of you have referred to yet.'

'And that is?' enquired Quentin.

'Has Sir Robert indicated to you the last very specific subject I discussed with him, before he handed over to you, the new team?'

Quentin and Charles looked quickly at each other,

'Not to either of us I believe,' Charles said, looking at Quentin, who was shaking his head.

'Interesting,' said Durov, 'Then I do not see the point in continuing this discussion any further, until I have a new meeting with Sir Robert. Perhaps you could arrange that?'

Charles and Quentin looked at each other before agreeing to Durov's request, and leaving the safe house for Westminster.

FCO, Westminster, London.

Quentin and Charles were seated facing Sir Robert who was looking less than happy and reasonable.

Quentin had opened with a short request for all information to be made available to them as a direct result of Durov's comment that morning.

He had also linked the request with their surprise that Sir Robert had decided, for whatever reason, not to include a specific item in the brief.

150

Sir Robert remained silent for a short time, obviously weighing up risk/reward factors in his mind.

'Quentin, I will tell you both what Durov said to me the other day, and it must be restricted to us until I advise otherwise. Is that perfectly clear?'

Both Quentin and Charles voiced their agreement.

Sir Robert then spoke with deliberation, 'Durov's words, if I remember them accurately, were as follows,

Within your Foreign Office you have a senior leak. The individual has been working over a number of years with our SVR. I do not know his, or her name. The quality of what has been given has been high.

I am sure you are now both aware of the seriousness of his statement, and the possible repercussions that will follow.'

All three were silent for a short time before Quentin spoke,

'Clearly we cannot carry on further with our questioning without including 5 or 6 at the earliest opportunity. Interview will merge into interrogation at an early stage, don't you think?'

'I agree with you,' said Sir Robert, 'I will therefore consider possible options and discuss further with you in due course,' as he started to write on his pad, 'I will not be hurried, Durov can wait. Perhaps a period of reflection by him will also aid us in the long term.'

Charles saw no point in adding, or detracting, from what had been said and agreed. His own thinking was in complete disarray at Durov's disclosure.

Wednesday 3rd December 2008. IISG HQ, London.

Harry was contacted by the Swiss Embassy at about 10.00am. He was asked if he could attend a meeting at the Embassy that afternoon at about 3.00pm, or, if not convenient, the same time on the Thursday.

He readily agreed to that afternoon.

Promptly at 3.00pm, Harry entered the Swiss Embassy in 16-18 Montagu Place, London W1, to be met by Jan Glaus, who took him to a small office on the second floor. Tea and coffee were offered which Harry declined.

As Jan opened the conversation, the door opened and a woman entered, introducing herself as Lina Eblin, who sat down in an adjacent chair.

Jan introduced himself as a member of the Swiss Intelligence Service, explaining, 'There are two sections within it, one being Federal, the other being Military. Slightly confusing I am sure, but there is action to bring everything under one name and control, which will, hopefully, be happening by the end of 2009.. I am in the Federal Division, and Lina is in the Military.'

He noticed a small look of surprise on Harry's face, and smiled,

'You are not the first, nor the last to register a little surprise!'

Harry hastily apologised, turning to Lina, and saying, 'My own experience with some of the Mossad female officers should not have made me look surprised. I am sure Swiss female officers are equally well trained and professional.'

Lina smiled, and replied, 'A well scrambled reply Mr Baxter, but I won't argue with you. Your observation is completely correct.'

Jan continued, 'Naturally, following your approach we looked up your organisation on our database, and as a consequence, your own background and career.

Without going into specific details, we know of your MI6 career to date, followed by your new current position in IISG, reporting to the UK and Europe Director, who was your previous Deputy Director at MI6.'

Harry nodded, 'With, I hope, confidentiality between my organisation and the Swiss Embassy, I can confirm what you have just said, and that continued confidentiality will be maintained.'

'Certainly Mr Baxter,' Jan confirmed.

'Having put that matter to bed, could you now please address me as Harry? I much prefer the informal address.'

'Certainly Harry,' Jan replied. Lina smiled, but said nothing.

Harry then explained, in outline, the IISG investigation involving Banque Roubert.

Both Jan and Lina listened intently as Harry covered the last few months, both in Europe and the Middle East, on the Banque Roubert challenge.

As he finished, Jan and Lina looked at each other before Jan spoke,

'In some ways it is a pity we had not spoken a few months ago, but there are a number of co-incidences that we now share.

Putting Banque Roubert on one side, I would refer to two very large European banks whose recent activities could be described as both illegal and criminal, and which involved regimes that, under UN and other international agreements were prohibited.'

Harry interjected at this point, 'Both French, I believe?'

Jan ignored the comment, and continued,

'Following on from that it was decided by the Swiss Federal Government that a necessary and urgent review of all Swiss banks and branches should be carried out, with particular emphasis in similar areas to the two European banks.

It was very clear from our initial investigations that a certain flexibility in interpretation had crept into the international Swiss banking protocols.'

He paused, 'Regrettably, profit to the exclusion of good practice being the driver. But this is not the first time such practices have surfaced.'

Lina spoke for the first time,

'As you can imagine Harry, intelligence is shared between the two divisions of our Intelligence Service at all times, and our Military wing looks at possible criminal activity linked to insurgent groups around the world, but with some particular emphasis on the Middle East and Gulf. That is where the co-incidences start to occur with us and your organisation.'

Harry spoke slowly, choosing his words carefully,

'If it is to our joint advantage to, shall I say, compare notes, in our investigation, which you indicate could be very similar to your own, there could possibly be some particular advantage to us both in sharing such information and intelligence, thus achieving a speedier resolution.'

Jan smiled, 'I fully understand your comment Harry, but such a decision has to be taken by the Director of the Federal Intelligence Service, so I cannot comment until he has reviewed the proposal. It is clear from my side, and I think Lina's as well', she nodded, 'that such a proposal could benefit us both, and I will submit it to the Director.

Once I have his answer, I will telephone you again.'

Harry thanked them both, and said he looked forward to their further contact. Returning to IISG HQ he asked to see the Director soonest for an update.

The Director listened closely as Harry brought him up to date with the content of the discussion at the Swiss Embassy, and the further contact that would be made, to confirm or otherwise, sharing of background intelligence, and a joint M.O. moving forward.

'Sounds positive Harry, but all will depend on their Director's decision, which I hope will give the green light. With our limited capacity any shared Intel will be of great help. Keep me up to speed, and good luck!'

Friday 5th December 2008. IISG HQ, London.

Harry's phone rang at about 11.00am. A Mr Volkov would like to speak to him, said the switchboard. He was connected.

'Morning Volkov, and what requires you to contact me?'

'I have been posted to our London embassy. You know how I am moved around from country to country. I was hoping we might have a coffee, and a talk whilst I am here.'

'Perhaps Volkov, but it would have to be agreed by my Director, who would certainly ask me why. I will ask, and leave a message at your embassy. Goodbye.'

Harry updated the Director whose reaction was clear,

'He's fishing Harry, and my first bet is he is here in London in all probability involved in the Durov asylum case. Don't rush Harry, you have enough to keep you busy. Keep him at a distance. When useful to us, then we'll see.'

About an hour later the Swiss Embassy were on the phone. It was Jan.

'Harry, things are moving following our discussion, and I was wondering if you were free this evening, as the Embassy is holding a cocktail party for various related Swiss and UK industries and bankers. Our Director will also be there, and it would be an opportunity to meet informally. If you are able to attend it will start at about 6.30pm.'

'Jan, many thanks for the invitation, and I will certainly attend. I appreciate your thought.'

Harry updated the Director again who smiled,

'Well Harry, small steps, but looks encouraging. I am sure you will be at your diplomatic best this evening. Brief me on Monday.'

Swiss Embassy 16-18 Montagu Place, London W1.

Just before 7.00 pm Harry entered the Swiss Embassy, where his name was checked against the guest list and then directed into a conference room where the cocktail party was being held. As he was offered a glass of wine, his shoulder was tapped by Jan Glaus.

'Good evening, Harry. Pleased you were able to make this evening. Let me introduce you to our Director, Alex Buhler, who is over there by the window.'

They walked over, and Jan introduced Harry to Alex Buhler, an academic looking man with glasses, who shook Harry's hand very firmly, whilst looking at him intently.

'Good evening, Mr Baxter. So pleased you could attend this evening. Could we have a short discussion after business matters have been dealt with our other guests?'

Harry nodded.

'Excellent, probably about eight I would think. Jan meanwhile will look after you, I am sure.'

At about 7.45pm Harry and Jan were joined by Lina, who, by her initial comments, was clearly aware of the planned discussion at about eight o'clock with the Director. They left the main conference room and made their way to the second floor, and entered what Harry presumed was the Director's office, who joined them within a few minutes.

'Mr Baxter, neither you nor I want to waste time, bearing in mind the various challenges facing us both at present. I am sure that by pooling various intelligence matters between us, under agreed confidentiality, it will be possible to hasten our joint actions against criminal banks and individuals.

Jan and Lina outlined to me your career and organisations, both current and previous,' at this point he smiled, 'so I am more than satisfied with your continuing security clearance. I will be communicating my proposal to your Director, and I am sure that we will, jointly, be able to bring these criminals to justice in national and international courts.'

Harry replied, 'I agree Director, and in addition we have recently, within a joint operation with another European country, uncovered a massive amount of data involving illegal transfers around the world from several administrations that I am sure can assist us both.'

The meeting over, with principles agreed, Harry made his move to leave, thanking Jan for his organisation, and telling him he would be fully briefing his own Director on Monday. Collecting his coat from the ground floor lobby, he found he was leaving the embassy at the same time as Lina.

On the spur of the moment Harry said, 'I would normally be going back to my apartment, but looking at the time I wonder if you would like to have dinner with me somewhere around here?'

Lina smiled, 'Nice idea Harry. Cannot accept this evening, but what about sometime next week? That is, if you ask me again!'

'OK, I will. As long as you let me know which days you will be free.'

'Will do Harry.'

Harry tubed back to Clapham, thinking that it was well over a year since he took a lady to dinner. Really out of practice!

**

Harry saw the Director as soon as he was in the office.

He advised him of the discussions with the Director of the Federal Intelligence Service, Alex Buhler, at which both Jan and Lina were present. Also, that Buhler would be contacting the Director IISG with proposals for future co-operation.

Harry also mentioned that he had referred to the recent successful trawl of data, (without mentioning DGSE), which would, in all probability, greatly assist in the investigations. Clearly, he would seek DGSE approval for such co-operation.

The Director had listened carefully as Harry outlined the general thrust, and the players, of the operation moving forward.

'Good work Harry, but we need to see the Swiss proposals, in detail, before we accept. It obviously gives some additional horsepower to help us in our project, and initially I cannot see any objections coming from DGSE. Pan European co-operation and all that. I look forward to seeing Buhler's proposals.'

At about 4.00pm Harry received a text from Lina, 'If the offer of dinner is still alive, then Wednesday or Friday. Your choice! Lina.'

Harry replied, confirming Friday, and suggesting he picked her up from the Embassy at about 7.00pm if that's OK? Which it was.

FCO, Westminster, London.

Sir Robert had called both Quentin and Charles for a meeting at 4.00pm.

He opened, 'I have been considering our future actions in light of the comments made to you by Durov last week. A general observation was also made about the early introduction of the Security Services, and I want to delay that at the present time.

I am of the view that we have to build a level of confidence with him, and in light of his recent disclosure to you both, believe the questioning should be done solely by Quentin, on a one-to-one basis.

Yes Charles, I see you wish to speak, and perhaps you are disappointed by my action.'

'Not at all,' Charles replied, 'Quite the reverse. I think, bearing in mind the change in events, that your recommendation is the one to implement soonest.'

Sir Robert looked pleased, as he turned to Quentin, 'Do you also agree?'

'Certainly,' he replied.

Tuesday 9th December 2008. IISG HQ, London.

The Director had received the communication from the Swiss Embassy covering the points the F.I.S. Director had indicated to Harry.

Certainly, the parameters allowed both F.I.S. and IISG to operate in a comparatively flexible mode, both in their UK relationship, and more particularly in Europe and elsewhere.

In discussing this with the Director, Harry said that he would contact Alain Dubois soonest to get an update on the data research. He needed to have some clear analysis before sharing any of it with the Swiss F.I.S.

Harry called Alain that morning.

'Alain, I know you have a mountain of data to go through, but certain things have moved on, and you and I need a bon meeting, OK?'

'Pas problème Harry, when?'

'This afternoon?'

'Bien, d'accord, what time?'

'2.30pm, here, or your office?'

'Your office Harry, I need a change of view! I will bring some data with me.'

They met that afternoon and Harry explained, with a degree of confidentiality, his recent meetings and discussions, which had led to a working proposal with another European country.

Alain smiled as Harry finished, 'And, would this other European country, peut-être, be Switzerland?'

'Why?' replied Harry.

'Because of your recent visits to Switzerland, and a particular international bank with money transfer problems between certain branches in the Gulf and elsewhere.'

'Under our usual rules of total secure confidentiality, I would have to agree! Is that agreed?'

'Agreed.'

Alain then proceeded to outline what their data research and analysis was revealing.

'As far as we can estimate, so far, at least the equivalent of £150bn has been laundered through IFS.'

'Good Lord,' said Harry, 'You'd intimated a significant sum on the telephone, but this amount is mind-blowing.'

'C'est vrai! But what is more interesting are the identities and locations of the senders and receivers, which we are slowly discovering. Pas mal, eh?'

'Not bad Alain? Terrific is a better word. With this sort of intelligence, we can blow them apart, whoever they are.'

'Or Harry, perhaps our governments might like to exert a little pressure on some of these people and organisations, in order to avoid complete exposure? With this we can empty, and clean, la poubelle!!'

'OK Alain.

As soon as you can, and I appreciate the complexity, please let me have some major donors and receivers, by country, and amounts, so that in a number of agreed ways we can start to exert some uncomfortable pressure on them. Let us agree joint actions, after I have briefed my Director, as he may need to brief some old colleagues, if you know what I mean.

However, I think the old firm will be happy for us to make a few waves, before they get involved. You understand?'

'Absolument, Harry. I will have a few general words with my Director. He knows how well you and I work together!'

Alain indicated some of the countries, donors and receivers, and promised to get back to Harry with some specific details within seven days.

After he had left Harry updated the Director,

'Let's be quite clear, this is a combination of financial and political dynamite, and therefore will have to be handled with extreme care, not only for political fallout, unless intended, but for, I would imagine, heavy mob retaliation. Any public exposure of governments, public figures, countries involved, Presidents, senior Ministers, etc, would no doubt result in a few fatal accidents occurring, whether media, political opponents, whatever.

As a game changer it's up there in the top three. How DGSE will respond is yet another matter. How we proceed is the key to everything, and also has obvious implications with, and for, the old firm.'

The Director nodded in agreement,

'Harry, this is way too broad a canvas for our size of operation, let alone technical and operation capacity. Your comments concerning the old firm are particularly relevant; withholding of strategic information, involving clear defence of the Realm, would be actionable under UK law, not something our U.S. HQ would wish for!

No, I need some thinking time on this, plus some discreet discussions with Washington. From your side Harry, keep the continuing dialogue and data with Alain going, but without any commitment at this stage. Discussions with me, USA, developing strategic plan, which we will share with them shortly, you know, a holding action. But we will work with them on this. Obviously.'

'I understand' said Harry, 'I'll just tell Alain we need to get all the ducks in a row before we move. Or, something similar he understands!'

'Fine Harry, let us meet Thursday p.m.; I should have been able to discuss things with Washington by then, and arrived at some sort of M.O. moving forward. If not Friday a.m.'

'OK. I'll keep Alain up to speed, and we'll probably have received some electronic data from him by then.'

Safe House, West London.

Quentin Horncastle met Durov that afternoon at 3.00pm. He thought he appeared more tired and strained than the last time they had met. Durov also indicated slight surprise that Charles was absent on this occasion.

Quentin opened, 'It was decided, at a higher level, that our discussion should be carried out on a one-to-one basis. Hopefully, this will expedite the process in terms of time, and also in interpretation of questions and answers.

Sir Robert outlined to me the essence of your statement to him, concerning a senior leak within the Foreign Office. Let us discuss this as a first item.'

'As I said to Sir Robert, I do not know the name of the individual, male or female, who always have an alias identity applied to them. In this case I believe the code name is Erebus.'

'Is there any other information, however slight, about the individual, that could assist us, in at least determining whether male or female?'

'Bearing in mind the code name is Erebus, God of Shadow and Darkness, perhaps male? Or called thus to cause confusion? I do not know.'

Quentin put that question to one side, and continued with a series of other questions in order to determine veracity, or otherwise, in Durov's request for asylum. One thing became very clear. Durov was in no hurry. He was a master in terms of the ambivalent response, and was under no pressure to reveal.

Thursday 11th December 2008.IISG HQ, London.

Just before midday Harry was trawling through the first batch of data he had received from Alain that morning. He was looking to see if there were any clues as to actions by Banque Roubert, whether Switzerland or Lebanon, which would indicate a trail of sorts.

He was interrupted by a telephone call from Volkov.

'Mr Baxter, I think there is something that interests us both. Could we not have a coffee, and I can explain.'

'Volkov, if you are just fishing, then don't waste my time.'

'What do you mean, fishing? I am not wasting my time, or yours.'

'OK, when?'

They agreed that afternoon, about 3.00pm, at Kensington High Street Underground Station. As a matter of course Harry updated the Director.

'Let's see if he is genuine, there might be something.'

The Director agreed, somewhat reluctantly.

Kensington High Street, London.

Harry and Volkov met as arranged, ordered their coffees, and sat down near the rear of the coffee bar.

'OK Volkov, you have the floor.'

Volkov looked confused, 'The floor?'

'Volkov, just tell me what you are thinking.'

'This is confidential between you and me.'

'Other than your two-page report to your senior officer in the Embassy, that is,' Harry said sarcastically.

Volkov ignored the comment and carried on, 'You have some good experience of Bratva, I know, and we are investigating the transfer of money they are making from drugs, prostitution, kidnappings and murders, political payoffs, bribery, etc.'

'Nothing new there then, Volkov.'

'We found out, from an informer under interrogation, that they are moving money in different ways, cash, western shares, and bank transfers. But bank transfers are not made from Russia. Cash is taken to near country, and then transferred. Bratva is not just in Russia. We think that some routes come through London. That is why I contact you. This is why I say it is interest to you and me.'

'So why no representation at a government level?'

'Because we believe, no know, that Bratva has connections into our government. We have to be very careful.'

'Interesting Volkov. How do you think IISG can help.?'

'You are civilian, not government, but with good connections. You can be more flexible, perhaps. That is why I contact you. If you find something that smells of Bratva, perhaps we can share?'

'Hmm. I hear you what you say, and first I have to raise this with my Director. I don't know what his reaction may be. Possibly No. I'll contact you, or leave a message at your embassy. OK?'

Friday 12th December 2008. IISG HQ, London.

Harry saw the Director at noon, who had suggested a sandwich lunch covering their joint update.

Harry opened with his discussion with Volkov, which caused the Director to raise his eyebrow on more than one occasion. Harry added his own observation, the first being that SVR was clearly on the same path, but apparently some distance behind, as of now.

'Put that to one side Harry, I'll come back to it shortly. Let me update you as to my discussions and agreement with Washington.

They fully understood our lack of capacity, and the increasingly broader canvas on which we are operating. I was able to convince them to increase our budget, bearing in mind, as I understand it, increased fees due to geographical spread and complexity. Having said that, it is difficult to second guess their reaction to Volkov's approach!

We need to 'partner', as much as we can, at this stage, to keep overall expenditure within limits, whilst also looking for potential additions. Obviously, we can expand carefully at present, subject to our current activity.

Now then, Volkov.

Tread very carefully. Indicate we might be able to consider assisting in a very judicious way, subject to UK laws, where data, provided by them, is analysed and verified by us in the legal pursuit of money laundering through the UK.

We will have to see whether SVR and the Russian Embassy will buy into that, but I'll also make sure the old firm is aware of what we are up to. SVR must be aware that we would keep our alma mater in the loop?'

Swiss Embassy, London. 7.00pm

Harry had changed his shirt and put on a different tie for this dinner date. He laughed at himself, considerably out of practice on the social front. Anyway, let's enjoy the evening, he thought.

He arrived at the entrance of the Swiss Embassy exactly at 7.00pm, as Lina exited at the same time, grasping his elbow with a, 'Good to see you again, Harry, and where are we eating, I'm starving!'

'As I only had a sandwich for lunch, I'm with you on that! Now what cooking style do you like, French, Italian, Chinese, Swiss?'

'Let's go Italian, if that is fine with you.'

Harry hailed a cab, and they headed off to South Kensington to one of his favourites, Il Falconiere. As they were quite early, they were able to choose a quiet table in the corner, and order drinks, before leisurely ordering their food.

It was a classic 'getting to know you' scenario, giving enough to be interesting, but lacking much detail to avoid becoming too personal. Harry quickly dealt with his army and subsequent career.

'You probably know as much as me in your position,' was an easy way to wind it up.

Lina gave him some basic family details, Swiss German father and Italian Swiss mother, and one brother in the family business of engineering. Harry could see some of the family characteristics in her fair hair and very pale olive skin.

Harry certainly enjoyed himself, both for her company, and for the good Italian food. Lina apparently also enjoyed herself as well, with both keeping well clear of 'business chatter'.

They had coffee and liqueurs following the meal, quietly talking about anything and everything.

At about 10.15pm Harry looked at his watch, and said 'By the way where do you live? Not that I'm trying to cut the evening short, but I want to make sure that I get you home safely.'

Lina laughed, 'I have a small apartment, very close to the embassy, so not a real problem.'

'Excellent', Harry replied, 'More coffee, and another brandy? I'll book a cab.'

They talked quietly in the cab on the way to her apartment and Harry dropped her off at about 11.15pm. Lina thanked him, and before entering her apartment gave him a continental kiss on each cheek.

'Lovely evening and dinner Harry, have a good weekend.'

Harry left in the same cab. About three minutes later, a car, parked about 20 yards down the road, started its engine and drove quietly away.

Monday 15th December 2008. IISG HQ, London.

Harry took the call from Banque Liban at about 11.00am.

Jean Nemours advised he had an update,

'Following the two transfers to the bank in South Lebanon I told you about, we have been running security screening and checks of all our employees. Plus, we had set up additional hidden security cameras, both external and internal.

As a result of recordings taken on Friday morning at about 2.00am, we have identified who has been responsible for these transfers, and who was arrested by the police at about 3.00pm Saturday.

He was a young man, who we thought was extremely professional and responsible. He has admitted his crimes, and also being a member of Hamas. We hope that we will be able to recover some of the transferred monies, but that will depend on the co-operation of the bank near Gaza.'

'Good news Jean, and I hope you will be successful in getting back some of the transfers. When I am next in Beirut, I will advise you in advance, OK?'

'OK.'

Harry brought the Director up to speed via an internal email, and by return was asked to see him that afternoon at 3.00pm.

That afternoon 3.00pm

The Director was looking pensive as Harry entered his office.

'Let me update you Harry, following my off the record conversation with the old firm.

They are aware of Volkov's posting to London, and are convinced this is due to the asylum request by Durov. What was interesting was their ambivalence to your possible discussions with Volkov, no doubt hoping for some sharing by me with them. Of that, I am sure.

They then suggested something a little more structured than our ad-hoc conversations from time to time. They referred to Tom Denman who worked with you.'

'Yes, Tom. First class, thorough, dependable, solid as a rock. What was the reference?'

'They thought an agreed connection between the two of you would be of benefit to both them and us. I said it sounds good in principle, and would discuss with you.'

'No argument at all. Definitely agree. I couldn't ask for a better connection with the old firm.'

'Fine, I'll set that up, and suggest you contact Tom.'

Harry went back to his office, thinking that in the world intelligence game that governments have to play, working relations between public and private can often be more effective in reducing the timescale. This was one such game. It would be good working with Tom again. Like they'd never stopped.

Wednesday 17th December 2008. IISG HQ, London.

Tom Denman called Harry at about eleven,

'How about lunch, on me, if you're free?'

'I never say no to a free lunch Tom. Where and what time?'

They met just after 1.00pm at a small French restaurant and took a table near the back.

After the usual exchanges Harry commented, 'Well Tom, what goes around, etcetera, etcetera! Almost like old times. So, what is your brief, so I don't embarrass you with my questioning!'

Tom smiled, 'I trust you Harry, and I think, no, I know you trust me. Whatever we discuss, or say, to each other is held in confidence, subject to mutual permission being given to brief our respective bosses. How you and I speculate, or discuss, or act, on any matter is merely groundwork in our investigations. This is how I would interpret my brief.'

'Tom, no argument at all with your brief. I completely agree. Now what are we discussing initially, after we've chosen our lunch, for which I thank you in advance!'

With a working rapport established, both meal and conversation went well.

Tom indicated that deliberations involving Durov were very slow, with, it appears, some F.O. confusion as to the best course of action. Representations had been made by MI6 to be involved in the questioning, but this had been rejected. He confirmed that they were confident that Volkov was in London due to the Durov application.

Harry explained the Volkov contact, and the restrictions that the Director had placed on his response,

'Now that you and I can liaise, is there anything you can do to track what Volkov is up to? Do you have any friends in 5, who are probably doing that already, who might like to share that information?'

'Not sure Harry, but will certainly follow up.'

Their discussion was wide ranging, and they went their respective ways after lunch, with a working rapport fully engaged.

Friday 19th December 2008. IISG HQ, London.

Harry took the call in his office at about 4.00pm. It was Lina.

'No, it's not an official call, just social. I am having a small dinner party tomorrow night, and wondered if you were free? I'll be completely honest, one of the parties had to fly back to Switzerland, so I'm one man short! I hope you're not offended!'

'No, I'm not offended at all. A free meal. Would I say No? No! Very happy to accept. What time, dress code, formal, informal?'

Lina laughed,

'I was hoping you'd say Yes. Drinks at seven, Dinner at eight, dependent on my cooking! Oh, and informal, a relaxing evening, I hope.'

'Looking forward to it already, see you at seven.'

Saturday 20th December 2008.

Harry took a cab to Lina's apartment, arriving at about twenty past seven, to join a group of five people, a couple from the Swiss embassy, a couple Lina knew locally (French Swiss), and himself.

Accepting a glass of wine, Harry made small talk with everybody, whilst Lina kept dashing into her kitchen to check her cooking.

He noticed an obvious coincidence with the French Swiss couple who had previously lived in Lausanne, but resisted the temptation to find out if they had any experience of Banque Roubert.

Time passed quickly, and Lina called them into her small dining room just after eight. The meal was excellent, Lina serving a mix of Italian and French dishes, plus some Swiss white and red wine.

At about 11.00pm Harry made a move to leave, only to be told, quite firmly, to sit down, as the clearing up and washing had yet to be done, by him and Lina, after the others had left!! The others left shortly, and he helped Lina clear the table, and dry the wine glasses!

That done, Lina pressed him to another coffee and liqueur, which meant, after further relaxed conversation, it was 12.30am when he next looked at his watch. He called a cab which was promised in about fifteen minutes, whilst he thanked Lina for her very kind hospitality.

'I am, of course, expecting a similar invitation to dinner in your apartment,' she replied, smiling.

'Extremely unlikely,' Harry observed, 'it's not even large enough to swing a cat, and has no dining room, so my invitation would be for dinner in a restaurant of your choice, or in my little house in…....'

His voice trailed off, 'I'm sorry, that was said without thinking. I do have a very small house/cottage in the wilds of Sussex, not very exciting, but I find it a great place to catch up and recharge.'

His phone pinged. It was his cab. He thanked Lina again as she walked him to the door. He turned to give her a continental kiss on both cheeks, but somehow their lips met, briefly.

She hugged him, before looking up,

'I like you, Harry Baxter. Don't leave it too long before I see you again, and that doesn't mean in the Embassy chasing corrupt bankers!'

Harry took his cab back to Clapham, and about three minutes after his departure a parked car, about twenty yards from Lina's apartment, started its engine and quietly left. He had a number of thoughts going through his mind as he reflected on the evening, and its conclusion, which were still there when he switched off his bedroom light

**

Monday 22nd December 2008. IISG HQ, London.

Harry updated the Director further concerning the agreed M.O. with Tom Denman, which should certainly save time when sharing appropriate Intel. With the holiday period intervening Harry was going down to Sussex, not only to his cottage, but to see his friends.

'Let's hope nothing kicks off over Christmas and New Year,' he thought. But from bitter experience he knew it often does.

Too much of a temptation for certain countries and religions. Security and observation are often relaxed, not deliberately, but the time of year, family, celebration, often play a part. A slight relaxation across the board provides that opportunity, and tragically the consequences.

Tuesday 30th December 2008. Harry's cottage, Sussex.

His telephone rang at about 9.00am. It was the Director.

'Morning Harry, hope you've enjoyed your holiday break so far. Sorry to interrupt, but events move on in a number of urgent unrelated directions. We need to meet and decide next steps.'

'I could be with you by midday, traffic permitting.'

'Excellent, see you then.'

Midday. IISG HQ, London.

The Director had organised coffee and sandwiches, for what he described as a 'session'.

'Let me give you the headings, not necessarily in any particular order, Lavrov, Volkov, Durov and Quentin, International Bank corruption, Gulf deposits and Sheikh, Charles Urwin FCO, and MI6 overview on Charles Urwin.

Following recent activity, updates and discussions, I took some time off to try and think outside the box. And, I have come to this conclusion. Most, if not all, are related and interconnected in some way.'

He saw a look pass across Harry's face,

'Stay with me Harry, whilst I join up a few dots. You must also allow me to speculate as to why the relationships I am suggesting have occurred in this manner.'

Harry did not interrupt, and the Director continued,

'Let's take some easy ones to start with. Lavrov, Volkov, Durov, and Quentin Horncastle. Simple straight-line connections, Foreign Minister Lavrov, Senior Russian Diplomat Durov, seeking asylum in the UK, SVR Officer Volkov, trying to find out current Sitrep. If asylum granted, one in the eye against Russia, or a future cuckoo in the nest? Is Quentin up to the task? Yes, my contact assured me.'

This comment was made in answer to Harry's questioning look.

'Should special interrogation team have been tasked? If not, why not? I would certainly have them in place as a matter of course.

However, moving on, let's look at a number of international bank corruption incidents. These involving European banks sanction busting movement of funds, from countries like Russia through London to various havens in Cyprus, Estonia, and Latvia, and the Caribbean.. Other European banks sanction busting, dealing with Iran, Cuba, Sudan, Libya, Syria, & Burma. It is estimated that fines will be measured in billions of dollars for these crimes. And then we have a puzzle involving a Saudi sheikh and $350m. Do you see where I'm heading?'

'I think so, but I'm going to need some more data,' Harry replied, smiling.

'Anyway, to continue.

On a slightly different tack it would be fair to say that there is a significant difference of opinion between 5 and 6 as to the credibility of Charles Urwin. His recent experience at the hands of Albanians is viewed with some scepticism, but it appears to stand up. However, your Petro Dudnyk could challenge that with his own contacts reports.

My own view is to reserve judgement. We simply do not have enough corroborating evidence to decide one way or the other.

Quentin, on the other hand, is, certainly from an overall perspective, totally reliable and well experienced.

Cutting back to our dodgy bankers, I would not be surprised to discover a solid connection with one of them, with our missing Sheikh and $350m. Now do you see my line of thought?'

'Yes, I think so, but......'

'But what?'

'Well, in some ways the connections are convenient, forming and creating what you think is a possible linkage. If we are to follow through on this, all we have to do is prove your assumptions, which I will add, will not be an easy task!'

'Agreed Harry, so we will have a number of parcels to open and prove. The overall connections should, as a result, hopefully, become apparent.'

'Fine. And what is going to be our M.O. in moving forward with them?'

'With our various resources being limited we must use our connections to maximum advantage. Yours with Tom Denman at 6, Alain DGSE, Jack CIA, etc. Any success will be shared.

We need to have a clear outline as to how we will operate in 2009, hence today's meeting. We also need to show to Washington we have a clear strategy and action plan when I talk to them in the middle of next month.'

'Understood. Whilst I'm here, I'll start to put together some threads of an M.O. that we can discuss in the New Year. Focus, A, B, C, etc; regional implications, gaps in our armoury, internal and external resources, security issues, etc.

Incidentally, I have a meeting early in January with Alain Dubois. Update on analysis of data from IFS. And a further meeting planned with the Swiss team on some of their current home investigations. Usual updates with Jack DeCosta, and David Hadar. Keeping my friendships in good repair! No doubt it will all help?'

'Absolutely Harry. Get as much back-up data as possible from all concerned, that we can incorporate in the M.O. presentation to Washington. And, in case I leave before you today, here's to a safe, happy, and healthy New Year.'

'Many thanks Director, I'll drink to that and your good health, at the appropriate time!'

Harry made a rough outline list over the next hour before making his way back to Sussex.

During his journey back, he was thinking that often in these situations, one is required to put forward a costed scenario based upon certain assumptions, when in fact you have no real idea what scenario will eventuate, and which as a result could therefore render your assumptions obsolete. Not easy, but who said it would be!

***

IX

January 2009

Thursday 1st January 2009. Harry's Cottage, Sussex.

It had been a great New Year's Eve with his friends, and perhaps that final liqueur had not been such a great idea. However, once a year is allowed.

At about 11.00am he was watching some TV news and celebrations around the world when his mobile rang. He recognised the number. It was Lina.

'Happy New Year Harry, at least it's not raining, or snowing, up here in London!'

'And a very happy New Year to you Lina. Was not expecting a call from you. Thought it might be my boss with an update or three!'

She laughed, 'Well, may have an update or three for you within a few days, so will call to fix a date next Monday when everyone is back. Meanwhile, enjoy the rest of the break. Speak then!'

'Many thanks for the best wishes, Lina. Looking forward to a catch up soon.'

He put down his mobile,

Co-incidence? Funny, he had been thinking of giving her a call, but she'd beaten him to it. Similar to him, two single people, no near family, times like this always emphasised it. He realised he was looking forward to seeing her again, and not just on a professional level.

Might as well have an early sandwich lunch, then a walk around the village, and get an early night to catch up on the previous 24 hours!

After wishing everybody a Happy New Year, Harry was ploughing on with the basics of the M.O., when Jim Bolton appeared at his door.

'Harry, can I have a word?'

'Come in Jim, what is it?'

'You remember when we first met back in June last year, and I had been asked if we heard anything about Charles Urwin, and his disappearance?'

'Yes, of course, but he is now back in the FCO, safe and well after, I understand, being kidnapped by Albanians.'

'Well, from one of our other Intel connections, usually solid and reliable, the thinking is he had deliberately travelled to Russia to start a new life.'

'You are joking, aren't you?'

'Not at all. Before I raise the Intel with the Director, I thought I would run it past you, bearing in mind you had a lot of contact with Urwin.'

'That is certainly true, but my first question would be, why?'

'Well, the obvious first reaction would be that he has been providing Intel to the Russians for some time, and it was starting to get to him, so he decided to cross over.'

'OK, taking that as a first assumption, why the story of the Albanian kidnap?'

'That could be true, bearing in mind Bratva activity in Russia. They are involved in everything, drugs, kidnappings, assassinations, local and national government corruption, as you know.'

'Fair enough. How do you want to play this Jim?'

'I was thinking, bearing in mind your experience with Urwin, that I take this to the Director, but request you be there as well.'

'Fine Jim, set it up.'

That afternoon Jim and Harry sat in front of the Director as Jim covered what he had discussed with Harry that morning.

The Director listened carefully as Jim went through the report that he had received from one of IISG's field agents in Latvia. What was interesting was the source and verification. It was almost identical to the version that Petro had provided to Harry in October. What was different however was some of the detail.

The original assumption had been that Albanians, members of Bratva, had kidnapped Urwin in London, taken him to Russia for 'selling on', but this was not the case.

It was believed that initially Urwin had gone voluntarily to Russia, but had then been kidnapped by Bratva Albanians in Moscow, who, when realising their hostage was British, had deposited him outside the Moscow UK Embassy. Detail was still vague, with no idea as to why Urwin had travelled to Moscow, or why he had been kidnapped.

After Jim had finished his report the Director and Harry sat in silence.

Harry spoke first,

'If, and at this stage it is a big if, this is true, then why had Urwin gone to Moscow? Some undercover op, but I would have thought he was too well known by the Russian Government, including SVR and FSB, and certainly no records here in the FCO of his travel and route. Frankly it smells, but that's just my opinion.'

'Harry, I'm inclined to agree with you,' the Director commented, 'but knowing the amount of false Intel that is generated in Russia and Eastern Europe we must reserve judgement at this time. If further corroboration or denial arises, that is another matter.'

'I hear what you say Director, but it will certainly stay lodged in my mind. As you know, I have always held reservations when it comes to Charles Urwin, for a number of reasons. One of them is the usual defence mechanism that swings into action in the FCO on behalf of one of their own. Some of the previous others I'm sure you will recall.'

Jim smiled, but made no comment.

The Director then spoke,

'Alright Harry, I recognise your suspicions, but until further evidence surfaces, we must accept the status quo. Jim, see if any further discreet digging throws up any further details. I must emphasise discrete. Understood?'

Jim nodded.

Harry and Jim returned to his office,

'I'm going to see if Petro can throw any further light on this. From your side Jim, some discrete digging might throw up something. Incidentally, there may be some new strategy ideas and actions coming out shortly concerning our Saudi Prince and the missing cash. I'll brief you once all is firmed up.'

Harry sat reflecting on the content of the discussion with Jim and the Director's comments. In his mind things did not add up, no matter what was the current status quo. He sent a message to Petro asking him to call.

At about 4.00pm he received a call from Lina,

'I have suggested dates for the meeting I mentioned concerning updates. Thursday or Friday, your call.'

They agreed Friday, 11.00am, with Harry indicating he was appreciating the co-operation on behalf of the Director and IISG.

'Switzerland will be expecting similar exchanges when you have some mutually appropriate Intel Harry, so don't forget our conversation today,' Lina joked, but with an obvious serious undertone.

'Absolutely,' Harry replied, As I've said many times to many of my professional friends, actually we're all on the same side.'

Putting down his telephone Harry wondered what was likely to be the sort of updates being shared on Friday, recognising that most of the time it was only small steps down a fairly dark road. However, no point in conjecture at this stage.

Wednesday 7th January 2009.. IISG HQ, London.

Alain Dubois called Harry that Wednesday morning.

'A late Happy New Year, copain.'

'And the same to you Alain. Here's hoping this year will be a successful one.'

'We need to meet Harry. The data we now have from IFS is excellent, which you and I need to review and decide our next actions. Can we meet tomorrow Thursday?'

'Certainly, mid-morning, say 10.30, your office at the Consulate?'

'Parfait. À demain.'

Harry put down his phone, thinking that the meeting could provide some substantial Intel, and reinforcement, for his meeting on Friday with the Swiss. Perhaps the start of the building of the three-legged stool.

Agreements, permissions, et al, would have to be agreed, but he was sure that a working protocol could be achieved. He briefed the Director in a very general way, who had enough on his plate with ensuring US/UK working relations stayed on a mutually firm footing.

Thursday 8th January 2009. French Consulate, Cromwell Road, London.

Greetings over and coffee poured, Alain started to explain where, and in what detail, the latest Intel extracted from the IFS electronic files added to the previous analysis.

'Harry, you must understand there is a massive amount of detail within the data. Country of origin, pseudonyms of senders, oblique titles of accounts and description of services in receiving country, etc.

One thing, however, is very clear.

This is international crime on an unprecedented scale, aided and abetted by several international banks, obviously fully aware of what they are doing, and in certain cases assisting Middle East and Caribbean countries that have been blacklisted by the UN. Additionally, we have major transactions involving Eastern Europe and Russia to various tax havens in the Caribbean and Indian Oceans.'

He paused, looking at Harry in a questioning way, 'No comment?'

'Why should I be surprised?' replied Harry sarcastically, 'We've all known it's been going on for years. At last, we may be able to make an example of a few of them, invariably publicly concerned about their international reputation, which now, on this evidence, clearly stinks!'

'Besides bringing some of them to justice Harry, we must agree how this information is to be shared, and distributed. Currently we have you IISG, me DGSE, UK and USA Security Services, some European agencies, and, no doubt, eventually, the UN. I'm sure my Director will have his views as well as your Director, Harry. Very sensitive, but these escrocs must be charged.'

'With you all the way Alain, now show me some of the detail and patterns of these transactions.'

Alain had taken a number of situations, packaging together for example, transfers from Eastern Europe to Caribbean tax havens, another being European banks receipts from Middle Eastern countries, clearly early retirement plans for current leaders and associates. Add to that, transfers clearly involving international organised crime, no doubt including drugs, kidnappings and assassinations, etc.

After about two hours, Harry sat back in his chair, and exhaled, 'We are going to need a bigger team for this, and before that, a clear agreement and plan to start with between your boss and mine, tout de suite!'

Alain nodded in agreement, 'Tout à fait. I'll speak to mine, if you speak to your Director, and see if we can organise an early meeting. D'accord?'

'OK Alain, and let me have some detail by secure transmission. I want my Director to realise what we are dealing with, and where it will probably lead. We will certainly be treading on a number of toes, I think!'

'Pardon?'

'Sorry, just an English expression! I'll call you.'

That afternoon. IISG HQ, London.

Harry had briefed the Director, covering his meeting with Alain in some detail, particularly the analysis of illegal bank traffic, and now they were starting a critical discussion on next steps with the Director leading.

'Without compromising any security issues, I will need to raise this with Washington, particularly bearing in mind some of the banking transactions you've mentioned. In addition, there is one area we have not touched on yet.'

'And that is?'

'Overall security for our personnel, and related organisations such as DGSE. The people, organisations, countries, rogue states, governments, international organised crime syndicates, etc, are not going to take any of these disclosures and legal challenges lying down. Many of them would be considering elimination of intelligence gatherers, sanction seekers, and governments, pursuing redress.

Do not minimise the risk Harry, we would be in the firing line, literally, with some of the individuals and organisations we are dealing with.'

Harry nodded slowly, 'You could well be right. If any of these proceed, definitely eyes in back of head response! Incidentally have meeting with the Swiss tomorrow for update from their side. See if any dovetails in with any of ours, and Yes,' noticing the Director's concerned look, 'I will be very oblique and minimal at this stage in providing any observations from our side.'

'Fine Harry, keep me up to speed, and I will update you after observations from Washington.'

Friday 9th January 2009. 11.00am, Swiss Embassy, London.

Jan and Lina met Harry in Reception, and led the way to a small conference room.

Jan opened,

'Good to meet Harry. I'm hoping this could be the start of our intelligence collaboration. Let me update you.

From our limited investigations since we last met, we have been able to identify in certain Swiss banks transactions, that on first examination appear to be suspect. Whether from source, recipient account, or both. Naturally, Swiss banks are reluctant to provide information in the usual way, putting client confidentiality as a first hurdle. At this stage I cannot tell you how this information was obtained, other than to say Swiss technology was involved.'

The discussion continued, Harry on a few occasions providing a general overview of where IISG was following a similar path, albeit without the benefit of Swiss technology. In any case he was given enough data to share with his Director, following agreed or otherwise strategy from Washington.

At about 12.30pm the meeting drew to a close and Harry suggested a working lunch. Jan declined, but Lina agreed, a small smile crossing her lips.

They walked to the Duke of Wellington pub, a few minutes away, and sat at a small table near the back. After ordering drinks and food, they chatted generally about current news before Lina interrupted him.

'Well Harry, what do you think of the current intelligence we were discussing with Jan?'

'Well Lina, let's put it this way. At the moment we are scratching the surface, but dependent on some, yet to be announced, comms protocol, life could get pretty damn exciting.'

'How do you mean Harry?'

'IISG is moving down a particular road, but before we go further, we need approval from Washington HQ as to our M.O. with other friendly countries and agencies. And that is all I'm saying today. Now what would you like for lunch?'

Lina laughed, 'OK Harry, fish, and a small glass of white wine, thank you. What about lunch with me on Sunday?'

Harry pretended to scramble for his diary before replying, 'Nothing booked. Yes please, and at what time? Casual or formal? Please say casual!'

'Casual, 12 noon. OK?'

Harry briefed the Director that afternoon, who had yet to agree their M.O. with Washington, but background observations as to how the Swiss were now operating would no doubt assist in his discussions.

Sunday 11th January 2009.

Harry wondered if lunch was just himself and Lina, or whether it could include her friends. He hoped for the former, but he mustn't be selfish, he told himself.

He rang her bell at 12.15pm. Lina embraced him and kissed him on both cheeks.

'Good to see you Harry, come on through and meet my friends.' They were a Swiss French couple, Geneva based, but in London on business. Harry did not enquire what their business was.

Lunch passed well, with friendly conversation and observation. Just before 2.30pm Lina suggested they all go a walk in Queen Mary's Gardens, itself a short walk from Lina's apartment. The walk turned out to be brisk, the cold weather encouraging it. Two things then occurred.

As they returned, the Swiss French couple thanked Lina for lunch and caught a taxi as they needed to get to Heathrow by 6.00pm for a return flight to Geneva.

Secondly, Harry felt that they were being tailed. He couldn't put his finger on it, neither could he check without drawing attention to it. It was just a feeling. He decided to keep his feelings to himself.

They sat in Lina's lounge, trading small talk until Lina said, 'There's one special thing I want to discuss with you Harry.'

'OK, fire away.'

'You and I haven't known each other for long, but we are not teenagers, are we?'

'Right on both counts!'

'I know about your tragic loss in December 2007.'

She raised her hand to stop Harry interrupting, 'It is obviously known within the groups you and I deal with, and I can relate to your pain. However, there is also something you should know about me.'

She paused,

'In February 2007, a senior Swiss Air Force fighter pilot was killed on a training exercise when a collision occurred caused by a trainee aircraft. Both pilots were killed. The senior pilot was my fiancée.'

A short silence followed before Harry spoke,

'Lina, I can certainly understand your grief, and you have my support in any way to make life more liveable and enjoyable.'

'One cannot ask for more Harry.'

She came over to the sofa where Harry was sitting, 'Now give me a hug Harry, before I make some tea.'

Two previously undiscussed items were now on the table, and there was a distinct feeling that their relationship had moved on a step.

At about 6.00pm Harry looked at his watch, 'Well, I suppose I should be making tracks, Monday calls unfortunately.'

Lina walked him to the door, where she kissed him firmly. Not on the cheeks this time, hugging him firmly, which he reciprocated.

'Call me soon Harry,' were her parting words.

'Definitely,' was his response.

And, as he made his way south to try and find a cab, he had that feeling again. Was he being tailed, or was he just getting a little paranoid?

*

Harry was called to the Director's office at about eleven.

'Right Harry, let me brief you on my discussions with Washington. A somewhat muddy and unclear response, but I can understand that with the other relationships they have to consider, namely the CIA, and various political ones, of varying political hues, including the UN.

In essence, they will be having Board and Senior management meetings to try and establish some sort of M.O. for us to operate under. However, I have said that initially everything must be kept very tight to the centre to avoid security leaks that could affect our operations and relationships with agencies such as DGSE, the Swiss, 5 and 6, etc.'

Harry interjected, 'That's the area that gives me cause for concern. If we don't take good care, too many cooks in the kitchen. Could I suggest something?'

'Go ahead.'

'As nothing has yet been discussed by the Board in Washington could we not keep it very tight and under wraps here in the UK?

At the moment just us and DGSE, plus an embryonic one with the Swiss, and 6 with Tom Denman. That's broad enough, while we dig deeper into the data. My concern is, with too many people with access to what we are analysing, it could then provide a possible access route to undesirables.'

'Hmm,' was the Director's initial response.

'I can't really argue with that Harry, as at this stage we're still digging. I will make such suggestions to Washington right now, which will be on their desk their a.m. Let's keep it very tight, we can't risk unfriendly penetration.

There will be some very upset people, once authorities start to crack down on this international financial criminal activity, with many of them looking for opportunities to halt such investigations by various means.

You and I know, that destruction of electronic evidence is one, also probably linked with attempted assassinations of any number of key players, witnesses, and investigators. Things could get very hot, Harry.'

'Well, that's cheered me up Director! Must make sure my 9mm has had its latest service, and oil change!'

'Eyes in back of head time, Harry, and I'm not joking!'

That evening Harry did check his 9mm.

It had not been used since its last service, but reflecting on the developing scenario, one should perhaps follow the Scouts, and, Be Prepared!

Wednesday 14th January 2009.. Safe House West London

Sir Robert Fordcombe was getting increasingly frustrated. Durov was certainly not being co-operative. It was a classic stand-off.

Sir Robert wanted detail; Durov wanted asylum. What was irritating Sir Robert, was the impression given by Durov, that he had decided to play slow ball, and was in no hurry, whatsoever.

Sir Robert, whilst continuing to show patience, was nevertheless determined to move on the process.

'Dimitry, I think the time has come for an honest exchange of views linked with intelligence. By that I mean Intelligence concerning SVR activity in the UK measured against what you expect under the general heading of asylum. Do I make myself clear?'

'With clarity, Robert.'

'In which case, I would suggest that commencing next Monday, we will proceed on the basis that our meeting will comprise of three people, namely you, myself, and an officer from one of our Security Services. I feel that we must make suitable progress, otherwise opinion as to time wasting linked with your return to your embassy, I am sure will be raised.'

Durov smiled gently, 'With the intelligence I have, I am sure that opinions linked to either of what you have just said, would not carry enough weight to create such a response. I look forward to our meeting next Monday.'

'As I do too, Dimitry.'

Sir Robert returned to Westminster in a pensive mood.

He was certainly confused as to Durov's relaxed attitude, and wondering what would be the outcome of discussions with a Security officer in attendance. The decision of which Service should be present also raised questions, as both 5 and 6 would claim priority for questioning.

He thought a request to both for a single representation between them, but to satisfy them, that both would have access to the full recording. On his return that was put into immediate effect, with detail of the officer to be received by him no later than twelve noon Friday.

Thursday 15th January 2009. IISG HQ, London.

Harry made up his mind that morning. Enough of this self-analysis. Life surely is for the living, along with other great phrases?

He called Lina on her mobile, 'Hullo there. Just an idea, and if you've other plans that's not a problem, but........'

Lina interrupted him, 'What *are* you talking about?'

'I was just wondering, if you were free this weekend, if you would like to come down to my Sussex estate for a change of air and scenery? If this is not a good time I'll call you this evening,' he said hastily.

She laughed, 'Not a good time, but a nice idea. Call me this evening.'

Putting the phone down, Harry thought to himself, 'Well, not kicked into touch, and, Lina thought it was a nice idea. We'll see this evening!'

As he left the office that evening, he had that feeling again. Somebody was tailing him. Almost impossible to pick out among the usual numbers making their way home, but was able to narrow the field down when he got off the Underground at Clapham Common.

Walking to his apartment he calculated that the tail could be one of four, who all seemed to be travelling in the same direction.

He decided to change his route home, taking a slightly longer route, but which included a road lined with small trees. Using these as cover and line of sight interference, he was able to take up a position in a house porch to observe.

It being January, and well after 6.00pm, it was dark, and the road was not well lit. One man on the opposite side of the road was walking vey briskly, head turning left and right, clearly looking for something, or somebody. Harry was motionless in the dark porch.

Harry gave him a twenty-yard lead before the tail became the tailed.

Harry, from his side of the road, using the trees to his advantage, then saw the man stop at the end of the road, and look left and right. Harry continued quietly to the end on his side, then briskly crossed the road which caused the man to startle, turn away, and walk briskly back up the road.

The one thing that Harry saw, from a distance of about two to three yards, was an East European face, Albanian, Latvian, who knows.

This is getting quite frequent, he thought to himself.

As the Director said, 'Eyes in the back of the head time.' Who, or what group, were initiating the tails, only time will tell, unless they make an early mistake?

At about 8.30pm he telephoned Lina. She sounded pleased to hear it was him.

'Right Harry, now do you want to start from the beginning?'

Harry did just that, explaining that his country cottage in Sussex was not an estate, very small, but with great views and walks, and several local pubs that did good country food. Plus, a complete change from London.

'Sounds a lovely idea Harry, but I can't this weekend, but can the following weekend. Does the invitation last until then?'

'Of course. It's in the diary as we speak. Incidentally, could you agree to dinner next Tuesday? You can? Great. Pick you up at the Embassy at six? See you then. Have a good weekend.'

Harry felt a lot better.

Lina was happy to come for a weekend, and he would see her next Tuesday. Life was getting better, and slightly more normal, if such a status occurred in the game they played.

Friday 16th January 2009. IISG HQ, London.

Harry saw the Director at about ten o'clock, and briefed him on yet another suspected tail, possibly East European.

The Director was concerned, but questioned Harry,

'Absolutely sure, no real doubt?'

'None at all. Felt it started as I left the office, maybe more than one, who then lets number two take over to change profile. Definitely caught him on the hop by walking a slightly different route.'

'Take good care Harry, I don't want any accidents at this stage. The demands on us are too many, plus our limited resources. They are, I hope, going to be increased in the near future. But, unfortunately, not yet.

Have a word with your good friend Alain Dubois, and see if any of their personnel are experiencing similar surveillance. Next time a similar tail occurs, try and get some ID, photo, something that our friends can then run through their databases.'

Harry nodded, 'Will try, but as you know tricky, without resorting to some physicality!'

The Director frowned, 'I just said, take care Harry. Avoid action like that like the plague! Understood?'

'Understood.'

Coincidentally, when Harry returned to his office, he found a message from Alain asking him to call.

'Bonjour Harry, we need to meet and talk. We will have to agree and decide our joint response and action to a specific challenge. Is it possible today?'

'Certainly Alain, your office, what time?'

'Twelve, à bientôt.'

Harry advised the Director and then made his way to Kensington.

Alain was looking concerned when Harry entered his office, and very deliberately closed the door.

'En bref Harry, we have a leak somewhere within what, and who, we are currently analysing from our recent acquisition.'

'OK Alain. Let's take it very slowly from Day One when you started analysis, and definitely, more importantly, who was included in your internal distribution list under a Strictly Confidential heading?'

Alain looked a little defensive as he responded,

'First, naturally, was DGSE HQ Paris, with highest levels of security and very limited distribution. Ensuite, DGSE, New York and Washington. Why? Because of certain connections and monitoring of specific countries represented in the UN.

We think that a leak may have occurred there, no specific detail yet, but we have been monitoring certain UN representatives for some time, both on the ground, lifestyle, contacts, and naturally, mobile phone intercepts, etcetera.'

He fell silent at this point, while Harry adopted a questioning look.

'We do not have any firm confirmation yet, but....'

'But what?' Harry queried.

'It would appear that certain countries are ignoring specific UN principles in the acceptance of money transfers from particular countries covered by the Black List.'

'So, what's new Alain?' Harry enquired sarcastically.

'In one of our confidential internal reports, covering the access to the London transmission centre IFS, which included details of my participation and liaison with yourself, a mistake occurred on the distribution list. How and why, I do not know. Enough to know that one of the UN representatives received a copy at their New York office. We are certain that is the leak. No action has been taken as yet against that representative or country, ... other than electronic and physical monitoring,' he added hastily.

Harry sighed, 'Well, at least we have one suspect or country who could be behind some of my tailing suspicions.'

'Harry, I regret this situation, and apologise for this mistake.'

'Alain, mistakes occur, some true mistakes, some deliberate. All I hope is that your internal boys will come down heavily on the person responsible.'

'Harry, I can assure you that process started at least two days ago. But the important point is you must take extreme care with your own security.'

'Don't worry, I will,' Harry replied somewhat grimly.

'Now, how can we use this leak to our advantage? First things first. Which UN rep received a copy? Name, country, address, NYC. UK embassy, High Commission, consulates, etcetera. I'd like to know what sort of opposition we're dealing with!'

That was covered in some detail by Alain, before Harry then returned to IISG to brief the Director, who responded both angrily and concerned, for very obvious reasons.

When Harry had finished the Director sighed,

'Not something we both need at this stage Harry.

However, let's try and turn this to our advantage, plus working with your friend Alain, who at the very least, will, I am sure, be prepared to assist us 100% in tackling the country you just mentioned. However, and equally important is your security. It really is 360-degree surveillance.'

He fell silent for a few seconds.

''One further point. I may share some of this with our previous colleagues. Need some thinking time to consider benefits for us and them. I'll keep you posted before I take any action.

Meanwhile enjoy your weekend, but take damn good care!'

Harry smiled,

'I think your advice actually applies to both of us, because they know the name of our organisation, and probably who's the boss!'

'You may be right,' the Director replied wryly.

Harry drove down to Sussex that evening to prepare for the following weekend with Lina. He had to admit that his checking for any 'tails' had increased, but his journey was uneventful

He spent his weekend with long country walks, a pint or three at his local pub, and running through many permutations of thought as to possible actions and responses based upon discussions and intelligence from Alain.

Getting more like a hornet's nest by the week, he thought, but don't relax for a minute, you can't afford that at this stage. The opposition don't take prisoners!

Saturday 17th January 2009. Eastern Europe.

At a discrete hotel located in Taganrog on the Black Sea, several well-known figures arrived individually in blacked out vehicles, entering through rear doors not visible to the general public.

No introductions were necessary. They all knew what they were there for.

The purpose of the meeting was clearly obvious, judging by collective facial expressions. They all had a significant problem.

Intelligence, by a circuitous route, had been sent to them individually, by a friendly Caribbean contact, who was also greatly concerned at the apparent knowledge now being discussed by certain European security agencies and related companies.

For the last few years, extremely confidential financial transfers, made between Eastern Europe, Central Europe, the Caribbean, and Indian Ocean, had taken place without let or hinderance.

Things had now changed, dramatically, and swift action was required. But what sort of swift action? That was the discussion, and decisions were made.

The Caribbean

That same weekend, in the Caribbean, two executive jets had landed after dark on a small island. Its population was always heavily discouraged to be curious about comings and goings at the strictly controlled airport. On this occasion about six or seven passengers were taken by blacked out limousines to a private estate on the coast, backed up by jungle, and patrolled by security guards.

Discussion over that weekend was almost identical to that in Taganrog. Action was needed. A clear message needed to be sent. Without any connection between the two groups very similar reactions were agreed. A very strong message was needed, both to international institutions, and also to certain individuals.

**

Tuesday 20th January 2009. Barking/Dagenham & Tottenham, London.

At about midday Guzim Troka took a call on his mobile. Recognising the contact, he switched to a security setting and briefly acknowledged by giving a three number numerical response.

An Albanian by birth he had entered Britain illegally in 2007. Yet another illegal immigrant in the UK, courtesy of a bribed European truck driver who had brought eight into the country to join an already established criminal Albanian network in this area of London.

Focussing on drug importation, distribution, and enforcement, including assassination, he was a trusted member, keeping a low profile, and as yet, not properly identified by the Metropolitan Police or Security Services. He received his instructions without question, just another severe warning to be given to someone, and if there were fatalities, they were of no concern to him. What he needed to do now was organise what was required to be achieved by the end of the week.

In another part of North London, Tottenham, Fedor Litvin, Russian, answered his mobile, receiving an instruction to join the caller in a nearby café, within half an hour. He recognised the voice of the Pakhan, so made sure he was early.

They sat at the back drinking Zavarka, a strong Russian tea, the Pakhan talking quietly, Fedor listening carefully. One thing Fedor clearly understood. He was being picked for a major operation.

He had been in London for about three years. Now a man of 23 years of age, continually tested as to loyalty and efficiency in his specific skill, namely that of assassinations. He was paid well, and among most of his fellow Russians was well respected, if not feared.

What was being outlined to him, was a requirement for a very strong message to be sent to a European Government, that interfering in matters Russian was not a sensible decision, and could result in fatalities.

Fedor guessed that the Russian government, in some form or another, was involved in this, but had decided that a non-attributable, or connected service of the state, should be used. Hence his briefing, action scheduled no later than the end of January, if possible.

Fedor said that in his opinion the schedule was too tight recognising the amount of reconnaissance that needed to be carried out, and the limited number of opportunities that would be available. However, he quickly added, noting the expression on the Pakhan's face, maximum effort would be made to try to keep to the proposed timing. However, opportunities for positive reconnaissance would probably be limited.

He was dismissed by the Pakhan suggesting that he should start his first reconnaissance as soon as possible in order to avoid wasting any time. The last words of advice from the Pakhan were, 'Failure is not an option to be considered by anybody.'

Fedor went back to his rooms thinking about the first recce. Maybe not him, but a fellow Russian, whose appearance was very similar to a first-year university student. Insignificant, bespectacled, smallish. Yes, ideal for safe first steps. He could pick up the trail after basic routine identified.

Be careful and precise. No reward for failure.

IISG HQ, London.

Harry had caught up with the Director that morning, who had obtained a brief update on the continuing Foreign Office examination of Durov's credibility within his asylum application.

What was very clear was that Durov was in no hurry, and apparently was playing a very long game with the Foreign Office.

First question was, 'Why'?

Surely, he had specifics to trade, or was he just fishing? Frustration from the F.O. was clearly building. Something had to break, and preferably sooner.

Harry couldn't really comment, just listened.

That evening Harry picked up Lina at her embassy at about seven before driving to one of his favourite Italian restaurants, where he was always made to feel very welcome.

They briefly discussed the coming weekend and time of departure, before Lina raised an item that had originated from their HQ in Bern.

'I was wondering if you had picked up anything from……' as Harry interrupted her.

'No Shop!'

'No Shop?'

Harry laughed, 'English expression. Meaning, when we are socialising, and someone starts talking business, then that is described as talking Shop, and is not accepted in a social situation.'

Lina laughed, 'Alright, No Shop!'

In this case, that was a pity, because, as events showed later, time could have been saved.

Wednesday 21st January 2009. Safe House, West London.

Sir Robert Fordcombe entered the drawing room accompanied by both an MI5 and MI6 officer, wishing Dimitry Durov a positive 'Good Day'.

Sir Robert had been unable to persuade either Service to stand down on this occasion, both Heads insisting on representation. Durov looked at the trio with a faint smile on his face,

'Sir Robert, good morning,

I see you come with reinforcements today. Or, should I call them Persuaders? No that is unfair. They look fair and reasonable men to me.'

'Dimitry, more than enough time has passed with your reluctance to share your thoughts, observations, and intelligence, for the UK Government to look kindly on your application for asylum.

Today, we need to fully understand your motivation and reasons for your application, and whether there is sufficient merit within your disclosures to support such a process.

I am instructed to inform you that there must be no further delay in this area, and also, if satisfactory progress is not made, then Her Majesty's Government will have no hesitation in returning you to your country's Embassy here in London.

Is that completely clear, and fully understood by you?'

There was a short but significant pause before Durov replied, in a quiet but resigned tone,

'Yes, Sir Robert. I fully understand, but I am putting my trust in your government that my asylum application will be granted on the basis of my detailed intelligence briefing.'

'Dimitry, I trust for both our sakes that that your intelligence brief is both current and verifiable. If so, then I would see no objection to your asylum.'

'Then shall we begin Sir Robert?'

Thursday 22nd January 2009. Russian Embassy, London.

His SVR Senior Officer, to whom he reported, was moaning, in very strong language, about Dimitry Durov.

He was a long serving SVR Officer, operating under the guise of Culture Secretary, this giving him some considerable freedom of movement in London and elsewhere.

The main thrust of his language was the absence of any intelligence concerning Durov.

This in itself was a veiled criticism of Volkov, and that all requests to the British Government for information were either being ignored, or even worse, were indicating that no information was currently available.

'You must proceed as quickly as possible, with your existing contacts here in London, to find out any information concerning the traitor Durov.

I do not need to remind you of the consequences for failure.'

His expression certainly confirmed his words.

Friday 23rd January 2009. FCO, London.

Sir Robert Fordcombe was chairing the meeting that included the MI5 and MI6 officers who had been at the debriefing at the safe house on Wednesday.

After agreement of interpretation by all of them, there followed what could only be described as an embarrassed silence. Sir Robert spoke first.

'Gentlemen, on the basis of what we have heard from Durov on Wednesday I can only defer to your specific knowledge and experience in this area. In my mind, at this juncture, I have only two questions.

One, is his intelligence true, and if it is, two, what is to be our reaction and process?'

The MI6 officer spoke first,

'Let us assume he is genuine. If he is not, what is his motive when he is applying for asylum? Access to our strategies, both home and external? Would never happen. My own interpretation is this.

Durov described in detail the senior F.O. official who has been passing confidential and 'UK eyes only' policy intelligence to the Soviets over a number of years.

However, we know that that individual has our complete confidence in security terms, and what has been passed is designed to confuse and adversely affect foreign policy considerations by Russia.

The other F.O. official referred to however, is, as yet, not identified by us, and certainly presents a most significant challenge. Currently only identified by Durov by a code name, this will, I am sure, present a challenge to my colleague,' nodding at the MI5 officer, who in turn nodded his head in agreement.

Sir Robert observed that he would be preparing a report for the PM, subject to approval by both 5 and 6, which should also carry any interim recommendation as to whether asylum is likely to be granted, subject to further intelligence briefings from Durov.

Sir Robert and the two officers also discussed additional elements of intelligence provided by Durov, which would require further investigation and clarification over the ensuing weeks.

The meeting broke up, the two officers to liaise within a week, following further internal investigations and data research by both agencies.

Sir Robert sat alone in the meeting room collecting his thoughts. They ranged far and wide. Motivation. Loyalty to Queen and country versus loyalty to a foreign power whose prime motive is destruction of democracy.

He recalled a comment of Sir Winston Churchill, 'It has been said that democracy is the worst form of Government, except all those other forms that have been tried from time to time.'

He thought about an F.O. official, living a constant lie to bring about the collapse of the U.K.

Traitors on the one hand, and the constant fight on the other, whether it is political, religious, cultural, or whatever, of persons or groups who must be faced. Yes, Defence of the Realm. That had been his motivation and career. Work to be done.

He shook himself as he stood up, and walked briskly out of the room.

18.00hrs. Swiss Embassy, London, and Sussex.

Harry picked up Lina and they made their way through Friday's rush hour traffic in Surrey, before stopping for an evening meal in Sussex. They were both relaxed, but tired, after a usual week, happy in each other's company, talking quietly over their food in a country pub.

Arriving at Harry's cottage, warm due to Harry's central heating timer working properly for a change, they sat with coffee, drinks and some gentle background classics, as their working stresses gently dissipated.

At about eleven, Harry yawned, 'Let me show you your room. I'm sure you're tired after the drive down.'

'I won't argue with that Harry.'

Taking Lina upstairs he placed her overnight bag in the spare bedroom, properly prepared by him the weekend before, he thought meticulously.

He kissed her on the cheek and wished her a good night's sleep, with the parting comment,

'No rush to rise in the morning. Take your time. The forecast is OK, with bits of sun, but on the cool side.'

They both slept soundly, Harry up before Lina, preparing a modest but healthy breakfast as he said, 'because some walking was on the agenda today!'

Lina laughed, 'Don't forget I am Swiss. We have some quite big hills in my country, with some testing walks!'

'True, but I was only joking! I think!'

Harry took Lina for a gentle walk around his small village introducing her at his local shop, and the friendly pub (for coffee).

Just before lunch he said that his friends had asked them over for dinner that evening, a short drive away, which produced a very feminine reply concerning what she should wear, and if she had known that would have had an impact on what she had brought with her!

Harry replied, laughing as he did, 'It's just a very casual dinner, come as you are, jeans and sweater, really!' And that's exactly what happened.

It was a great evening, Classic steak and salad, a good red wine, and lots of good humour. Harry's friends clearly approved of Lina and enjoyed her company.

On the drive back in practically deserted country lanes Lina put her arm across the back of his seat resting on his shoulder. Arriving at the cottage Harry suggested a small brandy and coffee, Lina asking for tea. They chatted about things discussed over dinner with his friends, until Harry, looking at his watch, suggested 'lights out.'

Making their way upstairs Harry found his hand in hers, and stopping by the spare bedroom door turned to kiss her goodnight. Lina turned away, still holding his hand and gently pulled him towards the main bedroom.

Stopping outside the door Lina lifted her head and kissed him firmly, then saying, 'No Harry, neither of us needs to say anything.'

She turned and gently pulled him into the bedroom, making no effort to switch on any lights. With no external lights it was very dark.

Harry held her close, his heart pounding, conflicting thoughts scurrying through his head. Holding her hand, he slowly guided her towards the bed. They sat on the edge and kissed again before Harry gently pulled at her sweater. Her hand stopped him as she stood and undressed. He could just make out the form of her body as he too undressed and both of them slid beneath the bed covers. They held each other tightly as they kissed and made love. Her muffled cry against his shoulder triggered his own response. The physical and emotional release left them both sated and exhausted.

It was probably at about seven on the Sunday morning when Harry stirred.

The pale light of dawn was just starting to seep through the bedroom curtains as he gently opened his eyes to see Lina, her eyes open, looking at him.

'Morning Lina.' He smiled as he spoke. 'Did you sleep well?'

She smiled in response,

'The first thing an Englishman asks his lover when he wakes up is, did you sleep well? Yes, I did, and will you now please kiss me?'

Which he did, and which led to a somewhat delayed breakfast.

What Harry thought, and he hoped Lina felt the same, was the complete and immediate change in their relationship from previously.

Now there was a relaxed intimacy, without the understandably more careful, and in some ways more formal approach to personal boundaries. Now there could be complete honesty, cards on the table, face up. No skirmishing round the edges.

It was a lazy, comfortable Sunday, with a relaxed lunch at his local pub, before heading back to London, it had to be said, with a certain amount of reluctance from both of them.

Harry pulled up outside the Swiss Embassy, at which point both started to speak at the same time. Harry deferred.

'Harry, it has been a wonderful weekend, and I hope we can share many more like it. I hope you realise what I feel for you, and I hope you feel the same about me.

In our chosen career, life can be difficult for two people like us, but let's give it a try. That's what I want, and I hope you feel the same.'

Harry paused before replying,

'You have just said what I was going to say, almost word for word. I'm with you 100%. And yes, that's what I want, and I feel the same.'

Lina kissed him on the cheek, before saying, 'Call me tomorrow, and think of me before you put your lights out tonight!'

Harry drove back to his flat, both euphoric and sad, if that's possible. And yes, he did think of Lina before he put his lights out.

**

Monday 26th January 2009. London.

Not all daily newspapers carried the item, but most did,

''Massive Explosion near Kings Cross Station, Saturday night, the 24th January 2009.''

Most headlines carried a photo underneath showing the huge gaping hole in the side of the building located in a street to the East of Kings Cross Station in London.

The copy was clearly speculative. Internal gas explosion, or a bomb? If a bomb why? All the usual questions and answers to fill a few column inches, whilst the police and security agencies struggled to find the real reason.

Towards the bottom of the page, and with no apparent connection to the headline item, was a reference to a diplomatic member of the UN, who tragically appeared to have been shot dead not far from the UN, having been caught in crossfire between two street gangs.

His country had been notified by their embassy, with condolences sent from the Secretary General of the UN, Bak Kim-Moon. New York police were pursuing their investigations into which criminal groups were possibly involved.

French Embassy, Knightsbridge, London.

Knightsbridge is always busy, shoppers, students, tourists, whoever. Alain Dubois spends probably half of his time in the Embassy, the rest on a floor in the French Institute in South Kensington.

His team, including specialist software and comms engineers, can work quietly in South Kensington, without getting under the feet of the diplomats at the Embassy, who in many cases would deny all knowledge of those activities.

A young man, possibly a student or tourist, was taking photographs up and down Knightsbridge, occasionally including the French Embassy. A more detailed examination would have shown a sizeable telephoto lens on the camera, itself an expensive Canon or Nikon.

Further observations later that day would have shown him close to the French Institute in South Kensington being equally active.

Stopping for a coffee that afternoon he was comparing his many shots with a photograph in his wallet. It was a passport size photo of Alain Dubois. Apparently, no luck today, but keep taking photographs.

IISG HQ, London.

Harry was sitting in the Director's office discussing the destruction of the IFS office situated to the East of Kings Cross Station. The only intelligence so far, was the Press, reporting on what had happened on Saturday night. Large destruction of property but no human casualties.

Accident or deliberate? That was the question.

'Well Director, will your friends be able to fill in some of the gaps? Certainly, looking at the photographs I cannot believe that hole was caused by a gas explosion. Also, collateral damage to upper floor and roof. Way too large, plus knowing the sort of comms kit they had there, as advised by Alain Dubois, it certainly wasn't caused by an electric fire setting off mains gas.'

'You could be right Harry, and yes, I will be tapping a few elbows over the next few days to see what the thinking is. Meanwhile usual precautions and vigilance. We don't know how far these incidents spread, in more ways than one.

May I suggest you get up to speed with Alain Dubois to see if he has any particular thoughts on this?'

'Will call him today.'

He called Alain at about two that afternoon,

'I'm sure you've seen the papers Alain?'

'Oui. What a big hole in that wall! And the roof. That was not a gas explosion, was it? That was definitely materiel.'

'Any thoughts, or intel, as to why, who, whatever?'

'Not at the moment Harry, but will telephone you if I receive anything.'

'Many thanks Alain.'

That afternoon at about four thirty he called Lina.

It was strange, but they were both slightly nervous with each other, and the conversation was a little stilted. However, they agreed to meet on Wednesday, both saying they were really looking forward to that. Harry came off the phone, wondering if Lina was having second thoughts, whilst Lina was also thinking that Harry may have had a change of heart.

Tuesday 27th January 2009.. Barking and Tottenham, London.

Guzim Troka was paid well. The media photographs were dramatic, and indicated a finality for International Financial Services, or, if not, a long period of absence before resumption.

He received his cash at a local Albanian café, no doubt part of the ever-increasing proceeds collected daily by the local drug gangs, via the face-to-face suppliers and couriers.

Fedor Litvin's assignment was moving at a considerably slower pace. When an assassination is planned, a professional recce is essential. When and where (time of day and location) it is carried out is critical. The ever-increasing spread of surveillance cameras in the capital was obviously restricting potential locations, pushing dark early morning or night time as the more likely.

Choice of weapon was another, and non-traceable. The current weapon of choice was the 9mm Baikal IZH-79, manufactured in Russia, modified in Lithuania, with or without a silencer, with ammunition, sold across the streets of London for about £1200, by Lithuanian gangs.

Fedor's Baikal was a silenced weapon.

His reconnaissance was moving slowly, hardly surprising given the locations of the designated target. The photographer was being careful, tailing and photographing must not appear too obvious, or too frequent.

Police are now very seldom seen physically on the streets, unless an incident has been called. Police patrol cars are the preferred option.

Fedor decided, that as time was now critical, he would have to take some part himself. What he wanted to see was habit. Did the target have one? He carried out a three-day tail himself, and recognised it.

Alain Dubois did have one, and it was not really a major surprise. Old habits die hard. Coffee, black, strong, French style. The single shot of coffee, but taken more than once a day. Really a harmless habit, but noticeable.

The French Consulate on busy Cromwell Road, London, was exactly opposite the Natural History Museum, a magnet for tourists and students. Both road and pavements busy at most times.

However, when leaving the Consulate on foot, turn left down Cromwell Road, and after about 100 yards, turn down the first left into Queensbury Place, where at number 17, the French Cultural Centre was located.

Alain used to stop at a coffee shop on Harrington Road, just South of the Cultural Centre, to pick up his choice as he walked between Consulate and Cultural Centre. That was his habit.

And that was what Fedor was looking for.

Queensbury Place was also one way for traffic from Cromwell Road. This meant that no traffic including police cars could enter Queensbury Place from the South, only from Cromwell Road in the North.

He formulated a basic plan in his mind. Then started to look for weaknesses. The only one he could see, on reflection, was Alain's habit.

Tuesday 27th January 2009.. FCO, London.

Sir Robert was reviewing his notes following the last meeting with Durov compared with the recording made at the time which had now been transcribed in the form of a script.

He had asked Quentin Horncastle to meet him to discuss elements that had arisen, and whether a further meeting between Horncastle and Durov might produce more clues or evidence.

After a brief explanation as to what had been achieved recently Sir Robert raised the question of a further meeting between Durov and Horncastle. In addition, he also asked if Quentin thought that the inclusion of Charles Urwin at that meeting would assist or otherwise.

Quentin was obviously gathering his thoughts before replying,

'To be honest, I'm not sure whether the presence of Charles either increases or decreases Durov's readiness to expand in any of these areas. As you are aware, Charles' cynicism, or general attitude, can also be a deterrent to people when one is hoping for openness, or transparency.'

'I'm minded to agree with you Quentin, but thought I would raise it with you.

Although we are moving forward and making some progress with Durov, I still require significant amounts of additional verifiable intelligence before I can recommend asylum. I shall be contacting both 5 and 6 to pursue this area with increased vigour.

Facts are required, but clearly some pressure needs to be brought to bear.

Durov has to recognise that our patience is limited, as indeed is our hospitality. I'm sure you understand that?'

'Clearly Sir Robert.'

Wednesday 28th January 2009. Swiss Embassy London.

Jan Glaus, Lina's Federal colleague in the Swiss Intelligence Service, tapped her on the shoulder, as he caught up with her walking down the corridor towards the coffee machine.

'How are things on the military front?' he joked. 'Activity certainly seems to be getting busier on the Federal side. Can we have an update when you're free?

'If you are getting a coffee, which I think you are, why don't we have aa update in the empty meeting room?' nodding in the direction of the room they were just passing.

'Fine. Black, or white?'

Jan opened, as they sat down with their coffees,

'The Swiss Government has been putting pressure on various international banks, located in Switzerland, specifically concerning international receipts and transfers, where it is felt inadequate safeguards and acceptable processes are applied concerning sources and recipients.

Firstly, we believe inadequate testing as to source of funds, and secondly, no real challenge as to destination and professional credibility of receiving account.

This has been highlighted by lists provided by certain European and International Governments, with clear evidence of either criminal groups or members of known corrupt regimes.

Bearing in mind some of the related activities and investigations being carried out by IISG, with obvious links to CIA, MI5 and 6, and DGSE, I thought it right to update you on what is happening at a Federal level.'

'Thanks Jan. Can you let me have any specific details so I can cross check against what IISG has given us? That would be useful.'

Jan continued,

'Just an observation, and yes, you can tell me to mind my own business, but I did see Harry Baxter picking you up from the Embassy last Friday evening. Friends, as well as a professional relationship?'

Lina smiled slightly, 'Yes, you're absolutely right, Jan.'

'In what way?'

'You mind your business, and I'll mind mine!'

'Touché!'

They both laughed, and continued their discussion on suspect banks, a number of which demonstrated a clear absence of probity.

That evening, at about 6.30pm, Harry met Lina at the entrance to the embassy, standing by the cab door he had arrived in.

Once the cab drove away from the embassy, they both turned and kissed, before Lina broke away and laughed. Harry, however looked somewhat surprised, to say the least.

Lina held his hand firmly,

'No Harry, nothing to worry about, I was just thinking about the very obvious question that Jan put to me today!'

Lina then explained the brief comments that she and Jan had exchanged earlier in the day, before murmuring in his ear,

'It's only three days since our weekend, but I've missed you,'

'That makes two of us,' Harry murmured in response.

They went to a quiet restaurant in South Kensington, and picked at their food, both a little nervous in their new relationship.

Just after ten, Harry, looking at his watch, said, 'Well, a working week, so I suppose I'd better get you home soon, otherwise more people will be talking, or asking more questions!'

Lina smiled, 'Alright Harry, let's get the coach to get Cinderella home.'

Getting into the cab Harry was giving the driver the address, when Lina pulled his arm and said, 'No Harry. Not mine, yours.'

Thursday 29th January 2009. Safe House, West London.

Sir Robert, accompanied by Quentin Horncastle, greeted Durov politely, one could say formally, and certainly not with any hint of informality.

'Let me open Dimitry.

We have now spent a period of time, how can I say, in trying to establish some sort of rapport in your request for political asylum. If this is to be granted, then provision of solid verifiable intelligence must be forthcoming from you. I dislike repetition, but for the recording of all our discussions, then my statement it must be made. Do you understand?'

'Certainly, Sir Robert.

I have also been giving some thought to the question of verifiable intelligence, which will be exchanged for my political asylum. Let us begin before my memory fades,' he said, smiling slightly.

'As you will recall, I was not able to bring with me any data confirmation, whether hard copy, or disc. My mobile telephone, I am sure, will have provided some information before being cancelled by the embassy. Most will have been in code.

However, there are two areas where I think I can be of assistance. Namely, the two Foreign Office officials who were, and are, providing intelligence on a regular basis to Russia.

I believe you are already aware of one of them, who was recently retrieved from Moscow.'

Sir Robert and Quentin exchanged a quick glance, but made no comment.

Durov continued,

'The view in Moscow was that such a defection from the British Foreign Office would certainly weaken the UK's position in its relationship with the USA. Additionally, focus on potential damage, internal security and vetting, would mean greater internal self-examination with resulting damage to strategy and thus, operational efficiency.'

Durov fell silent at this point, looking keenly at Sir Robert and Quentin.

Sir Robert spoke first,

'Before you proceed further, I must stop you there. Whilst your interpretation of Moscow's view is fully understandable, it is, in my opinion, considerably wide of the mark in real terms.

However, as we are now moving into the clear realm of verifiable intelligence, we must include both of our security services, which I will organise for ten o'clock tomorrow morning.

I look forward to continuing our discussion at that time.'

Sir Robert and Quentin did not speak until they were in the car returning to the Foreign Office. Silence persisted for a few minutes.

'Well Quentin, your view?'

'Very confused, to be honest Sir Robert.'

'As am I, Quentin. Let us see what the inclusion of the Security Services produces tomorrow. Clarity, or more confusion?'

IISG HQ, London. 12.00 noon.

Harry was called into a meeting by the Director.

'Any further intel from Alain Dubois concerning the damage to IFS?'

'Only their opinion it was definitely a bomb of sorts. Certainly, IFS are out of business for some time, in more ways than one.'

'Yes, keep the connection up to date with Alain, something extra may come out of London gossip. You know what I mean.'

Returning to his office he called Alain. He repeated what the Director had requested.

'Pas Problème, Harry. Anything I hear, you will hear very quickly.'

However, in the great scheme of things, unfortunately it is not always good, or useful, news.

Friday 30th January 2009.10.00am, Safe House, West London.

After murmured greetings, Sir Robert, Quentin, MI5, and 6, sat in a semi-circle facing Durov.

Sir Robert opened,

'Following our meeting yesterday, officers of our Security Services are now present. Will you please start again, using as far as possible, the same introduction?'

Durov nodded, and repeated, almost verbatim, what he had said the previous day. On at least two occasions the Security Services looked at each other without registering surprise.

He then continued,

'The second Foreign Office official, who is identified under a specific code name, not known by me, has been operating for a number of years, and has a direct link with SVR HQ. His/her intelligence is considered consistent and reliable. As far as I am aware he/she has no interest in seeking asylum in Russia.'

The room fell silent as this initial information was absorbed.

The MI6 officer spoke first, 'And you have no idea whatsoever, who this Foreign Office person is, male, female, his or her area of expertise, country focus, etcetera?'

'No, but let me say this. Bearing in mind the intelligence provided, detail, scope, UK government policy etc, it is of a sufficiently high standard to indicate seniority. And, as far as I am aware, there are no female Foreign Office officials at what I would describe as this particular intelligence level. You understand what I am trying to indicate?'

'Unfortunately, yes,' the MI6 officer replied.

The questioning continued, this time from the MI5 officer,

'Recognising your appointment and position at the Russian Embassy in London, surely you would have been given a full background on all Russian sympathisers in the UK, plus known agents?'

There was a slight pause before Durov replied,

'I had only recently taken up my position at the Embassy, and had not received a full briefing and disclosure of what you are referring to.

All I had received were the usual updates on the embassy, current items of contention between the embassy and the UK government, subject limits as to direct discussion with the ambassador to ensure his neutrality of knowledge, etc.'

He paused before continuing,

'However, I do remember that I was given a short list of Trade Union officials, with known sympathies for Russia. Some I remember, perhaps this could help?'

The MI5 officer dryly observed, 'We probably have a full list, names, addresses, telephone numbers, and names of favourite restaurants. So, I don't think your list will add anything we don't already know.'

The room fell silent again, before Quentin spoke, quite slowly. but with a clarity that no one could misunderstand,

'It appears to me, and I am quite prepared to be challenged or corrected, is that the quality of the intelligence you have access to, whether in hard copy or memory, is slight.

My question is this? With such a light weight approach and offer content to H.M. Government for political asylum, why would any government in our position grant such asylum?'

Durov replied with equal clarity,

'I referred yesterday, and today, to your Foreign Office official who has been safely returned from Moscow.

That is one area of focus. The second is the longer-term individual, male in all probability, who has been providing excellent intelligence over a number of years.

I also have excellent intelligence concerning our London Embassy, and related activities in the UK, plus my country's relationships with Eastern European countries and China. I'm sure you appreciate the depth and scope.

If I was returned to the Russian Embassy I would disappear, with no benefit to either you, or me.

So therefore, Sir Robert, in front of a number of witnesses,' nodding at this point in the direction of the intelligence officers, 'please confirm your best interest and intent to provide me with political asylum.'

Sir Robert, on this occasion, looked like an animal caught in a vehicle's headlights. In front of witnesses all he could do was agree with a small inclination of his head, but at the same time, with somewhat gritted teeth, and an icy smile.

*

Sat 31st January /Sunday 1st February 2009.. London.

During gentle discussions, late on the Wednesday evening, when they had returned to Harry's apartment, Lina had insisted that they spend the weekend at her apartment. There was no argument.

After meeting at the Embassy that Friday, they had enjoyed a quiet meal at a nearby French restaurant before returning to Lina's apartment in York Street. On the Saturday morning Lina was up and preparing breakfast, before scolding Harry for his lie-in.

'Come on Harry, a bright but cold day. A brisk walk round the park. We both need some fresh air.'

Harry agreed, and they strode out towards Regents Park at about ten o'clock. They took the Outer Circuit of the park, giving them about 4.5 kms of brisk walking.

Harry had to admit he would need to do this more often, exaggerating his puffing at the halfway mark. The one thing that was obvious to them both, they loved it!

They chatted as they walked, taking in the various views of the park and the differing skylines of London. However, without mentioning his thoughts, Harry was struck from time to time with the repetitive, and irritating, feeling that he, or they, were being followed.

He couldn't put his finger on it, or identify specific cases as he looked around, but he couldn't deny his suspicion. He didn't mention it to Lina. No point in ruining a good walk!

However, as they left Regents Park through Clarence Gate, Harry received a hard stare from two men walking in the opposite direction. They were talking English with an East European accent, and both made a point of staring at him at the same time.

Lina did not see them as they were directly behind her travelling in the opposite direction. There was no obvious reason for the stare. Harry made no comment to Lina. Am I getting paranoid? Harry thought. No, that stare was deliberate.

They made their way back to Lina's apartment, and made tea. They spent the weekend simply enjoying each other's company, the weekend passing all too quickly for them, but becoming more relaxed in their relationship as time passed.

***

X

February 2009.

Monday 2nd February 2009.. IISG HQ, London.

Harry saw the Director on Monday morning for an update, and as a final item, also mentioned his suspicions as to possible trailing, purely as a general item, and his own unsubstantiated feelings.

The Director, with a raised eyebrow, observed,

'Bearing in mind Harry, the various groups and situations currently on our radar I'm not actually very surprised. It was bound to happen sooner or later.

However, I will say this, and you must take this as a clear directive. from me, no argument. With the matrix we are dealing with at present, there is a clear and very obvious risk and danger. Some of these groups do not take prisoners.

Therefore, you need to crank up your own security profile, and protocols. Assume the worst. Safe rather than sorry. Understood?'

'Understood. I will also have an update with Alain, and see if there are any indications in his areas.'

'Good. Keep me posted.'

FCO, Westminster, London.

At about the same time in the Foreign Office, Quentin Horncastle was just starting to update Charles as to the content and decision of the meeting with Durov in the Safe House the previous Friday.

Charles listened with no comment until Quentin had finished.

'I can't say I'm surprised at the conclusion.

Durov is no fool, and, as far as I can see, he has played Sir Robert and the Security Services quite well. He obviously has a considerable amount of Intelligence of value. Clearly, he is not about to reveal any in depth, until he has his own personal position secured.'

'I agree Charles, but only time will determine depth and value of his Intelligence.'

'Yes Quentin, but if you or I were in a similar position, how differently would we play out the scenario?'

'Very true Charles.'

In another part of the Foreign Office Sir Robert was putting together his final document, for presentation to the Foreign Secretary later that day, justifying and recommending Asylum status for Dimitry Durov.

'Let us hope' he thought, 'that the intelligence revealed will provide a significant degree of balance against the ever-increasing attempts of penetration by both Russian and Chinese Intelligence.'

IISG HQ. London.

Harry called Alain about midday and suggested a lunch meeting if possible.

'Pas probléme. One o'clock High Street Kensington. Anything specific?'

'Yes. A number of things. Update, Sitrep, clarification and knowledge, parties involved, ranking, etcetera.'

'Bon, see you at one.'

As Harry put his phone down it rang again. It was Tom Denman.

'Hello Tom, how are you and the old firm?

'OK Harry, but would like to have a catch up with you soonest.'

'Fine Tom. When?'

'Any chance this p.m.?'

'Certainly, is 3.30pm OK?'

'See you then.'

High Street Kensington, London. 1.00pm.

Harry and Alain shook hands and sat down at their table in the rear of the restaurant, Harry noticing that Alain seemed less convivial than normal.

He opened their conversation with a brief description of his experience of a gentle walk in a London Park the previous Saturday, but which had a questionable finish.

He commented on the hard stares, which perhaps suggested he had been identified, and which in one way also confirmed his continuing sense of being tailed.

Alain then responded, quietly, and initially with an apology.

'Harry, I must apologise. The leak that happened previously concerning the distributed report of IFS data, it is now almost 100% confirmed, that this occurred either in New York, or Washington. The UN in NYC leaks like a sieve, and is our first choice following the recent shooting.'

'No apology necessary Alain.

With the huge mix of interrelated international crime syndicates, vested political interests, or relationships between politicians of every hue and organised crime, it is hardly surprising that you and I, and democratic governments, are often on the back foot.'

Alain nodded, and Harry continued,

'The one thing we have to do Alain, is take stock, review where we can best deploy our limited resources, ensure our own security, and that our working relationships across the board, top to bottom, left to right, are as secure as possible.'

He then smiled,

'Do that and we have then probably covered about 50% of our current challenges!!'

Alain smiled sadly,

'Yes, you're probably right Harry. Let's order and discuss a few of our current challenges.'

Later, as they left the restaurant and shook hands, a tourist, with a telephoto lens camera about fifty yards down the street, was taking photographs, before turning through 180 degrees and taking another, this time with both men in the frame.

IISG HQ London. 3.30pm.

After enquiring about each other's health with a smile, Tom opened up,

'Harry, we are tracking a number of situations, some certainly linked, others clearly working independently. None particularly pretty. Certainly, some very heavy Russian SVR elements plus Bratva, some related East European operators, and the usual, slightly more discrete, but very active, Chinese MSS elements.

To put it bluntly we have our hands full, or somewhat overstretched.'

'No arguments there then,' Harry replied, 'Join the club, or should I just say Snap! I had a meeting earlier today with Alain Dubois. You remember him? He helped us in a fairly non-conventional way a few years ago. Of course, you do!!

Well, a very similar pattern to us all. We can't handle all the threads. We need to agree the important ones and focus. That's basically what Alain and I agreed.

Frankly Tom, that's what you and I must do as well. Agreed?'

'Absolutely,' replied Tom, as he opened his briefcase.

FCO, Westminster, London. 4.00pm.

Sir Robert was welcomed by David Milliband, Foreign Secretary, into his office, with the usual question, 'Tea, or coffee?'

Sir Robert declined, as he placed his written recommendation on the Foreign Secretary's desk, with the soothing words,

'My fully detailed recommendations for your review, in due course, concerning Dimitry Durov's asylum application. It is felt, by me, and naturally both Security Services, that his application should be approved and agreed.

Over the next weeks and months, we are confident that a significant quantity of valuable intelligence will be obtained, providing our Security Services with information and data that will enable Her Majesty's Government to finesse its Foreign Policies, to its own advantage, certainly against Russian, and possibly, Chinese Governments.

I therefore look forward to your comments, and hopefully approval, Foreign Secretary in due course.'

'Sir Robert, I look forward to reading your recommendation, and will obviously reply to you, hopefully, in the near future.'

Sir Robert left the Foreign Office, feeling, on the one hand, that approval would in all probability be given, on the other hand the unknown value of Durov's Intelligence was yet to be farmed.

Quentin and Charles were deep in discussion, which, judging by their respective verbal positions, could also be described as a fairly heated exchange, in which neither was backing down.

'Charles, I really must insist that you allow me to finish outlining my proposal for distribution.'

Charles replied in a very measured tone,

'If I considered that the basis of your proposal had some legitimate and authentic content that would stand up to professional analysis, then I would certainly have allowed you to finish.'

A period of silence followed before Quentin spoke,

'If we are to confuse Her Majesty's enemies, then I believe a certain number of false trails must be laid. Otherwise, what is the point of deliberate confusion on our part?

I certainly subscribe to the very necessary credibility that has to be applied, otherwise there is little point in the exercise.'

'If you say so Quentin. I can only hope that natural selection will ultimately prevail. Perhaps with, or as a result of, margin notes from our Foreign Secretary.'

Tottenham, North London.

Fedor Litvin was now under some considerable pressure.

He was being pushed by his Pakhan as to progress, and completion. He was also told that if completion was not achieved by Monday/Tuesday the 9th/10th February, then he would be replaced.

Emphasis was placed on *replaced,* meaning that his reputation would be considerably reduced, if not destroyed, plus termination of assignments, and payments.

This was certainly focussing his mind. Non-performance would mean a significant, if not terminal change to lifestyle, and employment. Not something he wanted to consider. His reply to the Pakhan confirmed completion no later than the 10th.

Friday 6th February 2009. Safe House, West London.

Sir Robert shook Durov's hand before opening their conversation.

'I have received confirmation from the Foreign Secretary that your application for political asylum has been approved. However, we must now proceed, with some urgency, in terms of the intelligence that you say you are able to deliver.

This will require a move from here to another safe location, where you will be able to discuss and prioritise full details with both of our Security Services, 5 and 6.

I cannot, at this time, reveal the location of the new safe house, other than to say it will not be in London, and may involve more than one location.

This will take, at this stage, an unspecified period of time, only to be determined by the Security Services.

Do you fully understand what is now involved?'

'Completely Sir Robert, and I welcome your news.'

'Good. You will be relocating sometime over this weekend, and I will be visiting you during the course of next week.'

Sir Robert then quickly left, after advising the Security detail of the new Safe House decision, not the destination, merely that travel would occur over the weekend.

Durov was left to reflect on the future knowns, and more particularly, the unknowns.

*

Monday 9th February 2009. Kensington London.

For February it was not a bad morning for weather, but very, very cold.

Alain Dubois had decided to pick up some of his favourite coffee that morning before going to the French Cultural Centre, located towards the bottom of Queensbury Place in Kensington, a very quiet one-way street, running from North to South.

The IT recovery team were based there, on the top floor, still involved in deep analysis of the data secured from IFS the previous October.

Fedor Litvin, starting his tail that morning, had decided that if the opportunity presented itself, then shortly after sunset would be the best time.

Murky conditions, some street lights coming on, but not at full power. He had decided how he would carry out his instruction; his silenced 9mm automatic Baikal.

Following Alain Dubois at a safe distance was not a problem, but a day long operation is, particularly when one has no idea of the length of time any activity may take during any given day.

Plus, no prizes are given out, when, and if, loitering becomes obvious.

Later that afternoon, at about twenty past five, Alain appeared at the entrance of the French Cultural Centre, turning right to walk up to Cromwell Road.

Litvin, on the opposite side of the street, partially screened by a parked car, aimed at Dubois, walking briskly in a northerly direction, who was then briefly blocked by two parked cars, causing Litvin to pause.

228

Then a partially silenced shot was made, and Dubois fell to the ground. However, after a few seconds he rose to his feet. Across the street Litvin was lying on the pavement, motionless.

Dubois was joined a few seconds later by a man who obviously knew him. They shook hands, Dubois then immediately returning to the Cultural Centre. About ten minutes later the wail of a police car was heard turning into Queensbury Place from Cromwell Road.

Alain Dubois was always grateful for assigned backup protection, not frequently required, but obviously there when needed.

*

A newspaper report, a few days later, referred to the death of an unidentified man by shooting in Queensbury Place, London.

No assailant was known, or reason for the shooting, but police were continuing their enquiries.

In Tottenham, a Russian Pakhan was wondering what alternative solutions were still available, and at what cost. He needed to speak to some of his countrymen. Failure was not an option.

Tuesday 10th February 2009. IISG HQ, London.

Harry took the call from Jack DeCosta at about 2 o'clock that afternoon, Jack requesting a tight secure connection. He sounded serious.

'Harry, I'll be sending you some additional details later, but first thing to advise is that I will be in London tomorrow. Can we meet Thursday a.m.?'

'No problem Jack. What's happening?'

'Besides talking with you, I will be having a briefing meeting with SIS on Friday. However, I think that in terms of flexibility, IISG will be more appropriate with what is currently concerning us here in Washington.'

'Such as?'

'Two areas of activity in the Caribbean and West Indies involving massive financial criminal activity, and in some locations direct connection with the international drug trade.'

'Oh, fairly minor stuff then,' Harry joked in reply, before adopting a more serious tone,.

'So where do IISG fit in this dodgy matrix? You need some big guns for this, although I do know some of the drug trade background from my previous employer.'

'That's what we need to talk about on Thursday, Harry. No doubt you will let your Director known I'm visiting?'

'Definitely. I look forward to reading you report later today, and of course, you buying dinner on Thursday evening! Only perhaps, it might be my turn. I've forgotten!'

Harry went and briefed the Director on Thursday's meeting, and advised he would copy Jack's report to him on receipt.

That evening, Harry was walking down Pall Mall to meet up with Tom Denman for a catch up, and was also wondering if Jack's visit had percolated through to Tom. As he crossed the road, he suddenly recognised his old bête noir, Charles Urwin, walking towards him.

Charles was obviously lost in thought, and suddenly focussed on the somebody standing in front of him, namely Harry.

'Good Lord, it's Baxter. Good evening. But as you are now in different employment, I'm wondering whether I should even be talking to you.'

'And good evening to you, Mr Urwin. From what I've heard, and, of course, it is not confirmed or corroborated, you have certainly been in the wars in the recent past. Naturally, I hope you have fully recovered and back to your usual self.'

Charles looked less than pleased at Harry's comments, and brusquely terminated the conversation by moving away, saying,

'Thank you for your concern, Baxter, may I wish you good health.'

The exchange had probably lasted all of ninety seconds, but Harry had noticed the usual Urwin acerbic and rude response.

He met Tom Denman at about 6.30pm, and they took a small table in a wine bar, just off St James's.

Harry opened,

'Had a call from Jack DeCosta today, who will be in London tomorrow seeing both of us this week. Any ideas as to content?'

'Not yet, but understand I will be briefed tomorrow.'

'One area Tom, that has been raised internally, no details yet, is the Caribbean. Any current headlines with you?'

'No, just the usual drugs and money concerns, and related activities. Nothing much changes. Some newly appointed gang bosses, after an accident, or murder.'

Harry had read Jack's report before meeting Tom, but decided that nothing would be discussed with Tom until after his meeting with Jack, and his agreement.

Other areas of mutual concern were discussed, London gangs, continuing attempted penetration by the Chinese MSS across various levels, and inter country squabbles and security concerns in the Gulf and Middle East. The problem was that when one challenge was dealt with, another one replaced it immediately.

There was always a continuing form of repetition.

Harry and Jack DeCosta walked into the Director's office at 10.00am that morning. After the usual informal catch up the Director opened,

'I've read your report Jack, and if only fifty percent is confirmed then we both have a very large and sticky situation to deal with. Please give us an idea of how the CIA are planning to respond to this, and where you think IISG UK fits within the matrix.'

Jack took a deep breath,

'I just want to give you a few basic numbers to start with, so you have some real idea as to the amount of criminal money involved.

An international body, the UNODC (United Nations Office on Drugs & Crime), estimated that in 2007/8, almost $1.2 trillion was laundered by international criminals, particularly drug traffickers.

The estimate for 2009 is $1.6 trillion.' He paused,

'When you realise, and are aware of, the international web involved in this traffic, our international relationships and agencies are stretched to breaking point in trying to firstly, penetrate, and then to break up and bring to national or international courts, the head honchos.'

I'm sure you don't need reminding of the forced labour, summary justice delivered to small cogs in the wheel, and the frightening expense to all the various countries health services, dealing with what could be described as something of epidemic proportions.'

Jack fell silent at this point. The Director spoke first,

'Frankly a world embarrassment of epic proportions. Whilst IISG would like to play a part in the response, you have to remember we have limited resources, admittedly as a bolt-on to our US parent.

The UK's Security Services I know are stretched, but I know will want to play a part in fighting this. I understand you are seeing them this p.m.?'

Jack responded,

'Yes, I'm seeing them this p.m., but I had a specific thought about IISG.

With significant criminal activity in the Caribbean and West Indies, and some of your personnel not known in that quarter, I was wondering if we could use a partnership, of our local guy with one of yours, to get some solid Intel to put in front of the local Government, to persuade them to take some very positive action.

No reaction would produce a whole lot of pressure from the US and UK, and no doubt some embargos, not as yet defined.'

He smiled grimly,

'With the sort of people we are dealing with, we know that various local and regional politicians are well looked after to turn a blind eye. Others, due to the risk of physical beatings, or worse, ignore what is happening in order to protect themselves, or their families.

We have to highlight not only the international criminals, but also the criminal politicians, and civil servants, who are part of this obscene web.'

There was slight pause before the Director spoke,

'If you are looking to IISG to provide some team support to your man in the region, let me stress now, that we do not have any surplus capacity bearing in mind our current commitments.

At this stage, I would say frankly, address your proposal to 6. The region falls under their remit, and in comparison, to us, has a considerably larger resource from which to deploy.'

Jack looked disappointed at this comment, but agreed that he would certainly raise the issue at his meeting that afternoon.

Jack then proceeded to highlight certain areas in the international drug trade; the distribution channels involving the route of cocaine from the Andean region in South America, then through Venezuela, and into the Caribbean, and thence to either the USA, or various countries in Europe.

Along this route, controlled by corrupt officials, distribution gangs, and international criminal groups, it was estimated that over the last twenty years this represented a value well in excess of $100 trillion.

Linked to all of this was the matter of money laundering.

A very large and significant value assigned to this area. Some being trade based, some directly linked to terrorism financing, and some connected to basic corruption in a significant number of different administrations.

Jack paused, before saying,

'Not a great travelogue for the region and its reputation, and one hell of a challenge to our operations. Add to that mix the influence and connection of the world's largest criminal organisation, namely the Russian Bratva, then the multiplier almost runs off the page.'

The Director nodded in agreement, but did not comment.

After a short pause Jack spoke again,

'Can I just outline why I commented earlier about resource?

In most countries we are talking about, where the US and GB have embassies or consulates, their intelligence personnel are on the ground, and frankly, are already probably, if not definitely, well known locally.

However, if we were able to put an unknown two-man team on the ground, in a major country, with support from embassy or consulate, then our chance of success would obviously increase. Do you agree?'

'Possibly,' was the Director's response, 'But may I suggest we discuss this after your meeting with 6?'

'I copy that,' Jack replied, 'Could we meet tomorrow?'

The Director, Harry observed, agreed a shade reluctantly.

Harry telephoned Alain Dubois that afternoon.

'So, how are things with you Alain, still trying to find things to keep you busy?'

Alain laughed, 'Bien, I had an interesting interruption the other day which I will tell you about when we next meet. It seems certain people don't like me very much. Possibly some of our recent electronic names are getting a little nervous.'

'Reason for the call Alain, is to arrange to meet early next week to discuss certain Intel received from our US cousins. Could we make Monday? Here, say 10.00 am?'

'Pas problème. See you Monday.'

Friday 13th February 2009. IISG HQ, London.

Jack DeCosta came straight the point as he and Harry sat in the Director's office that morning,

'Your old company was very polite and listened to what I had to say, although initially did not appear too enthusiastic when I outlined my two-man proposal.

However, one of the senior guys present asked what your reaction had been. I said resource issues was an initial response, and second was 'Let's discuss after your meeting with 6.'

However, the name of Tom Denman came up as an existing agreed contact with Harry. Why not use that as a short-term operation was suggested.'

Here the Director interrupted, 'And how long was thought to be 'short term'?'

'Four to six weeks on the ground should give an opportunity to establish some positive Intel, plus further clarity and identification of some of the various players.'

The Director raised an eyebrow at Harry, 'What do you think Harry?''

'I suppose it's possible with some backup from our Embassy, but that connection must remain totally under wraps. No meetings, and telcon and data connections must be via here, the UK, or USA. No direct links whatsoever, and with no opportunity for the bad guys to hack into our comms.'

He paused,

'By the way, Tom Denman is damn good, and I would be more than happy to work with him. You know what I am saying Director.'

'No argument there Harry. But,'

Turning to Jack, 'I will obviously have to talk to Washington before we proceed further. We already have resource issues here, plus outstanding investigations, which not only have to be considered, but also processed. I'm sure you understand Jack?'

'Of course, Director, and if there is anything I can do, both in my shop, and yours in Washington, then just holler. OK?'

'Fully understood Jack. Thank you.'

After Jack DeCosta had left, the Director and Harry continued their discussion, albeit with the Director advising Harry that the main issue was, and is, resource, both physical and financial.

Perhaps, some of the financial shortfall could be covered from the CIA, through IISG USA, but whether the current physical resource could be stretched further was the unknown. Recruitment was not a fast operation, for obvious reasons.

'Leave it with me Harry, I need some thinking time.'

'Understood Director. If you need anything from me, just shout.'

'Oh, I will Harry, have no fear of that!'

They both smiled, both understanding pressures like this are never easy to resolve. Whatever business you're in, business is people.

At about five that afternoon Lina called,

'Harry, short notice I know, but pack an overnight bag and meet me at Heathrow tomorrow morning, no later than nine. We're off to Switzerland for the weekend, and no you don't have to bring skis, or climbing boots. Must run. Don't forget your passport! See you tomorrow morning!'

'OK, but....'

'No buts, see you tomorrow!'

Weekend 14th/15th February 2009. Switzerland.

Harry and Lina met as agreed, or *ordered,* as Harry said with a smile, as they waited for their flight to Zurich.

'I was very surprised to get your call yesterday afternoon, I thought we were planning a weekend in London.'

'Yes, we were. But you know surprises are often the best thing. Well, nice surprises anyway! Wanted to show you a little of my country. We are going to Lucerne, on the lake. I hope you will enjoy it.'

'I know I will. As you say nice surprises are the very best.'

They arrived at the hotel at about 3.45pm that afternoon. It was the Hotel Schweizerhof, a classic hotel, with views over the lake to the snow-covered mountains.

They both started to slowly unwind, taking a short walk along the lake as the sun fell behind the mountains, and appreciating the warmth of the hotel on their return.

Dinner that evening was a leisurely affair, with Lina choosing various Swiss dishes for Harry to experience, and politely approve or otherwise, washed down with Swiss wines.

Harry had no complaints, other than saying he would definitely need a good walk on Sunday, to burn off a few calories!

They drifted off to their bedroom at about eleven, after coffee and liqueurs, both, for some reason, feeling a little sensitive or nervous.

In the privacy of their bedroom Harry made a comment,

'It's a little difficult to explain, but I have this push pull feeling currently with respect to you and me.

One side of me is very happy that you and I met, and the relationship we have.'

'But?' Lina interjected.

'No buts, but a concern that something, whatever that something may be, could arrive and kick both of us very heavily in the teeth, and destroy what we have currently.'

Lina did not respond immediately, when she did, she spoke quietly,

'Harry, with our similar careers, and age, I think we have to take that risk, otherwise what do we do? Say Ciao, and meet occasionally for dinner? No, I don't want that, and I don't think you do?'

Harry said nothing, but walked over to Lina, putting his arms around her and holding her in a close embrace with his mouth close to her ear.

'Lina, you are the best thing that has happened to me in a long time. If you are happy to take the risk I referred to, then that makes two of us.'

He pulled back slightly before kissing Lina firmly, then taking her hand and walking over to the bed where he put out the bedside light. On this occasion their love making carried a new understanding.

Sunday 15th February 2009. Lucerne Switzerland.

At about 7.30am Harry tapped Lina on her shoulder, who rolled over and moved close to him with her head on his shoulder. He tapped again and she opened one eye, and murmured, 'Yes?'

'I was just wondering if you had slept well?'

This time Lina opened both eyes, whilst her spare hand grabbed her pillow before hitting Harry, accompanied by the comment,

'If you think that an Englishman has to ask his lover such a question every time, then perhaps you should discuss this matter with one of your French friends!'

Needless to say, matters, including breakfast, were delayed, but they were out on the lakeside by 10.00am.

Lina certainly knew how to walk, and Harry appreciated the walk, the views, Lina's commentary of Lucerne, the mountains, in fact everything, including a lakeside lunch in a Swiss pub.

Time passed all too quickly, leaving for Zurich at about 4.00pm, catching the London flight just after 7.15pm, arriving London Heathrow at 8.00pm local time, then taking a cab back to Lina's apartment.

They sat quietly together, both recognising that their relationship was now different, difficult to define, but had certainly moved to a different level, which in its own way made them both feel more secure.

Harry reluctantly said goodbye at Lina's apartment, and made his way back to Clapham, and a fairly cold bachelor flat.

He called Lina before switching out his light, saying that he was hoping she would have a good night's sleep, and regretting he would not be able to ask her that, in person, in the morning!

She growled in response, before laughing.

Monday 16th February 2009. Safe House. Location classified.

Durov had been brought to the Safe House the previous Thursday the 12th February 2009. He had been informed that de-briefing would commence the following Monday the 16th, with both 5 and 6.

Dimitry Durov was actually enjoying his relocation to the new Safe House. It was located in a country setting, surrounded by woodland, and large rustic fencing with a very solid main gate.

Security was high, but not obtrusive. Firstly electronic, with a 24-hour team in attendance, plus a small well-trained group, also on a 24-hour basis, ready to deal with any person, or group, trying to gain physical access.

On this particular day, officers, from both 5 and 6, had arrived to start the detailed discussions/interrogation of Dimitry Durov in order to determine whether the Intel obtained totally justified his request for political asylum.

Their opening remarks were designed to indicate such a qualification, and to emphasise that whatever had been said by Sir Robert was still to be confirmed, or otherwise, by the two security services.

The quality would be in the detail.

Harry sat down with Alain Dubois at about 10.00am, and did not waste any time in his briefing of Alain with the elements of his previous discussion with Jack DeCosta.

Alain listened carefully, and raised an eyebrow or two when Harry was covering Dollar numbers in the drug trafficking area and financial crime levels, using Caribbean bases.

'Pas surprise' was his only comment on more than one occasion, and then a questioning look when Harry spoke about the possible deployment of himself and Tom Denman, subject to agreement from IISG HQ Washington.

Harry continued, 'It depends on what is to be the focus, drug shipments, or money laundering for drug payments, through the Caribbean. We certainly can't do both.'

Alain interjected,

'Don't forget Harry, we, DGSE, have some operations in the Caribbean in our French islands Martinique and Guadeloupe, and would also like to see some tough justice against these escrocs.'

Harry smiled,

'I was hoping you might be interested. All you have to do is convince your boss that you need a *vacance* soon! Any assistance would be more than welcome.

To be honest our attempts to counterbalance some of this with the CIA will only have, I think, a slight impact, but the plus side will be drawing it into public focus, and then, hopefully, some action by the UN, and other interested parties.'

Alain nodded,

'Agreed Harry, and although I might not be able to join you *en vacance,* I know that DGSE would want to provide assistance and intelligence if they can.

However, another small matter occurred a week ago, so I'll update you on what happened On Monday the 9th late afternoon.'

Alain then explained what had happened in Queensbury Place just outside the French Cultural Centre, which caused Harry to look more than a little surprised.

'So currently, we have no idea as to the nationality of the hit man, but the thought is East European?'

'Yes, no documents, passport, driving licence etc, except a photograph in his wallet of a young woman with a Slavic look who we think was his girlfriend.'

'Well Alain, you were damn lucky, and thank God for your security. I have to admit the numbers of East European and Russians, currently in London, are obviously giving considerable concern to all the authorities due to the increase in organised crime in London, and other major cities.

Let's face it, even you, our French friends of DGSE, started calling London, Londanistan, in the late '90s, with their concern over the numbers of Islamic radicals in our capital!!'

Wednesday 18th February 2009. IISG HQ London.

The Director called Harry into his office just before 5.00pm.

'I've just had a long discussion with Washington concerning Jack DeCosta's suggestion.

In principle they agree that joining forces in this way may provide a period of time when unknown elements on the ground could achieve some penetration of criminal groups, funding routes, and sources, etcetera. That in turn would translate into hard evidence to be presented to Governments, UN, etc, etc.

The challenge is how to be most effective on the ground, and also to avoid any competitive elements, from anybody, getting in the way!

Washington will consider their position in the multi-discipline operation, and come back to me with a proposal within a week. They certainly didn't rule it out, and obviously, building an operational relationship with the CIA is definitely a very good thing.'

'Sounds good Director, I look forward to your further news in due course.

Incidentally, DGSE, according to my meeting with Alain on Monday, would be happy to co-operate, particularly with respect to their French islands' presence in the Caribbean. If we have a multi-pronged agency attack against these international criminals, then that could perhaps speed up the whole process.'

'At least we are building a multi-agency concern and action plan Harry. I'll revert as soon as I have some draft proposals and clearance from Washington.'

Thursday 19ᵗʰ February 2009. Tottenham London.

The Pakhan was not in a good mood. His recent efforts and results were not appreciated by people who paid for a clear message and assassination.

The lack of success, with respect to the attempted shooting of a DGSE agent in London, had brought heavy criticism to bear, with threats of summary justice unless this mistake was quickly resolved. He knew exactly what this meant.

He needed a new recruit, one who would be prepared to put his own life on the line in order to be considered for higher things in Bratva. He would start the selection process the following week.

Friday 20th February 2009. IISG HQ London.

Harry was mapping out some possible alternatives on paper, clearly dependent on what came back from Washington as to location, scope, timescale, etc.

At least he and Tom Denman would have some basics to consider when they next met. All a bit hypothetical at present, but at least some options for possible dovetailing with Tom's parameters.

If, and it seemed highly likely, that both he and Tom would spend some limited time in the Caribbean, then he would have to brief Lina carefully.

Purely 'intelligence gathering' would be an appropriate description he thought. Yes, accurate, but without much definition.

Monday 23rd February 2009.. Tottenham London.

The Pakhan put out an urgent message to a number of his Boeviks(Commandos). Bring me at least three Torpedoes (contract killers), within two/three days.

No hopeful amateurs, only real professionals.

Wednesday 25th February 2009. IISG HQ London

That morning the Director had received draft proposals from IISG Washington. Several detailed pages covering security concerns, inherent country risks in the Caribbean, benefits, and associated risks for operatives on the ground, countering those would be the obvious plus factor of a working relationship with CIA, etc , etc.

The main challenge was how to insert the IISG and MI6 agents on the ground. They would need a solid local connection for a verifiable introduction. Several alternatives were proposed.

The Director sighed as he reached for his phone to call Harry. Putting all the positives to one side, there was still a very high-risk element in whichever alternative was adopted.

He and Harry spent a considerable time that day in exploring and dissecting the various options, bearing in mind that whatever was the final choice, agreement with 6 would also be required.

That afternoon Harry summed things up from his side.

'A few things Director.

One. Will 6 play ball with IISG, or want to call the shots? Excuse the pun!

Two. How will the CIA respond to two outsiders stirring the pot on what is essentially their turf?

Three. And which in some ways is the most important. Can we get a solid credible intro on the ground, for Tom and myself working under aliases?'

'Yes, you are right Harry. Let's get a meeting with our old firm and Tom soonest. I'll leave that to you.'

'Wilco Director.'

The Director looked slightly pained at Harry's response, before smiling and commenting, 'A simple Yes would suffice Harry.'

Harry telephoned Tom that afternoon and opened with the suggestion of an early meeting to discuss possible M.Os.

What was very clear from Tom's response was that certain senior figures would now be involved in analysis and deliberation before approval would be given.

Decision by committee, Harry thought, as he listened to Tom.

If the original proposal was to be adopted, then flexibility on the ground would be essential. It was highly unlikely that natural progression would occur.

Harry could almost detect a tone of embarrassment in Tom's voice as it became apparent that senior personnel in 6 would now be involved in establishing the M.O. Which, he thought, would probably be torn up in the first 24 hours, due to unforeseen circumstances!

He reported back to the Director who listened carefully to Harry's summary.

'Hmmm,' was his first response as Harry wound up.

'I'm not really surprised Harry. Remember they do not have the same level of flexibility that we enjoy, currently.

Egg on faces this side of the pond, wherever we are operating, would no doubt bring about more control, and as a direct consequence, reduced flexibility.'

The room fell silent.

'Leave it with me Harry. Perhaps an informal conversation between myself and an old colleague might open up the channels.'

'Happy to do so Director. Will contact Tom again when you give me clearance.'

'Fine Harry. However, with so many cooks in the kitchen, we need to have solid clarity as to lines of responsibility, and dependent on the situation, who can say Yes, or No!'

Thursday 26th February 2009. London

Around lunchtime the Director met up with an old friend and former colleague, Paul Neville, in a quiet bistro near Regents Park.

After the usual pleasantries and food and drinks order, the Director came straight to the point.

'Paul, you are fully aware of what IISG UK is currently involved with both our US HQ, yourselves, and maybe DGSE. Clearly, because of our initial involvement, IISG is going to be feet on the ground in the Caribbean, with Harry Baxter working with your Tom Denman.

Because of our prime position with regards to intel and initiation of this proposal, we want to ensure we are not, repeat not, going to have an M.O. decided by one of your senior committees, plus frequent interference.

I am being bluntly frank, as you and I, over the years, have seen a number of operations which have suffered badly from what I have just said.'

Paul did not reply immediately. When he did, he was obviously choosing his words carefully.

'Norman, as you and I know, unfortunately, not all decisions taken within my department are subject to strict operational considerations.

Personalities are involved, linked with considerations as to how results will appear to a higher reviewing authority, or the public, which can have implications on current career, and, no doubt, possible progression.

Coincidentally, I do have some knowledge of your proposed operation as a 'review' meeting was called the other day to consider Tom Denman's position, reporting line, and more specifically, defined physical limits of activity and response in the Caribbean.'

He paused,

'You have to appreciate Norman, and I'm sure you remember,' he smiled at this point, 'that your current organisation has greater flexibility than mine, this therefore producing certain constraints that unfortunately cannot be ignored.'

'I obviously recognise that Paul, but to be honest my main concern is if 6 wants to establish the basic parameters of the M.O. If that is the case, then I could guarantee now that it will not work.

Obviously with elements of IISG USA involved, plus CIA, then we need flexibility on the ground with as little, long-range interference from Westminster as possible. Obviously, you will be kept up to speed by Tom Denman, and I am sure similar comms protocols will be established between US and UK IISG offices and your own.

My main point, therefore, is to remove any potential obstacles before we have the liaison meeting with your people.'

Paul nodded, smiling as the waiter appeared with the main course, 'Noted. Let's eat and discuss some more specifics over the coffees.'

Norman agreed.

Tottenham North London 18.30hrs

The Pakhan was not in a good mood. He was 'interviewing' the 'torpedoes' one by one, and so far, was not impressed. He lectured each of them about their 'duty'. The likely result of poor performance, or non-compliance, with the often-unwritten rules of the 'brotherhood'.

Eventually his choice was made.

The last, a Romanian, aged 28.

Previous operation about 18 months ago. Successful, but a close call with the London police. It had been a difficult operation. The target had been well protected. Patience had eventually paid off. However he had only avoided arrest by fleeing from the UK with a false passport and name, Andrei Ionescu, that had brought him back into the UK about three months ago. Since then he had been keeping a very low profile.

The Pakhan dismissed the other two, and arranged for a further briefing meeting with Andrei in two days' time.

Saturday 28th February 2009. Tottenham North London.

The Pakhan was briefing Andrei Ionescu on his target.

He provided a general outline of where the order had been issued. The international brotherhood that controlled much of the world's illegal operations, including drugs, extortion, kidnappings, political pressures and final retributions, and expedient assassinations.

All designed to impress Andrei, and cultivate a sense of importance in his mind that the assassination he was to carry out was indeed necessary and urgent, and would lift his 'ranking' within Bratva.

Andrei was impressed, not only by what he was required to do, but also by the stated fee. He readily agreed, and was given details of the target, name, address, and company.

Finally the Pakhan warned Andrei of the consequences for failure, repeating the threat that he, the Pakhan, could not protect Andrei if he failed.

***

XI

March 2009

Sunday 1ˢᵗ March 2009. Clapham Common London.

That weekend Harry and Lina spent, what Harry described as a 'cramped' weekend, in his apartment. However, some walks on the Common and bistro meals eased the 'cramp'!

On Sunday over breakfast, Harry, in a very general tone, indicated that there was a possibility of him going to the Caribbean for a short period, in order follow up on various investigations concerning money laundering linked to the drugs trafficking trade routes.

'When is this likely to happen?' Lina queried in a concerned tone.

'Sometime in the next few weeks,' Harry responded. 'But it really is just purely intelligence gathering.'

'Harry, we both work in similar worlds. Intelligence gathering can still, occasionally, be very painful!'

Harry replied in a joking tone, 'You know me, I'll take my Factor 30 or 50 with me, and be totally protected!'

The conversation changed to a brisk walk, and where for lunch, so Harry felt that the gentle fly on the water had secured a holding action, at least for the present.

Tuesday 3ʳᵈ March 2009. Foreign & Commonwealth Office, London.

Sir Robert Fordcombe was sitting listening to two intelligence officers giving him an update on their recent de-briefing experiences with Dimitry Durov.

Sir Robert was getting impatient.

Successful, would not be a word he would apply to the de-briefing he had received so far. He interrupted them,

'It is now almost a month since you were deputed to carry out, and I must emphasise the phrase, a thorough de-briefing, of First Secretary Dimitry Durov.

So far, we appear to have received extremely basic intelligence, the majority of which is probably Intel that is already in our possession.'

The MI5 officer interrupted at this point,

'What is very clear Sir Robert, is that Durov is dragging out this process for a reason, as yet not identified.

Intel that he has divulged so far is concentrated in one area, namely a focus on recruits achieved within the UK, as yet, no links to specific areas, specialties, European or world links, activities, or groups.'

The MI6 officer then observed,

'With respect Sir Robert, my own view is slightly different.

If, to put it in its simplest construction, Durov is being asked to provide both internal UK, and external Intel, at one and the same time.

Progress could, perhaps be improved if he was focussed with either of us individually, as opposed to jointly?'

Sir Robert sighed, and was silent for a few seconds.

'If I agree to your suggestion, I want it clearly understood that ALL Intel uncovered by both of you must be exchanged between you both preferably on a daily basis.

An extension to a maximum of three days will only be accepted if necessary to achieve resolution, or completion.

Is that clearly understood?'

'Understood, Sir Robert,' they replied.

In the safe house, Dimitry Durov was wondering how long he could drag out his 'interrogation' before ultimatums were issued, or the style of questioning was altered.

In his own mind the nuggets he had were too precious to be squandered too early in the process.

That afternoon. MI6 HQ London.

The arranged meeting between IISG and SIS took place that afternoon. There were four people from MI6 including Tom Denman, and two from IISG, the Director and Harry.

Of necessity, the meeting initially was wide ranging, both in terms of source and geography. However it quickly became more focussed when recognising limited resources and time availability.

Liaison with Embassies and appropriate personnel on the ground in the Caribbean both British and American were identified.

Jack DeCosta had provided a US CIA overview during his meeting with MI6, and the cooperation planned and extended to Harry and Tom.

What became very clear was the need for a tight focus on Who?, What?, When?, and importantly, for How Long?

Harry and Tom had not initially contributed much whilst the game plan had been outlined and discussed by their seniors. Harry decided at one point, that perhaps a verbal half brick into the pond might produce a response concerning IISG concerns as to the M.O. on the ground, and whether 6 wanted to call the shots.

The response surprised him and the Director initially.

MI6 stated that they were perfectly happy for IISG to 'run' the op, liaising with the CIA on the ground, and appropriate contacts via UK embassies. Also, that Tom would 'report' to Harry, as they had operated when Harry was in 6, to which Tom readily agreed.

At a later date both the Director and Harry agreed that this decision by 6 was probably/possibly due to gentle pressure from the CIA. Whatever, clarification had been established.

Harry and Tom would be travelling under assumed identities, all necessary docs, including, passports, health docs, debit and credit cards, etc, would be produced within 7-10 days.

It was decided that subject to agreement from the CIA, Harry and Tom would travel first to Washington and then Miami for meetings with the CIA, and then on to the Caribbean, starting in Trinidad. A provisional departure date was suggested, Friday, 20th March 2009..

Assumed identities could be familial links to current UK convicted criminals within the illegal drugs and distribution trades, but this was open to discussion/alternatives.

Harry and Tom agreed to meet on Friday the 6th at IISG to discuss 'further steps and details'.

Wednesday 4th March 2009. IISG London

Harry was called in by the Director at about 10 a.m.

'Morning Harry, any overnight thoughts on our meeting yesterday? Your first ten would be sufficient I think, for starters,' he said smiling.

Harry paused,

'Well, first things first.

I'm pleased they are happy for us to run the op, without, so far, any interference from their side.

Not being cynical, I suppose if we make a hash of it, then we, and the CIA, carry the proverbial can. Although I would anticipate the CIA putting a wrap on that if it happened.'

'My thoughts as well Harry.'

'Secondly, I'm very happy Tom is on board, just like the old firm. No problems there.

The only downside I see, is if the CIA want to take the credit for the op, but that is not my concern. As IISG is American, I'm sure they'll squeeze some joint credit agreement from them!

My interest now is the robust detail behind our aliases whilst in the Caribbean. I certainly don't want any leaks in that area!'

'My concern as well Harry. We need some solid irrefutable background to support that. Let's get some thoughts down on paper.'

Friday 6th March 2009. IISG London

Tom Denman and Harry sat down with two strong cups of coffee at 10.30am that Friday morning.

Harry sketched out his usual SMEAC, [Situation, Mission, Execution, Admin, Comms].

'It's certainly a good aide memoire in times like this,' he said smiling.

'No argument there Harry,' Tom replied.

On the basis of intelligence received so far, either through MI5, MI6, IISG, or the CIA, outline areas were identified, to be added to, or highlighted, dependent on groups/individuals, location, etc., and original source of Intel.

Dependent on the strength and quality of Intel then focus could be applied, once other factors such as current, or older previous Intel, are applied.

CIA input would be added to the matrix when Harry and Tom are briefed in Washington, which would be their first stop, sometime after the 20th March.

Among the people walking in the street outside Harry's office was one, Andrei, looking to see access, layout, adjacent roads and streets. Just the usual reconnaissance that hired killers carry out, calculating entry and exit against risk.

His next stop was Harry's address in Clapham.

Apartment was on the first floor. Residential area. Quite quiet. Normal access to street, and from there to main road, about 150 metres. No real access from rear. Various parked cars. Sparse street lighting. No commercial properties. Significantly quieter than office location, day or night. No argument. This was the best option.

Weekend 7ᵗʰ/8ᵗʰ March 2009.

Whilst Harry and Lina spent an enjoyable weekend in London, Andrei Ionescu made a trip to the country, to a small village in Sussex, and a small cottage in particular. Location, entry and exit to village, access to cottage front and back, neighbours, street lighting, all the usual details that affect entry and exit.

But one small, but very relevant, factor was overlooked.

Monday 9ᵗʰ March 2009. IISG London

The Director took the telephone call from a Senior Director of GCHQ, Paul Brent, whom he had met at MI6 liaison meetings in the past.

After initial catch up, Paul indicated that GCHQ could certainly assist with any comms from the Caribbean to the UK, and had made the contact on the suggestion from 6.

GCHQ had a strong working connection with the United States National Security Agency (NSA), and through that agreement secure connections, land or satellite, could be guaranteed for Harry and Tom, both data and voice.

The Director thanked Paul for his offer which would definitely be gratefully accepted, and which would certainly provide a solid comms base for Harry and Tom.

Putting down his telephone, the Director thought that it was encouraging to see the developing joint working agreements across members of the '5 Eyes'. Five countries, the UK, USA, Canada, Australia, and New Zealand, all sharing intelligence between them. Long may it continue, without political interference, he reflected.

Tuesday 10th March 2009. IISG London.

The Director, Harry and Tom, met that morning to firm up on identities, current activities, background cover, etc to be adopted by them during their Caribbean intelligence sourcing operation.

Bearing in mind likely criminal contacts, some solid background connections were needed to be able to withstand searching investigation by the local drug syndicates.

Harry and Tom would appear as an externally well-funded UK organisation (funded from 'East European' sources) looking for a direct relationship with the Trinidad drug cartel.

They would not be interested in any drug traffic routing to the USA, only for trans-Atlantic to North Africa, or Western Europe, and then for European and UK distribution.

Two separate assassinations which had occurred in London drug gangs families provided a foundation for their background. They would be cousins. Names, relatives, past marriages, etc, between families etc, and current members of the families still serving long term jail sentences, formed the baseline for their identities.

Some changes to appearance would have to be created, in Harry's case, designer stubble, with a different haircut. In Tom's case, slight change in haircut, but now wearing glasses. All changes would be evident on their passports, along with their new identities.

In Harry's case he would be Barry Foster. Tom would be Ron Hall.

Both surnames could be traced back to two criminal families.

Friday 13th *March 2009. IISG London.*

Harry and Tom met the Director at about 11.00am.

'We have now received all the various documents for you both, including passports, driving licences, addresses, bank a/cs etc, which we had organised previously. You now know your aliases so would suggest you get used to them as quickly as possible.

Background is detailed which you must study in your office, not to be taken out. Is that understood?'

Both acknowledged the instruction.

'I suggest you spend the rest of today getting up to speed in all areas of the documentation.'

Both nodded in agreement and went back to Harry's office.

'Well Ron, after lunch eyes down for a full house detail session.'

'Agreed Barry. A period of silence would be most welcome.'

They both laughed, and left for a snack lunch.

Weekend Sat 14th *- Sun 15*[th] *March 2009. Sussex.*

Harry and Lina left early for Sussex that Saturday morning, Lina having stayed with Harry in Clapham the Friday night.

For March it wasn't a bad day, still quite cold, but good time was made, and they arrived at the cottage at about 11.30am.

Central heating was turned up, and they walked to the village pub for an early lunch. Sitting at a small table, not far from a blazing log fire they were both, it had to be said, at peace with the world. This was capped as they left, when the landlord offered them some glorious lamb chops from a local farm, which Harry eagerly bought, plus a bottle of his best red wine.

'Guess who's cooking tonight?' he joked.

'By the way you do realise that today is the Ides of March? Not a great time for some historical figures we were told as children.'

They spent a leisurely afternoon before Harry started preparing the chops, and apologising that the pudding would only be ice cream.

However the good red wine made up for any discrepancy.

*

At about 2.00pm in London, Andrei left to drive down to Sussex. In his boot he was carrying two weapons, a 9mm Baikal handgun, and a 7.62mm light assault rifle. Choice would depend on distance, light, and profile.

*

That evening Harry and Lina sat quietly enjoying their lamb chops, salad, and red wine. The atmosphere was, to say the least, totally benign. Two people, comfortable in themselves, and their developing relationship. Harry was thinking it had been a long time since he had felt so relaxed, and in a word, comfortable.

At about ten they started to clear up, Harry collecting bits and pieces together to put in the rubbish…..

*

Andrei had arrived in Sussex at about 4.30pm, about an hour before sundown, although no sun that Saturday. He had parked his car in a small copse just outside the village, not visible from the road.

He deliberated on which weapon to use, the 9mm would be preferred choice if he could get close enough to the target, the rifle if distance forced its use. He waited patiently to see what visibility would be like that evening, which would also affect his choice.

At about 9.00pm Andrei left his car and using as much natural cover as he could made his way towards the cottage. He could see internal lights were on, and the occasional movement of persons inside, although identification was not clear at his current range. He had decided on the 9mm Baikal.

In Harry's small garden, a hedge at its southern edge provided a small barrier against mixed trees adjoining arable land. This would be his location and exit route to his rear. The distance from the hedge to the back door and window was no more than fifteen yards/just over 12 metres. He lay down on the hard and cold ground his Baikal clasped in a thin plastic glove in his right hand.

Just after 10pm he saw Harry and a woman through the kitchen window, and almost immediately the backdoor was opened, and Harry appeared with a bag obviously destined for the dustbin about five or more paces to the right of the door.

He lifted his Baikal to take aim as a large dog landed on his back accompanied by a savage growl and barking.

He rolled over and tried to hit the dog with his free hand, but all that produced was a twice bitten hand. The dog continued to growl and snarl, so he crawled towards the copse as quickly as he could, where having reached cover, he stood up and made his way back towards his car.

Harry had stopped when he heard the barking and snarling, thinking to himself, 'dog chasing cat, or something bigger!'

He recognised the barks.

His neighbour, Mrs Roberts, had a lovely big Alsatian, Wellington, known as Welly, normally as soft as grease, but, who doesn't like cats and strangers! Probably out for his short 'walk' before curling up in his very large basket.

'Probably chasing a big tabbi!' he thought.

Dumping the bag in the bin, he returned to the kitchen and his duties, not realising what a close shave he had had. Sometimes, ignorance of the facts, or situation, can be a blessing in disguise.

Andrei, his left hand bleeding quite severely, made his way to his car, and returned to London to deal with his damaged hand. He had overlooked one small relevant factor. A neighbour's dog.

He would now have to report back to the Pakhan. A discussion he was not looking forward to.

Monday 16th March 2009. IISG London.

That afternoon a flurry of high security communications involving IISG Washington, IISG London, MI6, etc, formed the basis of a meeting at 5.00pm.

Essentially the green light was given to action the operation of Harry and Tom in the Caribbean starting in Trinidad. Duration was, at this stage left loose, but certainly a joint review at the end of thirty days would be held as to progress, Intel obtained to date, and background on contacts made, both hostile and friendly.

As considerable pressure was building in Washington, Harry and Tom would be flying, firstly to Washington, for briefing meetings with IISG and CIA, then to Miami, for a meeting with CIA covering recent Intel in Trinidad, and a comms check with the NSA.

Departure was scheduled for the weekend 21st - 22nd March 2009.

Tottenham, North London. That evening.

Andrei had contacted the Pakhan for a meeting, scheduled by the Pakhan for 9.30pm. The atmosphere was icy, and Andrei, with his heavily bandaged hand, was certainly not feeling confident as he outlined what had occurred.

The Pakhan listened in total silence.

When Andrei finished, his last words asking that he be allowed to continue with the assignment, the Pakhan said not a word for at least a minute. Just a hard stare at Andrei.

When he spoke his words carried a clear menace,

'I allow you to continue. But, not in the country. You must stay in London. Understand?'

Andrei clearly understood and verbally agreed.

Tuesday 17th March 2009. IISG HQ London.

'Preparation is at least 75% of any successful operation, if not 100%!' Harry thought, as he put his alias mode check list through an initial review, several, if not many more, to be done before departure on Saturday. No doubt Tom would be doing the same sort of preparation, and as they would be travelling separately, flight time is also a very good opportunity for mental revision!

That afternoon the Director called Harry in for a 'Sitrep' meeting in advance of his departure on Saturday.

'Well Harry, in one way a little like old times with you and Tom working together again,'

Harry nodded, as the Director continued,

'But, let me emphasise one important point. This joint operation, is the sourcing and collection of intelligence, to assist both UK and USA intelligence agencies and companies, such as us, to combat a world-wide form of cancer affecting a multitude of countries.

I cannot stress too strongly the risks that you and Tom are likely, or possibly, to be exposed to. It is intelligence gathering, pure and simple. That in itself is risky enough, so I am insisting, on behalf of IISG USA, UK, and 6, that both of you maintain strong vigilance, and in the event of a hazardous situation clearly developing, carry out a tactical withdrawal.

Is that fully understood Harry?'

Harry nodded,

'Yes Director, but sometimes these situations do not give a warning,' But seeing the look developing on the Director's face, he added,

'I'm sure Tom and I would recognise, at the same time, if a tactical withdrawal was called for. Have no fear Director, I want to collect my pension at some time!'

The Director nodded his head, 'Just make sure you and Tom are on the same wavelength at *all* times,' he emphasised.

That evening Harry picked up Lina at the Swiss Embassy for a meal at a local French restaurant. He decided he would tell her of his departure on Saturday 'for the collection of some local intelligence working with Tom'.

Lina looked concerned, but realised that in the careers both followed, intelligence gathering was nothing new, and without it and subsequent response, everywhere would be hazardous, and a lot less safe for people at large.

Harry made light of the situation, confiding in her that a colleague from his previous career would also be travelling with him with the same brief.

When Harry walked with her to her apartment, he was expecting to go back to his Clapham flat, but her tight grip on his hand took him into her apartment.

Wednesday 18th March 2009. London.

Andrei Ionescu was re-doubling his efforts.

Harry Baxter was the defined target, and to ensure his own success and promotion he needed to be ultra-professional. Discrete tails both in Central London and Clapham over some weeks had shown a pattern.

Not rigidly defined, but consistent enough from time to time to confirm a pattern both in general movements by Baxter, but also Baxter and his girlfriend from the Swiss Embassy.

Having established a discrete log, Andrei Ionescu was considering possible options dependent on location, day selection, and time.

Spring was not far away, with better light conditions for people in general, but not for a person planning an assassination. An early decision was vital, not only for timing, but also to remove any negative and possible terminal response from the Pakhan, either to his 'career', or worse.

He decided that the next weekend the 21st/22nd March would have to be used for this. How? Time? Method?

Bearing in mind the urgency of the Pakhan's order, it would have to be either dawn or dusk, with poor light conditions, and a silenced 9mm Baikal handgun. Masked, on foot, no more than two silenced shots. Location, Clapham, dark dawn, or dark dusk.

He decided that Sunday would be the day. Morning or evening.

*

At 10.00 a.m. that morning, The Director and Harry entered their old offices, a slightly strange feeling which quickly passed as the meeting with a formal agenda got underway.

Besides Tom Denman and his boss, were two analysts with specific focus on the Caribbean, and one further specialist with current identification of gangs and persons in Trinidad & Tobago. Such data was also transferred during the meeting to Harry's memory sticks, password protected.

It was also advised that both IISG and the CIA in Washington would be providing additional background Intel as up to date/current as possible. Similar shared data would be extended in Miami by the CIA.

Harry and Tom were quizzed as to their aliases, 'Barry' being complimented on his developing 'designer stubble!'

The meeting continued over a sandwich lunch, backup verbal commentary being provided on the intel provided , plus some numbers as to various gang strengths and history, gang conflict/top dog syndrome, etc. Local corruption levels and incidence in government, police, etc.

The meeting ended at about 4.00pm and the Director and Harry made their way back to IISG HQ. The Director was silent in the cab, but once in his office spoke in a very measured tone.

'Remember what I said the other day Harry. Don't push your luck if you find yourself on thin ice. Cut and run. That's an order. Is that clear?'

'Absolutely Director. And I'll make sure it's the two of us!'

Shortly after that, Harry received a call from Lina saying she was taking a cab, and passing his office at about 5.45pm, on her way to his flat. Would he like a lift? He readily agreed!

They talked quietly in the cab on its way to Clapham, both appreciating the elephant in the room, but which, in a strange way, was strengthening the bond between them.

The cab dropped them off at a local Italian restaurant where they were known by the owner, and ate quietly appreciating the pending situation. They both realised they had reached a point in their relationship when words are almost not necessary.

They understood that unfortunately such gaps occurred from time to time. They were trained in certain specialties, and recognised the specific demands that created such separations.

When they went to bed that night they made love that was gentle and memorable. Afterwards, they held each other in that sated state that said it all without any words.

Fri 20th March 2009. Clapham London

On the Friday morning Harry booked a cab to take Lina to the Swiss Embassy, and on its arrival Lina held him very tightly, with words in his ear,

'Take good care Harry Baxter, remember me, and also remember what your Director said. If thin ice, Cut and Run. I'll be thinking of you.'

She looked up at him, her eyes moist, 'Now I'm off to the playground, so let me go, and hurry back as soon you can!'

Harry realising that they had definitely reached an important stage in their relationship, hugged her firmly saying quietly, 'Yes, I'll be thinking of you, often, whilst I'm in a different playground. And yes, I'll be back as soon as I can!'

Lina turned and entered the cab, giving him a cheery wave and gentle smile as it departed.

Harry went back inside his flat, feeling somewhat flat now she had gone. He shook himself, unlocking his briefcase and retrieving written data and memory sticks, plus a very small screen laptop.

His day was spent in detailed preparation, and finally packing for his departure on Saturday.

*Saturday 21*st *March 2009. London to Washington D.C.*

Harry Baxter (now Barry Foster) left early for London Heathrow airport, catching the BA flight to Washington leaving at 11.30am, arriving Washington D.C. at approximately 2.30pm, local time. He made his way to the Churchill Hotel, located near Embassy Row.

On the same day, 21st March, Tom Denman (now Ron Hall) had caught a BA flight from London Heathrow at about 12.30 pm to Boston, Massachusetts, arriving at about 2.30 pm that afternoon. He made his way to his hotel, the Boston Park Plaza.

They spoke briefly via their cell phones, and confirmed their meeting the next day at the Boston Park Plaza.

*Sun 22*nd *March 2009. Boston to Washington D.C.*

Ron Hall took a Delta flight from Boston to Washington D.C. arriving at about 11.30am, making his meeting with Barry Foster at just after 1.00pm.

A quiet conversation followed over lunch, before Ron left for his hotel, the Hotel Washington.

Monday 23rd March 2009. CIA. Washington D.C.

Barry had been notified by text that he would be picked up by car and driver XXXX, at about 10.00am that morning, registration number YYYY. Ron had also received a similar text.

Both collections proceeded without a hitch and made their respective ways to the CIA HQ, located in Langley, McLean, Virginia, a short distance from Washington D.C.

Having passed through Security, they were taken to a meeting room on the second floor, where they were both pleasantly surprised to be greeted and welcomed by Jack DeCosta.

'Welcome Barry and Ron. Great to see you again. Can't say that your stubble improves the view Barry, but needs must for what you are up to!'

'Thanks for your welcome speech, Jack. Top quality as ever!'

The other people present included two regional analysts, and also one officer with recent Intel secured, both electronic interceptions, and satellite tracking observations, covering land and maritime movements.

It was clear that interpretation, analysis, and discussion, would take at least two days, so jackets off, plus plenty of coffee, were obviously order of the day.

At about 6.00pm that evening, Jack called a halt.

'You guys need some sleep tonight, before another full day tomorrow. Suggest we take you back to your hotels, grab yourself a meal, and then hit the sack.

I look forward to seeing you both at about 9.30 a.m. tomorrow morning. Agreed?'

'Agreed', Barry and Ron replied.

Tuesday 24th March 2009. CIA Washington D.C.

9.30 a.m. seemed to come round very quickly that morning, but needs must. As Barry reminded himself, preparation was at least ninety percent of the battle!

Intelligence briefing continued, but now started to drill down on recent reports covering Trinidad gangs and bosses, plus intergroup rivalries and assassinations/murders.

Barry and Ron were generally aware of the lawlessness in Trinidad, but emerging details spelt out a much more continuous vicious graphic picture, clearly widespread across Trinidad's population.

They were told that Miami CIA, who they would be meeting later in the week, would have the latest intercepts, both electronic data and phone taps, for briefing the day before they left for Trinidad.

To put it bluntly it was not a pretty picture, quite the reverse, but definitive links, drug routing, financial transactions, source and delivery, were vital if this obscene trade was to be sanctioned.

During a break in the afternoon Barry commented to Ron,

'Not the easiest Intel gathering exercise I've been involved with Ron, and I would guess the same for you?'

'No argument there Barry. We'll have to watch our backs, doubly so, I think!'

'Definitely doubly agreed!'

At about six Jack DeCosta called a halt,

'I'd guess your heads ache now after all that good news, so in all seriousness I wish you guys the very best of luck and good fortune during your time in the Caribbean, and Trinidad in particular.

Plus, if it gets too hot, and I don't mean the weather, shout. We can help. Our CIA desk in the Embassy will respond to your signal that I am now going to give you. Memorise, do not record anywhere. OK?'

Barry replied,

'Jack, many thanks as always. Hope we don't need your assistance, but very glad it's there if needed! Plus, much appreciate your comprehensive briefing. Most of the mobs described sound fairly hairy, and yes, we won't push our luck.'

Ron and Barry then returned to their hotels to sleep, pack, and fly separately the next day to Miami. It would be fair to say that after that briefing neither slept particularly soundly.

Wednesday 25th March 2009. Foreign & Commonwealth Office. UK.

Sir Robert Fordcombe was reading a number of individual reports from MI5 and MI6. He was not impressed.

There was one basic thought or question within the Durov scenario that he could not either appreciate, or understand.

As a mental exercise he put himself in such a position, as a senior Intelligence Officer requesting asylum in a foreign country.

How would he wish the process to unfold? Slowly or quickly? Based on the value of Intel he was carrying mentally, he would want asylum confirmation as soon as possible. So why the hesitancy in providing important Intel?

Something was not quite right. But what was either the reason, or the reluctance?

Washington D.C. to Miami.

There were no hitches on either of their flights, Barry on United and Ron on American, to Miami, flight time just over 2 hrs 30 mins.

It had been agreed that they would be met by the local CIA, car and driver ID provided. They would stay overnight, Wednesday and Thursday, in a CIA safe house.

They were joined for dinner that evening by Pat Driscoll, local CIA chief, who, after a short brief as to activity on Thursday, hosted a relaxed evening, preceded by an initial remark concerning CIA Washington,

'There they deal with a lot of intelligence; you know the sort of thing. Might haves, might nots, maybe Yes, maybe No.

Whereas here, closer to the fun, we deal with the doing, implementation, that sort of thing. I'm guessing you guys fall into that sort of scenario. Right?'

'Right,' they both said. A relaxing evening was spent, followed by a good night's sleep, they both agreed, over breakfast on the Thursday morning.

Thursday 26th March 2009. CIA Miami.

The briefing meeting was held in the safe house, headed by Pat Driscoll who was joined by Bill Forbes, NSA (National Security Agency).

Pat Driscoll outlined to Bill what Barry and Ron had covered in Washington, and what his and Bill's emphasis would be.

He started by covering some recent Intel concerning specific gang operations in Trinidad in 2008.

The massive tonnage amounts of cocaine entering Trinidad are carried over by small cargo fishing boats, called pirogues, from Venezuela to the west coasts of Trinidad, and to a lesser degree, Tobago.

From Trinidad to Europe the favoured cocaine route is by sea, sometimes via Ireland, and thence to the UK and Europe, through organised crime distribution gangs.

Recently, a 60ft ocean sailing yacht was intercepted carrying the equivalent of $600M of cocaine, which if not captured, would have been flooding the streets of Britain. Surveillance was being carried out both on the ground and in the air, and still the foul trade continued.

A separate briefing was handled by Bill Forbes of the NSA, covering the arranged comms facility for both Barry and Ron.

This would be handled through a secure circuit of the NSA, picking up coded messages from both of them, transmitting through NSA handsets into the main network, for onward transmission to London or elsewhere. Unbreakable encryption on a single message basis, non-maintained, ensured that no legacy would apply to any message.

Finally a review was carried out on some of the current 'gangs' operating in Trinidad.

Position in the local hierarchy, numbers of personnel, estimated value of drugs handled on an annual basis, estimated number of murders and assassinations.

One important reference was made concerning Barry and Rom's likely discussion with gang members and leaders when that eventuated. Locations, any indications of habit (office, friends, 'soldiers', restaurants, bars, nightclubs, etc.)

Their M.O. would be simple. Buying cocaine, very significant funding from Eastern Europe direct to the Caribbean, or a multi stage, i.e. Eastern Europe to Western Europe, to wherever, and then to wherever. Just indicate preference.

Encrypted data was downloaded onto memory sticks, requiring codes for transmission or transfer, plus obliteration by code if required.

Winding up, Pat and Bill wished them the best of luck with firm handshakes, and a couple of cold beers!

Friday 27ᵗʰ March 2009. Miami to Trinidad.

That morning, the old team were travelling together.

Barry and Ron took the 10.00am flight from Miami International to Trinidad Port of Spain Airport, arriving just after 2.00pm that afternoon. Dark glasses were now the order of the day, brilliant sunshine and a temperature of about 30 degrees C.

They took a taxi to the Hyatt Regency and booked in.

The M.O. adopted by both was a serious business style, to the point of abruptness. Curt and short. Little humour shown.

However, need to draw attention to themselves, not as tourists, but clearly men on business. However, business not known.

Saturday 28th March - Sunday 29th March 2009. London.

Andrei was panicking. His tracking of Harry had hit a brick wall, both office and home. He had disappeared. Business, vacation, whatever. No sign whatsoever over the week, weekend, morning, noon, or night.

He had contacted the Pakhan, who listened in silence, before instructing him to check every other day. If no sign, then check again the following week. Updating the Pakhan was mandatory.

Saturday 28th March 2009. Port of Spain, Trinidad.

Barry and Ron spent some considerable time in the hotel's main lounges conducting serious looking conversations, before lunch and dinner, neither venturing out to the pool or terrace areas.

That evening after dinner, at about 10.30pm, they made their way to a nightclub, the Coco Lounge, by taxi.

They took one of the private booths located around the main lounge that can seat up to 5/6 people. Bearing in mind the usual crowd starting to fill up the club after ten o'clock, it would be fair to say they stood out, as two suited business men who have now taken off their jackets!

Having ordered their drinks, they chatted quietly between themselves.

Close on midnight a couple of men walked past their booth before returning and one stopping to enquire, with a smile,

'You wantin' a dummy man?'

'Are we wanting a what?'

'A dummy man.'

'No, but I might be interested in some gear.'

'How much?'

'I only talk to the boss.'

'Me the boss.'

'I just said I only talk to the boss. Understood?'

The two men looked at each other, but before leaving, said, 'Come Wednesday, this time, maybe boss man here.'

' Don't waste my time. No maybe. Boss man definite. Understood?'

The man nodded his head.

Barry did not respond, but briefly nodded.

They carried on their quiet conversation before leaving at about 12.30am, and returning to their hotel by taxi.

Sunday 29th March 2009. The Hyatt Regency Hotel Trinidad

Barry and Ron met for breakfast on the umbrella clad terrace at about 8.30am that morning. Dark glasses were the order of the day as they quietly discussed the previous evening.

'Perhaps an opportune opening. At least we'll get something, or nothing, to kick this off. Difficult until we meet some of these operators to determine whether we are dealing with the big boys or budding amateurs.'

Ron commented, 'Well, we have to put a fly on the water, and dependent how far up the ladder our contact is, then keep pushing to talk to the real players, or bosses.'

'Yes', Barry continued, 'bearing in mind the wealth of intel we have been provided with; the names of some of the known gangs, and numbers of likely members, it ought not to be too long before someone leads us to the top, the smell of money should be the unhealthy draw!'

Using their individual connections through the NSA secure network, they both updated their positions and status to London, leaving any points concerning contacts until later in the week.

Monday 30th March 2009. Tottenham London.

Andrei knew he had to update the Pakhan as to progress or delay. He made his way to Tottenham, aware that although his target had currently disappeared, this would still produce a negative reaction from the Pakhan.

He detailed the position, from both locations, office and apartment, frequency, and time of observations, and could only assume Baxter was away on business or holiday.

The Pakhan listened in stony silence, but finally realised that Andrei was unable to improve the current situation and carry out his order until Harry Baxter returned to London, from wherever.

'Update me here next Monday,' was his only comment.

Andrei was grateful for the instruction. He was still active, and had not been dismissed.

*

Tuesday 31st March 2009. Warehouse. Port of Spain Trinidad.

A conversation was being held by the boss with Kyle and Tyrell. They were the two men who had approached Barry and Ron on the Saturday evening.

Kyle was describing them, apparent nationality, appearance, attitude, and request. The boss was listening closely, then asked some questions. Were they police, US or UK? Didn't think so. Serious? Yes, and direct.

He paused, 'I meet them on Wednesday. You Kyle, come with me, drive the car. We will find out who they are, and what they want. Leave here about 11.30.'

That evening. Hyatt Regency Hotel.

Barry and Ron were sitting in the corner of the main lounge when they were approached by a suited Trinidadian, who, it had to be said, addressed them quite formally.

' Good evening gentlemen, can I join you?'

'It depends on your reason,' Barry replied abruptly.

The man took out his Trinidad Police Identity and showed it to both men, identifying him as Chief Inspector Michael Thomas, *Organised Crime & Intelligence Unit.*

'I would like to know what you were talking about with a man known as Kyle at the Coco Lounge on Saturday. You were observed by one of my men.'

Barry looked briefly at Ron before replying, brusquely,

'One of your men?'

'Yes, one of my men in my Unit of the Trinidad and Tobago Police Service.'

'And?'

'And we were wondering what two Europeans, obviously not tourists, were doing here in Trinidad.'

Barry thought quickly and spoke quietly,

'If you consider us to be a risk, at whatever level, then I suggest you ask us to join you for a discussion in your office. Do you understand?'

'Certainly, I have a car and driver outside.'

Barry and Ron followed him to the front of the hotel, where a police car was parked on a dark corner.

They were driven in silence to his HQ, and were taken to his office where they sat down at a small conference table.

'Your passports please.'

These were handed over, to be examined by the Inspector.

'Both of you are apparently frequent fliers, and your occupation description is very general.

Perhaps I should provide some personal and professional background?'

'Please,' Barry responded.

'I have what could be described as a working relationship with certain US agencies, attempting to reduce the amount of illegal drugs passing through Trinidad, en route to the USA.

Naturally, I am interested in any new arrivals, particularly business men, and their reason for visiting Trinidad. Assuming I do not receive satisfactory answers, then it is a fairly simple matter for me to ensure that they are on the next flight out of Trinidad. You understand?'

'May I now give you some background, Inspector?' Barry suggested.

'Please.'

'Both myself, and my colleague Ron, are employed and tasked by certain UK Government departments whose prime function is to chase, apprehend, and bring to justice, criminal funds that have passed through any UK financial operation, or organisation.

We are involved in such an investigation at present that has some significant financial end transmissions to Trinidad, we believe heavily linked to the illegal drug trade from South America to Europe. Essentially via Trinidad, to West Africa, and then Europe, including the UK.

The contact made to us on Saturday merely presented an opportunity for us to have a local discussion with a drug gang as to method of operation. Effectively, we are potential buyers. This in turn could hopefully expose some of the routeing of drugs to Europe and also payment from Europe to seller in Trinidad.'

Barry then expanded on the paucity of accurate intelligence concerning these criminal gangs, transport connections West to East, deliberate confusion created in the transmission of funds worldwide, and the apparent lack of success in stopping such a hideous trade.

Within this explanation Barry gave no indication of their US relationship or support, keeping to the bare bones.

'If what you say is correct concerning your reason to be here in Trinidad, it would have been much better if a formal request had been made in advance of your visit. In that way we could assist you.'

'I hear what you say Inspector, but with great respect the question of security of information, or confidentiality of operation, is not known to be very high here in Trinidad. I am sorry to say that, but that view is in general circulation in Europe.'

The Inspector looked as if he was about to angrily dispute that, but literally looked up to the ceiling and coughed, before quietly responding,

'Very unfortunately Mr Foster, you are correct in your view.

Here in Trinidad and Tobago, there is too much porosity. Too many things leak, and both of us know why. Too many gangs involved in illegal trade, drugs, murder, prostitution, and who have connection to civil service, and perhaps members of our government.

Perhaps the biggest problem in the Organised Crime & Intelligence Unit is maintaining security within the Intelligence area. It leaks, and you can imagine where it generally leaks to.'

He paused,

'I am not too sure as to my actions now. One is to put you on the first UK bound aircraft for an unspecified reason, other than undesirable; or to allow you to proceed with your investigation, but on the understanding of sharing what information you acquire with myself, only.

You will be taken back to your hotel in a cab, this I hope restoring some of your credibility if others are watching you.'

He smiled a little grimly at the end of that sentence.

'Take down this cell phone number. If assistance is required, call.'

Before they left, Ron asked him if he had been to the UK,

'Yes. Many years ago. Three years at a provincial university, and then a year exchange with the Metropolitan Police. Very interesting.'

Barry and Ron thanked him for his reaction and assistance and returned to their hotel, maintaining silence in the cab.

Barry, through his NSA comms unit, asked the Director for past reviews etc, on Chief Inspector Michael Thomas, *Organised Crime & Intelligence Unit, Trinidad & Tobago Police,* who had spent a year with the Met Police at Scotland Yard.

Check and double check.

***

XII

April 2009.

Wednesday 1ˢᵗ April 2009. Hyatt Regency, Port of Spain.

That morning Barry and Ron discussed the situation arising from their meeting with Chief Inspector Michael Thomas the previous day.

Barry opened with,

'Let's take a positive view of it.

We could be flying back to the UK, almost as we speak. Research into him may throw up some pluses, or minuses, which could either assist, or hinder our plans. Whichever, and whatever arises, let's up our own security, eyes in back of head, top grade!'

Ron took a slightly different view,

'First. We've got this meeting tonight. I have a concern on our security. I will certainly be carrying a weapon, just in case. These boys in Port of Spain are normally well-armed.

Second. Let's take a pessimistic view on our Chief Inspector, until we know otherwise. Just in case. OK?

They agreed.

That evening they left the hotel at about 11.00pm, taking a cab to the Coco Lounge and a private booth.

They were thinking that perhaps there would be a no show when Kyle appeared, followed by two men, one they thought would be the boss, the other his 'security'.

Kyle started to say something, but was pushed out of the way by the boss who sat down heavily, and stared at them.

279

After a few seconds he spoke,

'What you want?'

'Plenty top quality gear,' Barry said.

'Why you?'

'We have big funds for gear.'

'You English?'

'Yes.'

'Why I deal with you?'

Big funds, good deals. Both of us happy. Why not?'

'Maybe. Meet tomorrow. Kyle tell where.'

'O.K. What time?'

'Four, afternoon.'

'Fine. Would you like a drink?'

'No.'

At this point he got up and left, muttering something to Kyle in passing.

Kyle turned and said, 'Tomorrow, four here. I have car.'

Barry and Ron then went back to their hotel, at least feeling small progress had been made. Still no name from the boss man. Thursday is another day!

Thursday 2nd April 2009. 4.00pm. Coco Lounge.

Barry and Ron arrived by cab at ten past four to see Kyle standing by a car not far from the entrance. They walked over, Kyle seeing them, opened the rear doors.

They climbed into the back of the car, with minimum comment, and carefully watched direction and location of their short journey which took, it seemed, a devious route to a large warehouse.

They were led into a rear office, mercifully air-conditioned, to see the boss sitting behind a large desk. He waved them to two seats.

Barry and Ron had decided that as they were buying, they would push and lead in discussions and negotiations.

Ron opened, 'I'm Ron, this is Barry. What's your name?'

He muttered something in reply.

'What is your name?' Ron repeated.

'Joel.'

'Afternoon Joel,' said Barry interrupting, 'Can we get down to business?'

Joel spoke, 'Before that, how you pay. Where your money?'

Barry responded, very quietly, but with an edge to his voice.

'Let's understand each other Joel.

We have lots of money. You want to sell gear, and we want to buy a lot. Do you understand what I am saying, because maybe your business is not big enough for us. Perhaps we need to find out who the big players are, 'cos we are a big money player.

Is that clear Joel? Do you understand me? This place doesn't look much like big players. If you've got big player friends, can we meet them with you, or just an introduction by you?

I'm not wasting my time or yours. Can we deal or not? Yes or No.'

He waited for a response from Joel, looking at him directly, without blinking.

'OK' replied Joel.

'How much you want, and where deliver? Tell me that. I tell you price. Where you operate? UK.? Do people know you in UK?'

Barry nodded,

'You take our names, Barry Foster, and Ron Hall, families operating in this business for years.

And you tell me where I pay you. No cash, only money transfer. Understood?'

Joel nodded.

They then started discussing amounts, quality, etc, and it soon became apparent that Joel would have to call in some other players to perform to the levels they were asking for.

At about 6.00pm, Joel said Kyle would drop them back at their hotel and he would contact them sometime Friday.

Barry kept up the pressure, 'When Joel, morning, afternoon? Don't waste time, say midday. We've got other business to do.'

Kyle dropped them off at the hotel, making an interesting point to them.

'If boss not help, I know some big men who can. Not Port of Spain.'

'Thanks Kyle, but we are doing fine' replied Ron, raising an indirect eyebrow at Barry.

Later he reminded Barry of Kyle's comment, and his thoughts, 'Certainly no honour amongst thieves!'

That evening some data came back from London via NSA comms. First, some background information on Chief Inspector Michael Thomas.

Secondly, a report from IISG concerning a further interception of a major drug shipment being carried by an ocean going yacht, which had got into difficulties in heavy seas, requiring Navy rescue and arrest. Significant $ value in every case.

The background on Chief Inspector Michael Thomas made for good reading.

A man who had been asked to transfer from Trinidad Police to the London Metropolitan Police, in order to assist in the increasing numbers of West Indian criminals now operating in the Metropolitan area.

Diligent, resourceful, and objective, an officer of integrity. All very good words. However he had declined the opportunity, saying he wanted to attack the crime syndicates at source, who were creating misery for increasing numbers of the population.

Barry and Ron felt more comfortable now to exchange information and intelligence with him, such assistance would no doubt significantly assist in their own contacts with organised crime syndicates.

Friday 3rd April 2009. Hyatt Regency, Port of Spain, Trinidad.

Kyle passed by at about 11.00am. Meeting that p.m. at about 2.30. Different location, Laventille. He would drive them.

Laventille, Barry and Ron knew, was located in the eastern area of Port of Spain. It had the highest incidence of crime in Trinidad, most, if not all, connected to the drug trade. Also murders in Laventille were the highest in Trinidad, numbering about 250 per year on average.

Barry and Ron remained silent in the car as Kyle drove them to Laventille, stopping in front of a villa that looked considerably different to its neighbours. This one had cost money.

Walking across the shaded terrace they were stopped and frisked by two men, clearly checking for weapons.

Inside a fan whirred in an air conditioned atmosphere, coupled with subdued lighting over a large oval table occupied on one side by three men, the other side with two empty chairs.

The man in the middle waved them to the two chairs. Joel sat on his right.

'Understand you lookin' for plenty gear?', started the conversation.

Questions followed covering UK background, criminal families in the UK, why they are in Trinidad, and finally what quantity and how paid?

Barry led, but with Ron giving an impression as the money man.

The funds available are very large, East European, was as far as he would admit, but large quantities of 'gear' were wanted. Delivery to Western Europe was preferred route, or possibly central Mediterranean.

The discussion covered time to organise large shipments, obviously coming across from Venezuela, and more importantly method of shipping to Western Europe.

This was where Barry played the hard man,

'There have already been reports in UK newspapers and TV concerning yachts being arrested near Ireland full of gear. If that is your operation then we can forget any business now.'

'Is not us,' the man in the middle replied.

'If it is,' said Barry 'then you are in big trouble.'

'Is not us,' the man repeated.

'If it is, and you handle our consignment, and something like that happens, you know what will then happen to you.'

Barry let the thought sink in, before he spoke again,

'Our consignment must go by container, no amateur sailor route is acceptable. We will tell you which Med container port it must go to, either UK, Spain, or Italy. Understood?'

The man nodded, 'We meet next week. Kyle tell you.'

Barry and Ron were returned to their hotel by Kyle, and whilst being driven back, Barry threw a half brick into the pond.

'Kyle, you said the other day you had some other contacts. Perhaps we might speak to them as well.'

Kyle looked slightly nervous, but said,

'If you want, but different man contact you. OK?'

'OK.'

That evening Barry discussed the contents of the recent meeting with Ron, who thought that with ever increasing interception of illegal trans-Atlantic drug traffic, rates would certainly be on the increase, but also probably linked to violent measures between drug gangs to gain more individual gang control.

Saturday 4ᵗʰ April 2009. Hyatt Regency Hotel, Port of Spain, Trinidad.

That Saturday morning Barry telephoned Chief Inspector Michael Thomas' mobile telephone, via his NSA comms unit to update him on the recent meeting in Laventille.

Michael made no comment until Barry finished.

'Well, you've made some gang connections, we'll have to see what they offer you. The area Laventille is full of major and minor gangs. It sounds as though you are in contact with one of the major players, so please keep me up to date.'

Harry agreed, but forgot to mention the other potential source through Kyle.

As it was Saturday Barry and Ron spent a little time in the shade by the pool after a swim. Whilst they were lying on their chaises longues, one of the pool boys passed by, handing Barry an envelope from Reception.

Thinking it was an interim bill Harry opened it, to find on a blank card, a telephone number and the words 'Kyle contact', which he passed to Ron, with the comment, 'They are certainly not wasting time.'

That evening he telephoned the number and held a short staccato conversation, which provided an address and a suggested meeting on Monday. The number and address he passed to the Chief Inspector.

Monday 6th April 2009. Foreign & Commonwealth Office, London.

Sir Robert Fordcombe was holding an updating meeting with both Security Services officers.

Whilst maintaining an expression of professional neutrality, he was finding his control of his emotions more than testing, as they were increasing at a rate which he was experiencing, particularly stressful.

After some time the sole intelligence which appeared to have been shared by Dimitry Durov with the officers was limited.

As had been indicated before, certain UK individuals, Trade Union officials, with Soviet sympathies to a higher, or lower degree, had been named. Certain UK organisations with a greater than acceptable sympathy to Moscow, obviously due to improving trade links were also named.

Durov kept insisting that he only wished to discuss such matters with Sir Robert, principally, on account of the fact, that the intelligence he wished to share concerned *two* agents within the Foreign and Commonwealth Office.

To say that Sir Robert was both bitterly shocked and dismayed was not to minimise his reaction. He adopted the mandarin approach.

'Absolute rubbish,' he exclaimed. 'A preposterous claim, and what does he expect to achieve.? Trouble making of the highest order. Create divisions within Her Majesty's Government? Establish a witch hunt across a number of Government departments, sowing distrust and confusion?'

He paused to catch his breath and adopt his usual calm exterior, linked with his usual analytical style of response, or interrogation.

He was silent for a short time,

'I have decided, reluctantly, that the meeting with Durov and myself will proceed. Arrange a suitable date and time with my secretary for the meeting in the Safe House. You will both be present. Thank you gentlemen.'

He rose and left the meeting as both officers tried to speak. He waved them away as he left the room.

Monday 6th April 2009. Hyatt Regency Hotel, Port of Spain, Trinidad.

Barry and Ron took a cab to Barataria, about 7 kms from the hotel, arriving about 11.30am. The meeting was a complete failure, and a total waste of time.

Clearly some friends/acquaintances of Kyle trying to break into the big times.

As they had arrived they had seen the type of house where the meeting was to be held, so had instructed the cab to wait for them. They returned to the hotel, irritated, to say the least.

Back at the hotel Barry saw that he had received, via the NSA network, an email from IISG London. It contained data received from Alain Dubois DGSE, concerning further analysis completed on the IFS penetration in London. Included in the analysis were several repeating transfers from Eastern Europe and Russia to the Caribbean, including Trinidad. Some of the recipient accounts were clearly illegal, judging by numbering or individual fake names, or companies.

He and Ron discussed whether such data should be shared with the Chief Inspector, and decided that they would hold back at present.

North London. Tottenham. That afternoon.

Andrei updated the Pakhan. No sign of Harry Baxter whatsoever at home or work. Pakhan orders maintain surveillance. Report in 7 days.

Tuesday 7th April 2009. Hyatt Regency Hotel, Port of Spain, Trinidad. Morning.

Barry and Ron spent some time analysing the recent data received from Alain, via IISG. It became very clear that in order for further intelligence in the Caribbean area, and Trinidad in particular, to be extracted from the bare data, then cooperation with, and from, the Chief Inspector would be vital.

Barry called him, and asked if they could meet sometime that afternoon. 3.30pm was agreed.

Afternoon.

Barry explained, that in a criminal investigation in London, involving an international money transfer company, significant amounts of electronic data had been secured, which was being currently analysed and investigated. The data covered transmissions from and to various countries.

Initiating countries included several in Eastern Europe plus Russia; receiving countries included South America, the Caribbean, and certain Indian ocean countries and islands.

Some of the initial data, including the Caribbean, covered a number of banks and accounts; many accounts labelled as companies, some with no ID, just numbered. However individual accounts, whether as companies or numbered, were identified as being within specific local banks. Therefore a starting point for investigation.

The Chief Inspector having heard the background, smiled wryly,

'This information data is excellent. However knowing the operating style of some of these local or regional banks they will try to hide behind a screen of client confidentiality. I'm sure you appreciate this.'

'Absolutely. The same reaction occurs in the UK and Europe from time to time. However we have found that applying significant pressure to one bank, with the threat of legal or government intervention and adverse publicity has produced, eventually, sensible cooperation. Some other banks have then fallen into line. Is it not worth the try?'

He nodded, 'Certainly worth a try. If I can have details of specific banks, then I can consider which one would be a possibility to approach, and apply some pressure.

'By the way, I am happy with Michael, if you are comfortable with Barry and Ron?'

'Absolutely.'

After reviewing the bank data, Union Bank was chosen as the first for Michael to approach.

'Leave this with me to follow up. I know one of the Directors. I'll see what sort of reaction I get.'

Wednesday 8th April 2009. Hyatt Regency Hotel.

In Barry's room he and Ron were discussing further Intel contained in the recent communication from IISG London, via NSA comms, when he was interrupted by a call from reception at about 10.00am, advising that 'his visitor had arrived in Reception'.

Barry did not express surprise, leaving Ron whilst he went to investigate who this was.

Arriving in Reception his visitor was pointed out to him.

Harry opened, 'I think there must be a mistake.'

'No mistake' was the reply, 'my name is Duvan Cardona, I am from Colombia. You have been discussing some business with friends of mine.'

Barry looked at him without expression.

He saw a smart man, well dressed, with typical Spanish facial characteristics, carrying a little too much jewellery for his taste, who spoke English with a slight accent.

'Perhaps we should carry on this conversation with my colleague upstairs?'

'I prefer terrace please.'

Harry called Ron to join them on the terrace.

Seated in the shadows on the terrace Barry introduced Ron as to who the man was, who then opened the discussion.

'I think you want to buy big amounts of product I have direct connection with. Men you spoke with last week not have business connection like me. They contact me.

What amount you want, when, deliver to where? I need detail.'

Barry paused before replying,

'First we need to know who you are, who you represent, and whether you are a big organisation we want to do business with.

After that, if we have agreement, then we tell you amount, where, and when. Only by container. But only when we have agreed price. Do you understand?

'Yes.'

Over the next hour Cardona provided some details of his organisation, existing trafficking routes, quality and quantity of cocaine available, and at this stage a general indication of price.

Barry responded when Cardona had finished,

'I hear what you say, but understand from our position price is very negotiable. We may have more than one entry port into Europe by container. Is this a problem.'

'No. we deliver several ports in Europe. Guaranteed.' He said wolfishly.

'Let us meet Friday afternoon, four o'clock,' Barry said, to which Cardona agreed.

After Cardona had left, Barry contacted Michael Thomas on his private mobile, updating him on the recent meeting with Cardona, all references being oblique, and wondering if he had any background intel on the individual.

He promised to revert soonest.

Thursday 9ᵗʰ April 2009. Telcon with Department of Organised Crime & Intelligence Unit, Port of Spain, Trinidad.

That morning Barry contacted Michael Thomas on his personal mobile to hear what Intel he had uncovered on Duvan Cardona.

'If he is genuine, and I have a photo of him, then you have moved some way up the criminal pyramid. He is known as senior member of a particular Colombian syndicate noted on the LA-OC data files(Latin America-Organised Crime) which is also known to work with para-military and terrorist groups.

I know he comes to Trinidad occasionally, it must be one of his liaison meetings with dispatchers here, on behalf of the syndicate.

Obviously, he and his syndicate members will stop at nothing, so as I was also advised in London, whilst with the Met, tread carefully!'

'Agreed Michael, no argument! However, we have a meeting with him tomorrow, and I'm going to suggest our three preferred ports in Europe for container delivery. They are Valencia Spain, Genova Italy, and Liverpool UK.'

'Liverpool?' Michael queried.

'Yes, recent intel indicates quite a thriving container traffic through Liverpool for drugs, particularly cocaine. UK gangs have infiltrated the port, and are controlling distribution throughout the UK, and also then into mainland Europe. I want to see his reaction.'

Friday 10th April 2009. Hyatt Regency Hotel. Meeting Duvan Cardona.

Barry and Ron had insisted the meeting took place at their hotel, on this occasion in a private room, coffees and soft drinks available, no interruptions. They intended to try and dominate the discussions. They were the buyers, with choice. Having a two on one meeting meant they could effectively control , intro, demands, resolution.

A wide ranging discussion took place, covering quality of cocaine, amounts able to be container delivered to Europe per shipment, price related to quantity, period of time required covering order to delivery Europe, and consequences of non-delivery (payment, completion, recovery, etc).

Barry explained, in some general detail, the source of their funds, essentially East European, significant in value, and with suitable safeguards as to payment, ensuring no trace-back of source, and identity cover of recipients.

Ron covered areas of security required, monitoring of transmissions, penalties for loss of confidentiality, and a clear statement that severe action would be taken if this was not 100% secure.

The final question was, 'Did he fully understand what was expected of him?'

Duvan replied confidently that his organisation had several good years of well won experience, and that they could be confident of an excellent quality product, and delivery service.

He suggested that once they had decided on the quantity and destination of their first consignment they should speak again.

Barry responded, 'We do not intend to meet again. We know what is to be our first instruction.' He then described quantity, with Liverpool as the delivery container port. Negotiation as to price took over an hour, but agreement was reached.

Duvan raised no objections as to the quantity or container port, and said he would provide bank details within 48 hours.

After his departure Barry and Ron compared mental notes as to the specific items discussed. As far as they could determine most vital areas had been covered. Only time would tell if anything had been missed.

Friday 10th April 2009. Safe House, UK.

The meeting was scheduled to start at 10.00am.

Sir Robert, accompanied by the two Security Service Officers, greeted Dimitry Durov with a formal, if slightly icy tone that morning.

Durov responded in his normal tone to all three.

Sir Robert opened the meeting in a brisk manner, repeating what he had been told by both officers.

'Is that correct, and is that the main item for discussion this morning? If so, can we please move quickly to the credibility of your statement that I find extremely hard to believe.'

'Sir Robert, in the world of professional espionage that we both inhabit, there have been many instances of disclosure that have caused all of us to question its credibility.'

Sir Robert's face and nose crinkled in that manner that indicates the person has just recognised a bad smell, as he replied,

'As you spoke, I was thinking of the numbers that have fled your style of government and the treatment of its people, compared to those from this, and other close European countries.

However, enough conjecture, let us please focus on what you wish to say.'

Durov paused, clearly gathering his thoughts.

'The name of the individual is Charles Urwin, a First Secretary.'

Initially silence followed the disclosure as the two officers scribbled down the name.

Sir Robert, with a smooth, but sarcastic tone to his voice, responded very coolly, 'And what possible explanation can you give for making such an accusation? And I would suggest, that unless you have credible corroboration, confirmed by appropriate intelligence, then your hope for political asylum in this country could be short lived.

I trust you fully understand what I am saying?'

At this point the two officers both looked to Sir Robert for guidance.

Sir Robert spoke, 'I suggest a short break, and perhaps tea or coffee in separate rooms.

My first reaction is one of pure astonishment, but clearly having opened Pandora's Box, we will have to fully investigate. We will continue this discussion in a short while.'

Both officers left the room, no doubt to securely transfer to their respective directors, what was eventuating. And which, in fairly short order, would become pretty messy.

Saturday 11th April 2009. Hyatt Regency Hotel

That afternoon Barry received a non-attributable message on his mobile. Bank payment details from Duvan Cardona.

Via the NSA comms network, he advised IISG London that an initial contract was being created. Data would have to be provided in order to satisfy/confirm payment to the bank provided by Duvan Cardona. Plus check with DGSE re previous data recovered. Any recent transfers, and if so, from where, and when?

Monday 13th April 2009. Tottenham London. That morning.

The Pakhan was getting frustrated with Andrei, who reported that there was no evidence of Harry being in London.

Maintain surveillance was his testy instruction, with an implied threat that if nothing was achieved within thirty days he would be dismissed.

Somewhere in Essex, North of London. That afternoon.

A meeting was being held, which was included two criminal families heavily involved in the burgeoning drug trade and distribution in the UK, and onward transmission to Europe.

The third person was an Albanian. A senior local connection with the Colombian Syndicate.

An old contact from the Caribbean had been in touch, who had heard of two men negotiating with a major cocaine supplier for a container shipment to Europe.

He had raised the point of coincidence concerning their surnames being the same as the two families currently meeting. Cousins of the two families was the connection the two men had indicated. Quite a coincidence he had thought, hence raising it. The family connection involved two generations.

The Albanian provided both names, surname first, then the forenames.

A brief discussion followed, covering branches of the families, brothers, ages, offspring, etc. Eventually both families looked at each other, shaking their heads, and denying any knowledge of these so-called cousins.

Thanks were extended by the Albanian, who hurriedly left the meeting to communicate his findings to the Colombian syndicate.

Thursday 16th April 2009. Up to date Intel from IISG via the NSA.

That afternoon Barry received a comms update from IISG London, via the NSA, which unsurprisingly, gave him some significant cause for concern.

With the widespread interception of electronic comms by GCHQ, geographical focus on The Caribbean had thrown up a telephone conversation in Albanian from the UK to Columbia. Not a long conversation, in fact, very short.

The gist was, in Albanian slang, 'They're fakes.'

The Director had added, as a reminder, the high risk of his and Ron's covers being blown. Watch your backs!

He had also included some further Intel which covered the introduction of Albanians extending their reach and control beyond Venezuela down into Ecuador.

As a direct result of this, there would be repercussions and impact on the Trinidad drug traffic. Container shipments of cocaine from Ecuador sail North, passing Colombia, then through the Panama Canal and direct to Europe, to any one of four or five favoured container ports. Trinidad bypassed. No need for Trinidad, whatsoever.

Later that afternoon he was contacted by Duvan Cardona, who was asking for a meeting sometime Friday, for various details and updates on their European delivery. He agreed 4.00pm.

Friday 17th April 2009. Foreign Office, Westminster, London.

Sir Robert was chairing the meeting. The other three members in the room, were the current Chiefs of MI5 and MI6, and the Director of GCHQ.

It must be realised that there is often an air of friction between 5 and 6, and which obviously, from time to time, will also include the Foreign Office, with its own specialised brand of friction.

Sir Robert had prepared the most basic of agendas for the meeting. In prime position was the statement by Durov. The second and third were clearly a number of questions directed at the Security Services and GCHQ concerning known, or assumed, intelligence covering all aspects of Durov. The fourth was a rhetorical question as to resolution, but with an underlying edge as to paucity of intelligence to date.

The Security Service Chiefs had already scanned the predictable agenda, and were waiting for Sir Robert's first comments.

Sir Robert was fully aware that his own Ministry was clearly under the microscope as a result of Durov's statement, and the recent protracted UK/Russian incident involving Charles Urwin was still fresh in his mind.

'Well gentlemen, your observations and comments would be welcome.'

The MI5 Chief spoke first, 'Our current intelligence concerning Durov is very modest, mostly biographical from his previous appointments in Russia and elsewhere.'

Sir Robert sighed, purely sound, but an opinion, nevertheless.

The MI6 Chief was able to contribute a little more in his observations having been involved in the subsequent 'meetings' with Charles Urwin, after his release and return from Moscow. As to any additional suspects, at this stage, it was a clean sheet.

Sir Robert turned to the Director of GCHQ,

'Do you have anything specific that could assist us in this very painful investigation of trying to confirm or otherwise the statements of a Russian First Secretary seeking asylum.

As you are aware he is claiming that there are two traitors in the Foreign Office providing Intelligence to Russia's SVR. No details as yet have been provided.'

The Director responded by outlining what is a basic first step in such a set of circumstances.

'We can initiate this, by observation, physical', nodding in the direction of 5 and 6, 'and electronic, of the first and previous examination, namely Charles Urwin. Then broaden the net across links, such as close colleagues, friends. etc.

Time consuming of course, but could perhaps provide some additional Intel in due course.'

A general discussion on this proposal then followed, Sir Robert ending the meeting on an agreed action plan as suggested by the GCHQ Director.

Both 5 and 6 readily agreed, and would liaise closely with GCHQ, both in collection and analysis of any data and intelligence recovered. No stone to be left unturned.

Action this Day. Sir Robert had all fingers crossed metaphorically. The question now was how to deal, professionally, with Durov He had to admit to himself this was not going to be easy.

Friday 17th April 2009. Port of Spain, Trinidad. Armed Civil Disturbance.

In the afternoon Barry and Ron were sitting on the shaded terrace when they both heard the sound of shots being fired, obviously not too close based on the sound levels, but which continued for a good twenty minutes. In restricted streets an exchange of fire for twenty minutes is a long time.

In Trinidad, various areas to the East of Port of Spain, are controlled by individual crime gangs, involved in drugs, extortion, homicide, etc, which can spill out, from time to time, into an armed confrontation. This is either for maintaining, or extending, control of streets in specific neighbourhoods. Most of the gangs are made up of Trinidadians, but the profile was changing with both Columbians and now a new group, Albanians, moving into specific territories. Such basic conflicts are then bound to arise.

Increased levels of violence, murders, control of prostitution, kidnaps, no-go areas, all elements of a broken society, with no indication of any reduction or improvement. Only permanent decline.

Friday 17th April 2009. 4.00pm Hyatt Regency Hotel. Barry meeting with Duvan Cardona.

Barry met Duvan Cardona on the hotel shaded terrace. Ron was not there, unfortunately confined to his room with a bout of food poisoning that had arisen that morning.

Cardona came straight to the points he wanted to raise. There was some further adjustment on price he wanted to raise, plus shipping, which was becoming more costly, due to specialised packing, sheathing, and concealment to avoid detection, either by X-ray, or similar electronic systems.

Barry took a hard line, saying that he thought their previous negotiations had dealt with all aspects and he was not prepared to accept further increases at this stage.

Cardona's response was straightforward, if non acceptance then consignment would go to someone prepared to pay.

Barry haggled some more, and eventually they agreed a compromise, although it could be said, not in the best of humours.

By the time they had finished their discussion it was almost dark, and lights were illuminating various parts of the hotel, but not that particular area of the terrace. They walked towards the entrance to the hotel, stopping at a corner, where Cardona would turn left to the car park, and Barry right to the hotel.

They shook hands, Cardona leaving in the direction of the car park, as two well-built Trinidad males approached from the opposite direction. What happened next was completed in considerably less than ten seconds.

Barry was expecting them to cross the edge of the terrace and enter the hotel about twenty yards away. Instead in a few seconds time span, he was grabbed, knocked out, and now unconscious, carried quickly as a drunk might be to the car park, and bundled into the back seats of a car, no lights, but the engine quietly running. It left with no drama, and disappeared in an easterly direction down Wrightson Road in the direction of Laventille.

About an hour later, Ron, having recovered from his food poisoning to some extent, went looking for Barry with no success in the hotel, or on his mobile. Concern and worry kicked in.

He quickly returned to his room and turned on his laptop, opening his GPS tracker system. Both he and Barry were equipped with such trackers. It had been agreed at the outset of this operation that both men would be equipped with such a GPS device and receiving software. A small transmitting device was located in their trouser belts which enables appropriate transmission to laptop receiving software to track and determine location on a real time basis.

He saw that the tracker was stationary, in the Laventille area, approximately half way down Picton Quarry Road. His main concern was that this area is notorious for crime gangs, extortion, kidnapping, drugs, murder; the complete Devil's soup.

Ron contacted Chief Inspector Michael Thomas on his mobile. Within the hour Michael Thomas was sitting opposite Ron in his hotel room, receiving a very sketchy brief.

Ron explained the reason for his absence from the meeting with Cardona, and after attempting to find Barry, located him by way of the GPS tracker.

Michael sighed, 'Barry, I believe, no I know, has been kidnapped. Our major problem is by whom, but our priority is his release.'

At this point he was on his mobile to HQ, ordering the appropriate teams to stand to and await further orders.

Turning to Ron he said, 'The first thing we need is a recce of approximately where he is, and confirmation of exact location. That must be done quickly. Then,' he said grimly, 'We can decide on the M.O. to effect his recovery. '

Friday, that evening, about 9.30pm. Somewhere in Laventille.

Barry regained consciousness, his face running with cold water, and with an acutely throbbing head, to find himself tied to a chair facing two sullen looking Trinidadians.

A small bucket of ice cold water hit his face again, followed by a hard slap.

At that point one of the men spoke, 'You lie, you not UK gangs. You police.'

Barry had difficulty in speaking, 'Why do you say that. Not true. I am here in Trinidad on business. Buying for UK market.'

At this point an adjacent door opened and Cardona entered, walking over to stand in front of Barry,

'You are not who you say you are. I check on you with my UK contacts. You are not relations with UK group I know. So maybe police.'

Barry responded as firmly as he could,

'Let me explain. I am not police. Drugs are a big market in UK, and Europe. I now have large East European finance for buying. That's why I am here.'

'They say you are fakes.'

'I operate in London, there are many groups in London, and the UK. I know of the two families, but no connection. Ron and I have forged passports and documents to help us. We need contact with suppliers which is why we came to Trinidad.

Our East European finance is very large, which is also why we are here. Big money, big orders.'

Cardona had listened. He turned to the two thugs, and said something in the local patois which Barry did not understand. They nodded in agreement, as Cardona turned and left.

They picked Barry up, still tied to the chair, and took him into an unlit room at the rear of the house. He was left there in darkness.

11.30 pm Police HQ. Police Recce and Recovery Team.

Inspector Thomas had not been idle. Returning to his HQ with Ron, he had pulled together a small team of well-trained officers in the Organised Crime Unit, trained for such situations.

With Ron's tracking S/W giving a good indication of location, then physical confirmation of hazards needed to be identified, before any recovery action could take place.

In three unmarked cars, the team led by Inspector Thomas, together with Ron and his tracker, left just after midnight, and drove to the start of Picton Quarry Road in Laventille.

They arrived there at about 12.45 a.m., parking about 500 metres from the indicated house on Ron's tracker.

Two plain clothed officers then walked up the road to the open ground area on the right hand side, which extended eastwards towards groups of trees and bushes, and the back fences of three houses. Splitting up, one went in a clockwise direction, the other the reverse.

Moving very slowly, they joined forces at the rear fences of the three houses. The tracker had indicated the right hand one, all three sharing a fence height of just over two metres. What was obvious on the rear elevation, was that one ground room was curtained, the other two ground rooms were not. They then withdrew back along their original paths, and re-joined the team.

Having briefed the Inspector, and reviewed the latest tracking result, which indicated no movement, the team were prepped for a combined frontal and rear operation. Bearing in mind that the occupants will be armed, the frontal assault/diversion would start about five minutes before the quieter approach over the fence. All officers were armed.

The planned action would commence at 3.15am.

Saturday morning 18th April 2009. 3.15am.

The small assault team at the front of the house moved silently into position, the only disturbance at that hour was a solitary dog barking further up the road. A narrow path led from the side road to the front door, with a few small trees providing limited cover between road and entrance.

Two members of the team were carrying battering rams, and stood motionless awaiting the signal. It was given silently.

The smash of the rams, amplified by the surrounding silence, echoed as the door was attacked. It opened, and swung violently against its frame, hanging now by only one distorted hinge.

At the rear of the property the police team scrambled over the fence and ran silently towards the house, two focussed on the curtained room, the others on the adjacent windows. Almost immediately the sound of breaking glass filled the night.

The front door team ran into the house shouting instructions as it split into two groups, one to the first floor, the other on the ground.

Fractionally behind them, the rear team had broken through the French windows, and were now fighting with two men who had been sleeping on sofas. The fight was soon over, with both men handcuffed.

The last room, opened with a ram, contained Barry, slumped, blindfolded, and tied to a chair.

He was untied as quickly as possible, and helped onto a couch.

Ron had some fresh water for him, and then after a short pause, helped him into one of the police vehicles that were now outside, plus a number of curious neighbours who had been woken by the property assault.

No further persons had been found on the first floor.

Barry was taken directly to the Port of Spain General Hospital for a full check-up, and some rest. Ron and Inspector Thomas accompanied him, and after handing him over to the medical staff, confirmed they would return that evening.

Meanwhile Inspector Thomas had put out an APB for the immediate arrest of Duvan Cardona, Airports, Docks, etc.

That evening, at about 8.30pm, Ron and Inspector Thomas met at the General Hospital to enquire as to Barry's recovery, and to hopefully see him. The medical staff advised that Barry had been quite heavily sedated to aid recovery, and that it would be better to visit again on the Sunday morning at about 10.30 am.

As Ron and the Inspector were leaving the hospital the Inspector's mobile rang. It was an update on the APB. Duvan Cardona had been arrested at Piarco International Airport, attempting to board a flight to Caracas, Venezuela. He was now in transit to a holding cell.

'I look forward to an interesting discussion with him tomorrow morning,' said Inspector Michael Thomas. with a slight smile. 'With the evidence we have, through his meetings and negotiations with Barry, it should provide solid proof for a significant jail sentence. But small compensation for Barry's mugging.'

Sunday 19ᵗʰ April 2009. General Hospital, Port of Spain, Trinidad.

Ron and the Inspector met at the hospital and were given an update by Barry's doctor.

Barry had been examined immediately on his entry into the hospital, and his condition as a result of the beating he had received. As far as could be determined at this stage, no bones were broken, but there were large areas of severe bruising, including legs, torso, and head. Hair fractures could have occurred, but until X-rays were taken they had no confirmation, or otherwise.

Finally the doctor asked that the meeting with Barry was kept short in order to help his recovery.

Ron and David sat either side of Barry's bed, in the private room.

Barry was not looking good. His face carried severe bruising where he had been punched, and slapped. His body was covered by a smock, but the short sleeves showed heavy bruising on his arms. The bedclothes were raised above his legs, clearly a support cage to take pressure away from them.

He was awake, but clearly in pain.

'My apologies,' he said jokily with a weak smile. 'I can handle one, but there were two of them.'

The Inspector commented, 'Frankly Barry you were lucky. Take your time, and recover. Duvan Cardona has been arrested and is currently detained in our HQ. He will be tried, and will certainly go to jail for a significant period.'

'One down, and how many more to go?' Barry responded hoarsely.

Ron interjected at this point, 'I'll be reporting to the UK for both of us later today. Any general points you want to make?'

'No general points, just two specific ones.'

'Which are?'

Barry spoke slowly, and with a certain hoarseness,

'No word of my dust up to the Director. Understood?'

'Understood. And the second one?'

'The USA, UK, and Europe, should realise this is another type of World War we are trying to fight. It's too big for individual countries.

We need a First XI of committed countries prepared to fight together. Plus, we don't want any country that is only paying lip service involved. Anyway, I know I'm talking to the converted.' Barry smiled wanly at this point.

'I get your point Barry,' the Inspector said, 'We'll let you sleep now. Rest and recover, and do what the Doctor tells you to do. Right? Incidentally, there is 24 hour security outside your room. He is one of my best men.'

Barry nodded, 'Will do, and many thanks,' he said a little weakly.

***

Monday 20th April 2009. Foreign Office. Westminster, London.

Quentin Horncastle was just keeping his annoyance under control as Charles Urwin continued to irritate him with his verbal exposition of how he thought certain international matters should be resolved by Her Majesty's Government, namely the Foreign Office.

Quentin had appreciated Charles' intellect over many years, but, he had to admit that the level of intellectual arrogance, at times, stretched his tolerance to breaking point.

'Charles, I do not have to remind you, that as the present Government is not necessarily at one with your own views, it is vital that we maintain, although only so far as is required, a clear position of support for their stated policies. You do understand my position, I'm sure?'

'Yes, but with some reluctance.'

'Charles, you should understand that your reluctance is not solely confined to yourself.'

Sometimes, he thought, Charles really was a complete pain. But, there again, he was never boring.

Charles, concurrently, was thinking that the heavy mental load he carried, was, at times, a nightmare, to be handled with great care.

The Safe House. some miles North West of London.

Sir Robert was rapidly losing his patience.

He had sat down with Durov that morning, hoping that on a one to one basis, additional intelligence would be revealed. In the back of his mind he was also wondering if Durov was playing a double game.

Maybe some shock tactics should be employed by him in order for Durov to realise that political asylum is certainly not a given.

'Dimitry, I do not intend to waste any further time with our current conversation.

What is clear, is your continued reluctance, for whatever reason, to provide hard intelligence to justify the granting of political asylum by the UK Government.

I would suggest you reflect on this urgently, as the alternative is for the Government to consider allowing your Ambassador, or his staff, to have a face to face meeting with you. To date we have refused such requests. Location for such a meeting would be in London.'

At this point Sir Robert rose from his chair, and walked briskly from the room.

The same day. IISG HQ London.

The Director was reading a report from 6, updating him on the activities of 'Barry' and 'Ron' in Port of Spain.

The text was ambivalent and guarded at the same time.

It was clear that various contacts had been made with active drug dealers, from Venezuela and Columbia, using Trinidad as a shipment route to Africa and Europe. This, in itself, was providing additional Intel. What was also indicated was that similar traffic was being established from Ecuador, on a direct line/delivery basis to the UK and Europe, with no transhipment.

Somewhere close to the end of the report was a comment from 'Barry' which although short, summed up the current status, and what would be required in the future.

Correction, he mused; not in the future, as soon as possible.

The Director thought about this, and the countries involved. Getting such a group of countries to agree a common strategy could, or would, probably take a generation.

The other major hazard, impacting on the required strategy, was, that in some of the countries, there existed, and well protected, high level corruption, linked to merciless gang warfare.

Without doubt, a world size problem.

Wednesday 22ⁿᵈ April 2009.

Inspector Michael Thomas and Ron visited Barry in hospital that afternoon. Barry was certainly looking considerably better than 72 hours previously. Medication and rest was clearly working.

Barry opened with a smile on his face,

'The doctor says I can leave tomorrow. I've been running round the bed this morning to get myself in shape, and your man outside my door has given me some exercises to help!'

'Don't rush it Barry, but I expect I'm wasting my breath,' Ron replied.

'Just so you're in the picture, I had to send an update report to London, which will obviously go to your Director as well.'

He saw the look on Barry's face, 'Operation downsides have to be logged you know. Apologies, but no regrets.'

'Yes, OK, I understand ' Barry replied, 'If it had happened to you I would have done the same.'

They then heard some additional updates from Michael Thomas, concerning the general situation in Trinidad. He outlined some of the changes occurring with crime gangs, control, members, and developing relationships both internal and external in the country.

There was clear emerging evidence of shifts in local activity and the new incursion of international criminals, both regional and European, into Trinidad's drug market place.

Homicide was increasing by the month. Recent statistics had shown over 525 murders in 2008, the actual number being probably much higher. This occurring in a country with a total population of just over one million. He was not optimistic that 2009 would show any improvement.

He then surprised them both with a clearly off the record remark.

'It will not surprise you that there are many sections, individuals, or groups, within the Trinidad population who are involved in the criminal drug trade, importing, distributing, and transporting to the USA, West Africa and Europe.

Over the years I have submitted many requests, based on firm investigation and proof, to pursue both the leaders and followers in this evil trade. You will not be surprised at the very high proportion that were rejected.'

He paused, clearly collecting his thoughts.

'When you return to the UK, I will give you some data that could be used by your Departments, plus, I'm sure, various international partners wanting to assist in the eradication, or significant reduction, of drug trafficking.'

Thursday 23rd April 2009. IISG HQ London.

During the morning the Director had discussions with 6, followed in the afternoon with IISG Washington, providing a mutual update on activity in Trinidad, and the current status of 'Barry' and 'Ron'.

He was also advised that afternoon that Harry was making good progress. By then all agencies had agreed and confirmed that Harry and Tom should return to the UK.

Friday 24th April 2009. Port of Spain, Trinidad.

That morning, via the NSA secure link, Harry and Tom both received instructions to return to London soonest.

Harry had been released back to the Hyatt Regency that morning, so he and Tom were able to make a booking to fly back to London, overnight, via St Lucia, on a BA flight leaving at 19.15hrs, landing Saturday morning 10.15a.m. the 25th.

However, full operational cover was maintained until departure, this including a lunchtime meeting with Chief Inspector Michael Thomas. It was not a long meeting.

Michael Thomas handed Harry a small package.

'That is a memory stick containing all the information I referred to the other day. It is also contained in a lining that will not be picked up going through Security….. Just in case.

I hope that you will be able to use that information to good effect, and also share some of it with other appropriate agencies.'

'Michael, it has been a pleasure working with you, and I am sure this Intel will be very usefully deployed to good effect.

Plus, if you get over to the UK, please make contact, and we can certainly have good catchup, and good meal or three!'

That evening Barry and Ron caught the flight, which left on time, and as Harry admitted later, he slept most of the flight back to the UK!

Saturday 25th April 2009

Landing on time, and clearing Customs, Harry and Tom made their way to London, on the Heathrow Express.

Once in Paddington Harry telephoning Lina, to tell her he was back in the UK.

However, confusion arose as initially Lina thought Harry was telephoning from Trinidad! Once she realised he was back in the UK, she asked where he was. He confirmed, to then receive an instruction to come straight to her apartment! Which he did, arriving just after 12.30p.m.

Lina opened the door of her apartment, her face one big smile, as she hugged him fiercely. Unfortunately Harry could not hide a slight wince which Lina obviously felt.

'What's happened?' she queried.

'Oh, a situation where I was outnumbered two to one, and one of them wanted to make a point. Fully on the mend now, no real problem. Just my pride is a tiny bit dented!!'

She hugged him gently, 'When you've had a tea and some sleep you can tell me all about it.'

'Don't need the sleep, as I slept the whole flight! A coffee would go down well, and then I can bring you up to date. Great to be back. And, great to see you again.'

Harry gave Lina an abridged version of the last thirty five days, in very general terms, skipping quickly over the not so nice incidents.

Yes, the op had been worthwhile, and a good relationship established with the Chief Inspector for the future. He did not mention the memory stick. He did, however, stress the magnitude of the drug problem facing the world today. It definitely required a total re-think and new strategy by US and European, and other world Governments.

Harry did crash out on the sofa for about an an hour that afternoon, before suggesting they go out for an early dinner at one of their favourite restaurants.

Italian it was, and very good indeed, enjoying the food, their own company, and back home together. Perfect, thought Harry, as he fell into a deep sleep, after Lina had expressed some concern about his still obvious bruising.

'Looks worse than it is,' he countered with a smile, ' All I wanted were another three rounds, and I would have had him!'

Sunday 26ᵗʰ April 2009.

They spent a quiet, but comfortable day, before Harry said it would be necessary for him to go back to his apartment in Clapham that afternoon. He needed to organise himself for a meeting with the Director on Monday morning.

Yes, the time had passed too quickly for them both he agreed, before calling a cab and kissing Lina good bye.

'Call me tomorrow evening,' she said as he left.

'Guaranteed,' he replied.

Someone else had also made the trip to Clapham that evening. Andrei Ionescu.

Following up on the Pakhan's orders he walked down Harry's street at about 9.00pm. For the first time in just over a month a light was on in the front room of Harry's apartment.

Andrei's pulse quickened,

Check again on Monday night, he told himself.

**

Monday 27th April 2009. IISG HQ. London.

At 10.30a.m. Harry & Tom had a long meeting with the Director, to cover the most important elements of the Trinidad assignment. This meeting would be followed by a similar one that afternoon with the appropriate Officer at MI6. One specific element discussed that morning was the memory stick handed over by Chief Inspector Michael Thomas.

Harry had viewed some of the initial data, and on the strength of that had made another memory stick copy for MI6.

'I will be very interested to hear your reactions Director, after you have viewed some of the data on this memory stick.

Also Tom, I think your boss will be salivating at some of the names and connections in the same way. Organised crime and politicians as bedfellows. Not a pretty sight.'

The challenging question was effectively how could this intelligence be best employed? Analysis for starters. Then perhaps some specific focus for possible action.

That afternoon. MI6 HQ, London.

Effectively a replica meeting was held that afternoon, with a review of the assignment by Harry and Tom, and of equal importance the intelligence contained in the copy memory stick that Harry handed over via Tom.

Harry gave a couple of examples that he had viewed that morning, and the obvious repercussions that could arise from its disclosure.

Consideration of how to deploy such intelligence would, no doubt, take some time, bearing in mind the political and international repercussions when deployed.

Harry and the Director went their separate ways after the meeting, Harry back to Clapham, but only after the Director had said,

'Harry, you were damn lucky in Trinidad. Take it easy for a couple of days. You are not 100% fit yet, get some good early nights. Right?'

'Right Director. Wilco!'

'Yes, would be best, Harry!

See you tomorrow. A 360 degree update, review, and refocus due to new budget. By the way, that is good news! Sleep well!'

That evening. Clapham, London.

Harry called Lina and they had a short, but very sensitive conversation.

'Couple of things I want to discuss with you next weekend when we are down at the cottage.'

'Didn't know we were going to the cottage!'

'Thought I'd mentioned it. Anyway we are now!'

Lina laughed, 'Yes sir, any formal dinners?'

They joked between themselves for a few minutes, the typical verbal intimacy between two people comfortable in their relationship.

Outside, across the darkened street, Andrei Ionescu sees the lights and a person in Harry's apartment. Target positively identified, Harry Baxter.

That evening at about 10.00p.m., Andrei Ionescu reported to the Pakhan; confirmation target has returned, and is clearly identified.

Tuesday 28th April 2009. IISG HQ. London.

The Director had a review meeting that morning with Harry.

He was able to bring Harry up to speed with the general thrust of further deliberations and negotiations with IISG Washington.

Overall, with the close working relationships with MI6, CIA, DGSE, etc, Washington felt that this would justify an increased budget in the near future. The Director had been pushing for an increase in resources, manpower predominantly, due to demands both within the UK, and elsewhere.

Harry meanwhile had been expanding his analysis of the data on the memory stick provided by Chief Inspector Michael Thomas.

In one word, Explosive!

He dealt with a couple of examples to illustrate his comment.

One major crime syndicate, with the usual specialist services; including murder, disposal of opposition, local area control, drug transportation, intimidation and bribery of political figures, criminal courts, and local police force officers, to name but a few.

Description was detailed, by way of names, connections, and specific references to well known and reported crimes.

Another showed details of the relationships, (persons by name, significant players in business, politics, and obviously crime, in Trinidad), financial transactions from the region to Europe, including Switzerland, and actual dates of drug shipments from Venezuela via Trinidad to Europe, (in this case Spain).

The Director remained silent whilst Harry had outlined just two examples, within a significant cache of Intel on the memory stick.

'Hmm,' was his first response,

'I wonder what our old firm will be thinking as they start digging? I'm sure we will be having an early meeting with them to discuss how all this could be best used, both here, and across the pond.

Let me have a quiet think about this. An off the record conversation might be in order perhaps? I'll get back to you Harry.'

'Fine Director.

I also thought I might contact Jan Glaus at the Swiss Embassy to suggest we may have some Intel of interest for them, for follow up in some of their banks?'

'Hold that until I get back to you Harry.'

'OK Director. Incidentally I was going to see if Tom is up to speed in terms of the Intel. Off the record comm between us, naturally.'

'Just hold both Harry, until I revert.'

Harry nodded in agreement.

That afternoon the Director contacted Frank Stansfield at MI6. They had worked together over the years, in various locations, and activities.

They met at about 7.00pm, in one their old meeting pubs near Victoria Station, and tucked themselves into a corner in the upstairs bar and restaurant. It was not busy at that hour, and they would not need more than one hour.

The Director outlined what had been passed to 6, and the significant Intel that was contained on the memory stick recently handed over for analysis.

'I'm just lobbing some pebbles into the pond Frank.

This is definitely something that needs sensible analysis and then some joint actions between yourselves, 5, us, and probably the Swiss. Second phase would be joint submission, in fairly short order, with

Washington, to maximise any agreed strategy to try and combat this obscene cancer being spread around the world.'

They discussed the issue further in fairly general terms, and Frank agreed he would raise the matter internally with the appropriate team, and its Head. His contact with the Director would be maintained on a confidential/official basis, which ever was necessary.

Wednesday 29th April 2009. IISG HQ London.

The Director advised Harry that morning he could contact Jan Glaus at the Swiss Embassy as they had discussed.

'A few flies on the water, Harry. I know they will obviously be interested in the Intel, particularly chasing the tails of some of their friendly bankers.

Get them solidly on board in principle. What would be ideal is if a number of these contacts, players, and institutions, could all be hit at the same time, whether Europe, USA, wherever.'

Harry made his call to Jan Glaus. Meeting agreed Thursday 3.00pm.

Thursday 30th April 2009. 3.00pm. Swiss Embassy, London.

Harry met with Jan Glaus as arranged, and after Jan's sympathetic comments concerning his recent Caribbean trip and 'treatment,' Harry got down quickly to the scope of the Intel.

On the one hand Jan was not at all surprised with some of involvement by Swiss bankers, on the other hand disgusted, as they would have a very clear idea, or suspicion, as to 'product' and source.

Harry phrased the outline and direction how the Director wanted to action a collective response, Jan agreeing in principle, subject of course, to any specific Swiss Government caveats.

Harry returned to IISG with, at least, a general accord, and importantly, a similar enthusiasm.

That evening. Clapham, London.

Andrei Ionescu had spent the last three days tracking Harry from Clapham to the IISG London office, his lunchtime habit, and his evening return to Clapham.

What was interesting, was that Harry, in a small way, was starting to be predictable.

***

XIII

MAY 2009

Friday 1st May 2009. London.

Harry took his car in that morning.

He would pick Lina up after work, and then drive leisurely down to his cottage in Sussex, stopping for an evening meal just south of the Surrey border.

During the day he had continued his review of the substantial content of the memory stick, and had updated the Director on some of named politicians, banks, dollar or other currency amounts, countries involved, and suspended investigations that had occurred.

'It certainly is an ugly mix Harry.

I just hope that when this sees the light of day, if ever, some of these international crooks are put away for a very long term. And that is before we provide some publicity for a number of less than ethical politicians.'

That May evening seemed to herald the start of a good month, certainly with regard to the weather, as Harry and Lina dined in a small pub restaurant on the way down to the cottage.

Saturday dawned sunny so they went for a leisurely walk through the village , and up towards the Downs.

As they walked, Harry started talking in a slightly hesitant manner.

'When I was on flights and in boring hotel rooms in Trinidad, I had a chance to think about where I was going, and more importantly, where we were going.'

He turned to look at her. Her eyes looked sad, and her face had a questioning look.

'No, don't get me wrong. You know how I feel about you. I was just thinking of the way life from time to time gives you a warning. And, to be honest, Trinidad gave me a gentle warning, and a wake-up call.'

Lina cut in,

'Harry, you know how I feel about you, and I was not happy with your last assignment to Trinidad. Frankly dangerous.'

'I won't argue with that,' Harry replied, 'however Tom was there, and we were always a good two-man team.'

Then Harry suddenly blurted out, 'I want us to be together, and the question is, can we move in together?'

Lina put her arms around his neck and kissed him firmly.

'Yes.' She paused, 'Yes, please. Was that what you wanted to talk about when we were on the telephone the other day?'

'Yes it was, and I was nervous about raising it with you.'

'Absolutely no need,' she said, taking his hand, 'let's walk to the next village and celebrate.'

The weekend took on a different tone of light, form and colour, which was reflected in their lovemaking that night and Sunday morning.

They decided that Lina would stay the Sunday night in Clapham, taking a cab, or Tube, to work on the Monday morning.

They left early evening, and drove back to London, both happy in their relationship, and relaxed, now they were of one mind.

Harry wondered if there would be any adverse comments, or restrictions from the Swiss Embassy. Cross that bridge when we come to it, he mused to himself.

That Evening.

They arrived back a Harry's flat at about 9.45p.m, Harry handing Lina the front door key, saying, You open up, and I'll bring the bags in.'

In a reconstruction later, it was dark, only two old street lamps in Harry's street, and with it being Sunday it was quiet, being the end of the day, and Monday tomorrow, a work day.

Harry's car was not parked outside his front door, it was at least four or five car lengths further down the street, slightly murkier.

As Harry walked from the back of his car carrying two bags, two muffled shots rang out, almost immediately followed by a cat squealing.

Harry was hit twice, with what was determined later were a flesh wound, and a part broken upper left arm.

A woman at an adjacent house had run out on hearing her cat's loud squeal, but seeing Harry lying on the ground, ran back into her house to call Police and Ambulance.

With all this noise, Lina, who had gone up to Harry's first floor apartment, had run back down to the street. Running to a prostrate Harry she could blood seeping through his clothes, and a badly shaped arm.

Neighbours from various houses were now coming out onto the street, and expressing concern and nosiness in equal measure.

Why, who, not the sort of thing we get here, were the questions and comments being posed between neighbours, as eventually the wailing sirens of police and ambulance could be heard getting louder.

A late police report that night, also included the death of a young man who had badly misjudged speeding traffic, when he was hit and killed whilst trying to run across Clapham High Street towards the Clapham Common Underground Station.

It was Andrei Ionescu, who was running across Clapham High Street, when he was caught by a fast moving car jumping a red light, thrown into the air, and killed instantly.

In Tottenham, North London, the Pakhan was wondering what news he would be brought by Andrei on Monday.

**

EPILOGUE

Monday 4th May 2009. 10.00am. The Safe House.

Quentin Horncastle had received a final request from Sir Robert to hold one further meeting with Dimitry Durov in order to convince him as to the level of intelligence expected and required.

If Sir Robert is to finally sign off on his application for Political Asylum, then a quid pro quo must be visible.

Quentin maintained an affable approach to Durov, whilst they had coffee, and discussed, it had to be said in some detail, the UK government's expectations.

Durov, as always, was insisting on direct discussions with Sir Robert. The meeting ended, unfortunately, with no resolution.

Tuesday 5th May 2009. The Kremlin, Moscow.

Sergey Lavrov, Russian Foreign Minister, sat alone in his office in the Kremlin reviewing updates from a number of embassies around the world.

The one currently holding his attention was the one concerning the Russian Embassy in London. Attached to it were several additional comments covering recent activity and observations.

There was still total silence concerning Dimitry Durov, previous First Secretary at the London Russian Embassy. The Embassy continued to make repeated requests to the UK Government for access to Durov, but were constantly denied.

Once there was some intelligence, then eventually the traitor would be dealt with. The long arm of SVR/FSB would eventually strike, either sooner, or later, no matter how long Russia had to wait.

He sat back, his eyes somewhere focussed on the far distance, as he considered two options, one longer term, and one short term, both with plus and/or minus benefits.

With Charles Urwin now safely resident back in the FCO, he was reasonably assured of solid intelligence within UK Government thinking in a number of spheres of UK foreign policy. This could be of considerable benefit, when planning Russian response, and/or medium to long-term strategy.

The alternative short-term consideration would be much more dramatic. It could possibly bring about the fall of the current UK Government, and, perhaps as a bonus, install a new administration more sympathetic to Russian foreign policy.

It would, of course, bring about the removal of an intelligence source, by creating a situation where Charles Urwin is exposed for what he is. But the resulting damage and panic created by such an exposure would be catastrophic to the present administration, and put the United Kingdom firmly on the back foot, for a not inconsiderable period of time.

Notwithstanding the resultant political fallout arising from this, the long-term provider of intelligence, however, was still in place, and continues to be active in their submission of UK government foreign policy.

Added to this would be the complete loss of confidence by those countries currently sharing intelligence with the UK, particularly the 5 Eyes, which includes the UK, United States, Canada, Australia, and New Zealand.

Which one would have the longer-term benefit, he mused?

**

Tuesday 5th May 2009. 11.00am. Safe House.

The flap was building. The Security detail, noticing that Durov was not up at his usual time, entered his bedroom to rouse him.

He was dead.

Medical staff were called. Telephone calls were made to Sir Robert at Westminster, and Security HQ. Nothing could be done, except eventually determination as to death.

Sir Robert, on hearing the news, called an urgent meeting with 5 & 6, obviously anticipating the Russian reaction, and potentially, the huge damage that could be created by the death of a Russian diplomat whilst in UK custody.

An urgent post mortem was scheduled for Wednesday the 6th May.

Wednesday 6th May 2009. 4.30pm. Hospital. Post Mortem Team.

Tests and analysis had been non-stop throughout the day since 8.00am that morning. Security was rock tight both for team and results data.

Cause of death; Heart attack.

Overall condition of subject – apparently good for age.

Reason for heart attack? Evidence of general conditions to produce such an attack – none.

Later Analysis, however, that afternoon, had indicated minute traces of unknown substance in blood stream that *may* have caused heart attack. Composition? Unknown – further intensive analysis to follow.

Official reaction was for complete lock down, no comments on final Hospital report other than – Heart Attack.

One sealed copy by Police motor cycle courier to Sir Robert, who, upon reading it, called Quentin for a meeting a.m. Thursday the 7th.

Thursday 7th May 2009. Foreign Office London.

Sir Robert was reading the report again, when Quentin entered his office.

'Good Morning, Quentin. Nothing very good about it, I have to say. Read this,' he said handing the report to Quentin.

Quentin's brow furrowed as he read the details, looking at Sir Robert with a questioning look as he finished.

'What do you make of this, Sir Robert?' Quentin asked.

'Not very much at all, Quentin, I have to say.

Until we see more detailed analysis we are all fumbling in the dark. And that, by the way, includes all the various chemists and analysts trying to determine exactly what caused Durov's heart attack.

A very sorry business, and, which will, I am sure, turn politically ugly, once the facts are revealed to Moscow.'

They discussed some of the implications which would arise, but obviously, the fine tuning of their response would only occur, as Sir Robert said, 'In the fullness of time.'

Saturday 9th May 2009. Fulham, West London.

Quentin Horncastle, his wife and children, lived in a three storey Georgian style house in the best end of Fulham, situated on the west side of London. They had two young children.

About every two or three weeks they entertained an eclectic group of friends for dinner, with the dinner conversation rule of 'No Shop'.

On this particular Saturday, after the guests had gone, Quentin went into his study and unlocked a lower drawer in his desk. Inside was a locked leather case, which he opened. Inserting a small memory stick into the side of the small laptop, he punched in a specific code.

In his garden, in a small garden shed, was a sophisticated piece of technology, Russian made. Two small lights flickered. It was a satellite communication piece of hardware, with only one hard wired connected item, his small laptop, and with only one recipient, via satellite.

A small box appeared on the screen of his small laptop, 'SEND' or 'CANCEL'. He pressed 'SEND'. He closed and locked the leather case, then locking his desk drawer.

In the London Russian Embassy, located at No 5 Kensington Palace Gardens, a box on the night comms staff computer indicated an incoming compressed encrypted message.

An innocuous black Ford Transit van, parked no more than forty-five yards down the street from Quentin Horncastle's home, contained some very sophisticated electronic monitoring systems, plus two operatives who had downloaded the transmission, and which would be analysed and then decrypted by MI5 and GCHQ the following day.

After breaking the encryption, and following analysis, it would then be shared with MI6, and following further timely deliberations, investigation, consideration of potential arrest and caution, would ultimately be released to the Foreign and Commonwealth Office.

**

Friday 15th May 2009. MI6 HQ, Vauxhall Cross, London.

The C team were in a meeting. A total of five people, and, at this moment, no one was talking. A collective furrowed brow would best describe the quiet room.

The team leader spoke,

'On continuing and consistent evidence passed to us from our contact in Moscow, it would appear that we have our man securely, but not literally, in place, and doing well with respect to his reputation, and the quality of the intelligence he is providing.

However, as advised by 5, with this other player in the field, we are clearly going to hit a wall almost immediately, as intelligence provided by both appears, or is, contradictory. As a direct result suspicion will be generated of both players.

Question?

Is that something we can handle, or manipulate, or is that something we wish to neutralise? Both players will, as a result, be highly exposed.

Is that a risk we are prepared to take, particularly with one life, or both lives? This also makes the position of the current H.M. Government extremely delicate, and sensitive, in the event of exposure.

Should we consider closure of one, or both?

And, that does not take into account any subsequent damaging international political fallout for the government of the day that may occur.'

The room fell silent again.

**

Saturday 16th May 2009. Hospital. London.

Harry had been in hospital for almost two weeks. After the first week he was bored stiff, and getting impatient.

But to heal takes time, the doctors warned him. At times, in that half state of awake and dozing, he wondered what he could, would, or be able to do.

As an operative on the ground, wherever, was possibly not an option. Maybe, possibly, but who knows. If everything mended, why not? Running a show, and/or team from behind a desk, might, perhaps, if convinced, if forced, if nothing else was offered, could be.

His mind wandered over the last few years, highlighting the good, passing over quickly, those that were bad, and wincing mentally, at those that were really bad.

He drifted off to sleep again, and as he did, he involuntarily tightened his grip on her hand, causing Lina to look up from her magazine and smile, before she turned the page.

***

THE END, or JUST A PAUSE?

ABOUT THE AUTHOR

John Halfnight was commissioned in the Corps of Royal Engineers and spent his early years serving in the British Army in the Middle East followed by a commercial career in the UK, France, the Middle East, and the Gulf. From his various bases in London, Paris, Doha Qatar, Dubai UAE, and Jeddah KSA, as CEO or PDG, he operated extensively throughout Eastern Europe, Hungary, Russia, North America, Africa, Asia (including India & Pakistan), China, Hong Kong, Malaysia and Singapore.

He lives in the UK and consults with UK and foreign corporations.

True Lies is the fourth book in The *Harry Baxter* Series.

It was preceded by *Overt Lies*, *Covert Lies*, and *Cyber Lies*. The Harry Baxter Series is available on Amazon.co.uk & Amazon.com.

www.johnhalfnight.com

THE HARRY BAXTER SERIES

Overt Lies

MI6 operative Harry Baxter is called back from holiday to investigate whether an explosion at Buncefield Depot was an accident or deliberate. If deliberate, was it home grown or an act of international terrorism?

Overt Lies follows international intelligence agencies – MI6, MI5, Mossad, DGSE, CIA – as they determine the source and unwind the mystery of who bombed Buncefield terminal. Will the perpetrators strike again?

Following the Buncefield attack, Jihadists move their operations to the Gulf as security is tightened in the UK. They regroup, plan and solicit funding before returning to London to set up an attack on the heart of British democracy.

UK intelligence agencies MI5 and MI6 combine forces to thwart the attacks, consistently one step behind, desperate for Intel and fearful for public safety. Hostages are taken by both sides leading to a critical final standoff as the third attack is mounted in London. UK Security Services employ unconventional methods to resolve the nightmare scenario.

Covert Lies

Covert Lies, the second book in the trilogy, continues from where *Overt Lies* left off as it follows Harry Baxter (MI6) racing to help thwart a terrorist attack at the heart of the UK Government.

Harry is then posted to the British High Commission in Islamabad, Pakistan. He is involved in the rescue of a kidnapped UK senior diplomat, and is investigating the link between terrorist activity in the UK and Pakistani extremists.

Rogue players are providing supply lines of armaments to various terrorist groups, including Hezbollah, further complicating tensions in the Middle East and Gulf region. Vital working relations continue between British MI6 (Harry), American CIA (Jack DeCosta), French DGSE (Alain Dubois), and Israeli Mossad (Anna Harrison) in a heart-racing countdown to foil coordinated attacks against the UK and French governments.

Cyber Lies

Harry Baxter returns from Pakistan to MI6, Vauxhall Cross, London, to collaborate with MI5 as they desperately track both Russian and Chinese agents within the UK. Both countries are penetrating the major energy companies, destroying gas routing from Europe, and sabotaging power generation with the potential of turning out the lights throughout Britain.

As China prepares its plans and actions, Bratva, the Russian Mafia, is planning a multi-billion-dollar heist on the Energy Futures Markets around the world. As tensions build, the matrix of complexity resembles a game of three-dimensional chess as internal competition within the foreign intelligence communities creating a further level of risk in already high-stakes game.

The Harry Baxter Series is available on both:
Amazon.co.uk & Amazon.com

Front Cover Photo: Big Ben and the Houses of Parliament.
Back Cover Photo: The Kremlin Moscow.

Printed in Great Britain
by Amazon

14263625R00190